78

A FINAL DISCORD

Recent Titles by Tessa Barclay from Severn House

A BETTER CLASS OF PERSON
THE DALLANCY BEQUEST
FAREWELL PERFORMANCE
A HANDFUL OF DUST
A LOVELY ILLUSION
THE SILVER LINING
STARTING OVER
A TRUE LIKENESS

A FINAL DISCORD

Tessa Barclay

This first world edition published in Great Britain 2005 by
SEVERN HOUSE PUBLISHERS LTD of
9–15 High Street, Sutton, Surrey SM1 1DF.
This first world edition published in the USA 2005 by
SEVERN HOUSE PUBLISHERS INC of
595 Madison Avenue, New York, N.Y. 10022.

British Library Cataloguing in Publication Data

Barclay, Tessa
  A final discord
  1.   Crowne, Gregory (Fictitious character) - Fiction
  2.   Detective and mystery stories
  I.   Title
  823.9'14 [F]

  ISBN-10 : 0-7278-6249-9 (cased)
               0-7278- 9148-0 (paper)

Typeset by Palimpsest Book Production Ltd.,
Polmont, Stirlingshire, Scotland.
Printed and bound in Great Britain by
MPG Books Ltd., Bodmin, Cornwall.

One

The head waiter at the Belle Cascade recognized the Crown Prince of Hirtenstein at once. Not as a customer, of course. It was known to the gossips of Geneva that although His Serene Highness came from a well-regarded family, he had almost no money. So Etienne, quick-witted as always, understood that he was here as someone's guest.

He stepped forward, ready with the name under which the prince liked to be known. 'Monsieur Couronne?'

'Ah . . . yes . . . I'm here for M. Guidon . . . ?'

Good heavens, thought Etienne. Could it possibly be that the high-minded von Hirtensteins were thinking of borrowing money from the Banque Guidon?

'M. Guidon hasn't arrived yet, monsieur. Shall I show you to his table? Or would you perhaps like to wait in the bar?'

'I'll go to the bar, thank you.' Not too eager, that was the style to adopt, thought Gregory von Hirtenstein as he was conducted to the steel-and-glass balcony looking out on to the lake of Geneva, though his father and grandmother had been extremely eager – somewhat too keen, in fact, when they heard he'd been invited to lunch by this sedate and wealthy man.

'What can he want?' his grandmother had wondered. 'He's such a big noise in Geneva.'

'It will be about money,' said ex-King Anton. 'When you hear anything about Auguste Guidon, it's always about money.'

'Well, he's not going to offer to give us any, that's pretty certain, Papa. I don't remember ever hearing that he was giving money away.'

His grandmother sighed. The ex-Queen Mother of

1

Hirtenstein still had fond memories of the days when she didn't have to count every centime in her purse. But that was in another country, and besides the wench had been a lot younger then, as one of those bloodthirsty English playwrights had once almost said.

The Hirtensteins had been forced to leave their country because there had been a revolt. An aggressively reformist government came in, the Hirtensteins decamped to Switzerland: King Anton and his wife, heavily pregnant, and his mother. Alas, the ex-Queen had died soon after the birth of her son. So now they lived in a handsome little farmhouse on the slopes outside Geneva, where Papa taught horsemanship up to Olympic level, the ex-Queen Mother decorated the houses of the rich when she could land the contract, and her grandson earned a reasonable living from arranging concerts and recitals in the world of classical music.

Not by any means rich. No crown jewels carried away from their homeland when they left it so hurriedly, no bank accounts in offshore caches. So the sudden interest of M. Guidon was exciting, to say the least.

The Prince ordered an aperitif. While he waited for it, he rang his office. This was a tiny room up a staircase in the old part of Geneva, where Amabelle, his assistant, spent two or three days a week taking messages and keeping the books straight. She told him that she'd found the missing cellist, who had boarded the wrong plane in Paris but would arrive in time for the recital in Prague although not for rehearsals.

'Wonderful,' he sighed. The other members of the quartet would probably lynch the cellist. But he couldn't concern himself with that, for now here was M. Guidon, looking about for him from the doorway of the bar. M. Guidon, whom he'd never met but knew from his photographs in the papers.

'Monsieur Couronne! So sorry not to be here to greet you! A little crisis at the office, you know . . .'

'I understand,' said the Prince, saying a quick goodbye to Amabelle so as to shake hands.

Auguste Guidon was in his mid-fifties, looking up at Gregory von Hirtenstein from his 170 centimetres without rancour. The President of Banque Guidon didn't need to be

2

tall. Money and position gave him authority. His iron-grey hair was beautifully barbered, his suit was a perfect example of tailoring. The pale pink carnation in his buttonhole seemed to say that he could allow himself this little touch of softness because he was so tough in every other respect.

In contrast, the ex-Prince von Hirtenstein was some fifteen centimetres taller than his host, in a suit that was of excellent quality but about ten years old. He had an outdoors look, rather rangy and supple, due to winter devotion to cross-country skiing and to helping his father in the stables when he could. Some journalists liked to describe him as an eligible bachelor and went so far as to call him handsome M. Guidon showed no signs of being swayed by any of that.

'Shall we go in?' he suggested. 'Ricco will bring your drink – what are you having? Oh, St Raphael – I'll have the same, Ricco.'

They went into the dining room, where a few other very rich people were already sampling the efforts of the hotel's famous chef.

The head waiter fussed around them. An assistant stood by with menus. The wine waiter hovered. My word, thought Gregory, he really wants to impress me. Well, I'm impressed. But what's it about?

That became no clearer even after they'd chosen food and wine and were left in peace. Guidon began a conversation about the troubles of the European Union, a source of amusement to the Swiss because of course they didn't belong to it. Gregory went along with that, although he generally steered clear of politics. The aim of the Hirtensteins was to show no interest in matters of governance because the present regime in his homeland got edgy if they did. There actually were a few devoted royalists who wanted to see the monarchy restored in Hirtenstein, although his father always politely avoided meeting them.

After the EU, the topic was cars. Guidon was interested in vintage cars, had what he called 'a few examples'. Gregory talked about his Mercedes, a dear old thing his family had owned for fifteen years. Luckily the hors d'oeuvres arrived at that point.

3

It took until they were awaiting the coffee for the banker to get to the point. Somewhere in the middle of the dessert course he'd begun talking about his family, describing how it had held on to its land through the Napoleonic occupation of Switzerland until it finally emerged as a financial force about 1820.

Very well, thought the Prince. I was impressed already, so what comes next?

'My son was at school with you,' mused Guidon. 'Some years behind you, so you probably don't remember him. Gilles Guidon?'

'Ah . . . no . . . I'm afraid not.'

'You were taking piano lessons – rather good, I gather?' At this his guest made deprecating sounds, although at one time he'd thought he might make it as a concert pianist. 'Gilles is musical too. Plays the clarinet.'

'Really?' Now His Highness was interested. Was he about to be asked to help launch a musical talent on to the international concert platform?

The coffee came, and their liqueurs. Guidon sipped his Armagnac while he gazed past the head of his guest into some troublesome hinterland of his own.

'I hoped he'd follow me as head of the bank. Not yet, of course. He's got his career to make – start at the bottom, that's the right way.'

'I suppose it is.'

'He's not bad, you know. Another ten years, he could go abroad as our representative, speak for us at conferences . . .'

Gregory nodded. What was this all about? Clearly not a request to arrange a recital for the clarinettist. He waited, an expression of helpful attentiveness on his narrow features.

'The thing is,' said Guidon at last, 'he's not keen. He wants to get in front of the public. It's not anything our family has ever had to deal with before. We've always gone for reticence, dignity . . .'

'I see.'

'But this music thing . . .'

'There's nothing undignified about the clarinet,' said

4

Gregory, and then could have kicked himself for sounding so absurd. Yet it was true. What was wrong with wanting to make music?

'Mhm,' grunted Guidon. 'But jazz is undignified. Don't you think?'

A silence followed. Gregory was stunned. Then, alas, he found himself wanting to laugh.

The son and heir to the Guidon fortune, appearing as a jazz clarinettist? No wonder the father was shaken up. Now Gregory tried to recall the boy at school. The music department had tutors called in for most instruments, so he found he could recall the teacher for the woodwind section. Around him there had been five or six pupils. A very short, plump child . . . *Le perdreau?* The baby partridge? Had that been Gilles Guidon?

His hesitation had lasted a little too long. Auguste Guidon heaved a great sigh then said: 'I arranged this meeting because I need your help, Monsieur Couronne.'

Help? In what form? Was he supposed to call on the spirit of their schooldays – which had never thrown them together – and plead with the son to change his ways? Gilles would now be about – what? – twenty-five, twenty-six? A complete stranger to him, if the truth be told.

'I don't . . . er . . . see how?'

'Gilles has spoken of you sometimes. He admired you. At school, you know. You were of course a long way ahead of him, but he remembers how highly you were regarded. You played very well. He says he thought you might make a career . . . ? And even though that didn't happen, you are immersed in the music world.'

'But not the jazz world,' Gregory said quickly. 'Monsieur Guidon, what I know about jazz could be written in the empty space on a minim.'

'A minim?'

'One of those written notes with a little tail.'

'Ah. Ah, yes. I myself am not musical, you see. Not at all. And so you can imagine . . . I'm very much at a loss how to handle Gilles . . .'

'But it's not really a problem, surely?' He'd had time to

5

think about it. 'Lots of people have rather surprising hobbies. I mean, one or two big business types go hot-air-ballooning around the world. And I believe there's a duchess somewhere who collects Elvis Presley memorabilia. So you see—'

'But that's just the problem, monsieur. Gilles doesn't want jazz just as a hobby. He wants to become a professional.'

'Oh.' When he'd digested that, he asked: 'Does he play well?'

'How do I know?' the banker burst out in a tone of desperation. 'He plays with a couple of friends that he picked up in some club during the skiing season at Interlaken. They tell him he's great, I imagine – low-class layabouts who make a living on the outskirts of the tourist industry.'

'You've met them?'

Guidon looked offended at the mere idea. 'No, but I've seen them – they've been to the house now and again, for what I believe is called a "jam" session. They play in one of the old stables, where the noise won't disturb Rosanne and me. They really are the most unattractive types . . .' He took a big sip of his Armagnac for encouragement. 'Monsieur Couronne, what I wanted to ask you was . . . would you be interested in taking on Gilles as a client?'

'Me? But I just told you – I know nothing about—'

'Yes, yes, that was clear. But you understand business, don't you? Finding artists, drawing up contracts, that sort of thing. That's what you do, am I right?'

'Well, yes, of course. But only in the world of classical music.'

'Can it be so very different in the jazz world? Musicians have contracts, and when you need a particular instrumentalist you can find one. I could engage you to do that, couldn't I?'

Engage him. That implied paying him money. Gregory was by no means mercenary, but he had a living to make, and if the great Auguste Guidon was eager for his services, he ought at least to pursue the matter.

'What exactly would you want me to do?' he enquired in a tone that had some interest in it.

'I'd like you to . . . Could you find four players . . . You'd have to confer with Gilles on this and really, Monsieur Couronne, I'd want you to be a sort of . . . I don't know . . . Mentor? Guardian angel?'

Instead of being enlightening, this reply left him in more of a quandary than before. 'Guarding him from whom? And while he's doing what? I don't understand.'

Guidon looked as if he wanted to reach across the table and clasp his hand. 'Please, Monsieur Couronne, forgive me for being such a fool. I've never had to do anything like this before and really, I'm . . . I'm . . . at a complete loss!'

This was such a come-down on the part of a very self-confident man that Gregory was quite touched. He said: 'Let's go back to the beginning. And please, let's be less formal. Call me Gregory.'

'Oh – that's very kind – after all, sir, you are who you are—'

'Never mind all that. You said something about hiring four players. Why do you want four players? And what instruments should they play?'

'You'd have to ask Gilles about that. He has this ambition to equal the Quintette du Hot Club de France—'

'Good Lord!' Even M. Couronne had heard of them.

'Yes, well, you see how obsessed he is. His mama and I thought it would all pass over, but on the contrary, he's getting worse. He neglects his duties at the bank, at board meetings he doesn't pay attention, when I dropped in on him at his desk a week or so ago he was listening to something on his Walkman! It can't go on, it really can't. And so I thought . . . I thought . . .' He faltered into silence.

'Yes, go on.'

'It seemed to me that desperate measures were called for. So I made him an offer.'

'Yes?'

'I told him that . . . that . . . I would back him in setting up a quintet, pay for everything so that he could do what he's always longed to do – perform at the Montreux Jazz Festival.'

'Oh dear.'

'Don't shrug off the idea, Gregory, please think about it.

If you help him put together a group and they play – and if the audience shows their opinion . . . What I mean is, it's a test. Not spongers who tell him he's good because they can borrow from him, but a really knowledgeable audience—'

'Ah, I begin to see.' Papa was hoping his son and his fellow instrumentalists would be booed off the stage. 'That's a bit . . .' He was going to say 'savage', but amended it to 'extreme'.

'Well, it's the acid test. I begin to think it's the only way to bring him to his senses. I told him at the weekend that I'd pay for everything so long as someone sensible was in charge and after a long argument he suggested you. Of course, monsieur – I mean, Gregory – I was aware of your work in the area of the concert hall and the opera house. This is totally different, I know. And perhaps you think it beneath you?'

'Ah, now . . .' It was true that Gregory knew nothing about jazz. But he knew that some of his musical friends were extremely interested in it. Moreover, it so happened that he owned one single jazz record. It was of the great violinist Yehudi Menuhin improvising – jamming? – with Stéphane Grapelli of the famous Quintette. If someone whom he respected so greatly could take the time to make a recording with a jazz musician, surely a mere concert arranger ought to do what he could for this would-be jazz man?

'Let's talk about it. Can you explain exactly what you want me to do?'

'We have to find four instrumentalists to form the new "quintette". Gilles of course is the clarinettist. The most famous of the players in the original quintet were Stéphane Grapelli and Django Reinhardt—'

'Grapelli was a violinist—'

'And Reinhardt was a guitarist. However, Gilles is not trying to reproduce exactly the same ensemble. He . . . er . . . quite naturally he wants a group in which the clarinettist is important, so you and he would have to discuss what instruments to focus upon. But once you've agreed that, I want you to find the players, and I presume that has to be done through their agents?'

8

'Yes, I would imagine so.'

'So then comes the business side, what fees they're to have, how much per cent of the ticket sales, that kind of thing.'

'Yes.'

'I'd like you to supervise that. Gilles tends to get carried away over that sort of thing. Money no object – you understand what I mean, but of course once a business agent hears that Gilles's father is a banker, he might try some kiting, so I'd want you to use your head.'

'I understand.' This was all very intriguing to the Crown Prince, who had never heard the words 'Money no object' used in connection with any of his musical enterprises. He didn't say that he'd no idea how much a jazz player would expect. He was a fast learner, so he thought he'd be able to catch up on things like that. 'So I'm to discuss the make-up of the quintet with your son, and once he's decided on that I'm to hire musicians for him. And you'll make funds available?'

'Of course. Perhaps you'd like the two of us to draw up an agreement?'

'Wait,' said Gregory. 'I have commitments, Monsieur Guidon. Before I can throw myself into the project, I have to know the time scale. When would you expect me to begin on this?'

'Well . . . At once.'

'Ah. That might present difficulties.'

Guidon looked downcast. 'I . . . I would make it worth your while, Gregory.'

'Thank you. It's not the money, although of course that matters a lot. But I have clients who depend on me—'

'You have an assistant, though? I thought I was told you have an assistant?'

So the old fox had had enquiries made about him? Well, perhaps that was understandable. The anxious papa was about to invest what might be a considerable sum in the fantasies of his son. Naturally he'd want the man he appointed as overseer to have some resources.

'I have an assistant, yes, but she's only part-time.'

9

'You could perhaps extend her hours?'

'Well . . . that might be . . . I could discuss it with her . . .' He paused. 'Why the urgency?'

'Gilles wants to take part in next year's jazz festival.'

'Ah.' It was now October, a genial, warm October that made the citizens of Geneva feel they were still enjoying summer. The next festival in Montreux was in July, which allowed them eight months. Eight months to find the musicians, get them together often enough so that they developed a feel for group technique, to sign up suitable venues . . .

'I want him to do it,' said Guidon in something like desperation. 'He's frittering his life away. He goes through his work at the bank as if he's asleep, he spends half the night in his room listening to broadcast jazz music from here and there, he goes out to disreputable clubs to take part in impromptu performances . . . Really, Gregory, it's as if he's under a spell. My wife and I are extremely worried. We want to do something that could have a more or less immediate result.'

'Let me think about it,' said the Prince. 'It would mean reorganizing my own life for quite a time. And I have to point out to you again that I know nothing about jazz. It would really be better if you found someone who—'

'No, no, Gilles and I have been all through that. I can only go ahead with this idea if my son is in the hands of someone I consider dependable and that he considers acceptable. I beg you to take it on, sir. I . . . er . . . I would make sure you didn't suffer any financial problems.'

This, Gregory decided, was banker-speak for 'I'll see you make a good profit out of it.' Could he afford to turn the project down?

Between them, the Hirtensteins managed to make a decent income, but their various professions had their drawbacks. Ex-King Anton could only teach dressage if the roads were passable for the pupil's horse-box and sometimes snow caused difficulties. Ex-Queen Mother Nicoletta had to wait to be asked for her services as an interior decorator, and employment was intermittent. His own profession was subject to crisis – singers with sore throats, pianists with injured wrists, double-booking of halls by halfwit managers.

He thanked the banker for his assurances about money but persisted in saying he'd like some time to think it over. He wanted to ask his family what they thought. He and his host shook hands with a promise on Gregory's side to be in touch within a day or two.

At home that evening he recounted the conversation. Both his listeners were surprised, but his grandmother was immediately enthusiastic.

'Of course you must do it!' she cried. 'That family's so rich! And from what you say, they'll agree to almost any terms you like to put to them.'

'But, Grossmutti, what I don't know about jazz would fill an encyclopaedia.'

'Hm, hm,' his father said. 'It's rather vulgar, isn't it?' He looked into his glass of wine, searching his memory. '"Rooty-ti-toot, three times she shoot . . . " Er . . . I forget the rest.'

'I'm surprised you know even that,' Gregory said, hiding a grin. 'What opus does that come from?'

'I seem to remember it's from a song called "Frankie and Johnny" – the American cultural attaché used to have it on a record that he played for parties. Dear me, such a long time ago.'

'Who cares if it's vulgar?' cried Nicoletta. 'Greg isn't going to appear on stage singing it! You're going to be in the background, aren't you, my love, arranging the venues and talking about contracts. And Auguste Guidon is going to pay you an enormous fee for doing it, and he'll be in your debt for ever after because you'll have saved his darling son from wasting his life on all that nonsense.'

'Aha,' said her grandson. 'What if Gilles does so well that he leaves the bank and goes on tour with the band?'

'Nonsense. The son of a Swiss banker is never going to be any good at jazz. It requires soul, fervour, passion—'

'What makes you so suddenly an expert on jazz?'

The ex-Queen Mother of Hirtenstein was silent. Some fifty years ago, she had danced to American swing. Evenings when she had escaped the dullness of the little palace and with a companion – not her husband – had spent happy hours twirling and twining to the big-band sound . . .

By the end of the discussion it had been agreed that Gregory would talk to Amabelle to see if she could take over more of the office work. If she thought it possible he would then have a meeting with Gilles Guidon to find out what would be involved in finding his musicians. It had to be clear from the outset that Gregory knew nothing of the talent in that field, nor did he have any contacts.

He was reluctant about the whole thing. But there was a prospect of quite a lot of money – and his family needed that.

He telephoned his true love – so far away in London – that night to tell her the news. It gave Liz Blair a fit of the giggles. 'You're what? Getting involved with the City Stompers? Going to supervise performances of "The Darktown Strutters' Ball"? That will be fun!'

'Liz, don't. I'm really in two minds about it. I might back out if you make fun of me.'

'Now, now, don't be chicken. You can do it. After all,' she conjectured, 'you know how to handle agents and artists. The jazz community should be a lot less intelligent than opera-house managers.'

'You think so?'

'Oh, of course. They're always either drunk or stoned, from what I hear.'

'Liz!' He pictured her as he thought about what she said: fairish brown hair tied back from her face gleaming with nourishing cream, hazel eyes sparkling with amusement, that delightful body in some version of nightwear which – he knew from experience – could be either a T-shirt and bikini bottom or a filmy lace-trimmed gown.

'Well, even if they're sober and in their right minds, you can do it,' she said. 'It's just a harmless business venture, after all. Nothing to it.'

As it turned out, she was quite wrong.

Two

Next morning he talked over the idea with Amabelle. He took a delicious cake with him to the office up the old stone staircase in the Rue Sarcat. It delighted her yet made her suspicious. 'What's this for?' she demanded.

She was a plump young widow with two children to bring up. She gave two days, sometimes three, to the work for the Hirtenstein Agency, the hours arranged so that she could always fetch her son and daughter home from school. She was unassuming, efficient, and made good coffee.

This she now did, and they settled down to share the cake. He told her about the jazz project. Although at first she exclaimed in horror, she took to the idea a lot faster than he had. 'Guidon! Of course we must arrange to do it. One doesn't turn one's back on a man like Auguste Guidon! He knows all the best people, and his bank sponsors quite a few musical events.'

'But I can only do it if you take on ninety-nine per cent of the office work.'

'I worked that out already. OK.' She made rapid calculations with the calendar and her diary. She decided she could come in oftener and stay longer. 'And it's only for a few weeks, anyway, until you get this jazz band together for him . . .' Her voice died away. They both knew that musicians always took up more time than you thought they would.

'Well, let's hope so.'

'There are a few things on hand, I'll deal with those. Anything abnormal I'll call on you, and you must promise to keep your mobile switched on all the time.'

'Amabelle, you can't have your mobile switched on in a concert hall.'

13

'But you can if you're in a jazz club, because who'd know it wasn't part of the music?'

They had a little laugh at this sally, unaware that jazz fans can be as serious as Wagner enthusiasts. Greg was to learn things like this during his relationship with Gilles Guidon.

Which began that afternoon. He rang Papa Guidon to ask for the son's telephone number, was put through almost immediately to Gilles's office, and introduced himself.

'Oh, great to hear you! I really feel I know you already, of course, from school. *Le grand Grego* – there you were, ahead of me at La Sonnelle. Doing great things – much admired, I can tell you. I was so pleased when Papa told me you were considering our little plan. I hope you've decided to take it on, because if not, the whole thing—'

The Prince, taken aback at this flow of flattery, managed to catch a momentary pause for breath on the part of the speaker, and broke in. 'Yes. Thank you, so I'm ringing to ask when we might meet?'

'Oh, as soon as you like. Tomorrow, lunch? Or this evening – but of course you won't be free, busy as you are, although it would be nice—'

'Yes, yes, this evening – excellent – when and where?'

'Why don't you come to our little eyrie and I'll show you my "rag room". My equipment's all there – we can play some discs, give you some idea . . .'

The 'rag room' turned out to be the old stables of the Chateau Guidon. This was about halfway between Geneva and Montreux, on a steep slope northwest of Morges, about an hour's drive away. Greg knew the area and had passed the entrance to the place often enough to find it easily. But he was somewhat startled to be stopped a few yards in by gates and a speaker-phone. He announced himself and was asked to wait while the gates were electronically opened then closed behind him.

The length of the drive up to the house gave him the chance to admire the property. In the golden light of the westering sun, the hillside showed stands of pine and larch, silver-grey rocks, and the dark shadow of little gullies. There was a waterfall sparkling on the upper slopes. What it was to have big money, he reflected.

Gilles Guidon was waiting for him in the forecourt. The house wasn't really a castle, more a very large mansion that had been added to and altered as tastes changed and the family fortune increased. At some point one of the bankers had felt the need to rename the property, and a family with so much money and influence must be allowed such a harmless foible.

Gilles bounced up to the side of the Mercedes. 'So you found us! Great, brilliant, let's go to the rag room and we'll have a drink and get started on the planning. Papa agreed we could be informal tonight but at some other time he'd like to introduce you to Mama and show you round, if you'd like that. Here we go, through here, this arch is supposed to be the original for the coaches and carts before we had cars.'

Still babbling, he led the way from the forecourt, past the garages – which were extensive and presumably housed M. Guidon's collection of vintage cars – over a cobbled yard to some well-preserved stone buildings with the half-doors of horse stalls. Through one of these entrances Greg was now ushered, ready to undergo the chill and discomfort he found in his father's stables.

But no, the stalls had had their divisions removed, and had been linked together to give a large pleasant space, the stone walls painted white and adorned with posters and record covers, the lighting carefully designed to give the place a glow, warmth coming from efficient heating, and a big sound system and television taking up most of one side. The far end had a slightly raised platform, presumably for performances.

'Now, what can I offer you? Wine? Beer? Soft drink? Coffee? Got everything to hand, Nounou made us some sandwiches or I can ring for something hot if you'd prefer that, what about a Toggenburger, our cook does them with a special relish?'

'No, no, a sandwich will be fine. And coffee please, I have to drive home.'

'Of course, should've thought of that, coffee coming up

– please, sit, sit, push the cushions aside if you don't like them, Mama fusses about making the place comfortable so there's a bit of her touch here and there although she doesn't really like coming in here, too like living like a peasant although what peasant would have a hi-fi system like that, I ask you.'

He switched on a machine to make coffee, twitched a cover off a plate of substantial sandwiches with plenty of trimmings, and dragged a little table to the side of Greg's armchair.

'Now I want to get things straight about the kind of group I'm aiming at,' Gilles began. 'I think Papa told you I was trying to emulate the Quintette du Hot Club de France, but that's a fallacy, it just happened that I mentioned it to him when he said jazz was an American fad. I mean, of course everybody knows that there wasn't a clarinet in the quintet. It consisted of strings, you know – three guitars, a double bass and a violin.'

'Really?' Greg said, surprised. That was nothing like his idea of a jazz band. Trumpets . . . a saxophone . . . a drum kit . . . He was going to ask for more information but Gilles was surging on.

'I want my combo to have a woodwind sound. My clarinet, a bass clarinet, piano, double bass and sax. What do you think?'

'Bass clarinet? Can a bass clarinet play jazz?'

'Why not? A different sound . . . I can get an arranger to handle all that, but I didn't want to commit myself to it until I'd got the players. And that's where you come in, Monsieur Couronne. I've got some demos I'd like to play for you – some are audio only, some are videos. I want you to tell me what you think, and then when we've made a list I want you to go after them.'

'Go after them – in what sense? Where are they?'

'Oh, all over the place. But I want you to feel free to travel anywhere you fancy, Grego – I may call you Grego, mayn't I? I called you that at school.'

'Of course, please – but I must make it clear that I can't spend too much time on travelling. I gather that a lot of

16

jazzmen are American – I couldn't possibly spare the time to—'

'No, no, of course not, if you don't want to, that's fine, there are a lot working in Europe, there's a guy in Stockholm, for instance, but I don't think he'd want to join someone else's group, though never mind, there are a lot of good pianists and I'm sure we'll sort it out.'

It was a long evening. M. Couronne listened to jazz for the first time since he put away the record of Yehudi Menuhin and Stéphane Grapelli improvising. At the outset he was baffled. When he thought of 'variations' he thought of Bach and the Goldberg or Beethoven and the Diabelli. He thought of a plain statement of the theme and then clever versions of it in different keys, different rhythms. But on the discs and tapes that Gilles played, it was difficult to discern what the theme was at the outset, and sometimes even when the performance was halfway through.

It was a given that he knew nothing about jazz, but he knew many of the tunes that the bands were supposed to be playing. He heard them in sounds that drifted from speakers in department stores and hotels. 'Begin the Beguine', for instance. He could even sing the tune, if asked. But it took him until almost the last bar of one of Gilles's recordings before he caught the melody in it.

Well, he didn't have to be an expert on the music. Gilles would supply the expertise. He had to deal with the business side. He accepted from him a short list of fourteen, with marks against the names indicating which he thought the best. 'Start with Clifford,' he urged. 'I'd really like to get him. He's really good. He played with Stan Getz, you know, he's one of the best tenor-sax players around. He might need some persuading because he's been taking it a bit easy for the last couple of years, by all I hear. But the great thing about him, besides his playing, is he's black. I want the quintet to be ethnically varied, if you get my drift. So go and see him personally, so as to make sure of him.'

Wally Clifford lived in Bristol. M. Couronne saw himself flying to talk personally with him, journeying of course by way of London, where Liz Blair lived. A very invigorating

17

thought, but he felt obliged to say, 'But seeing people personally might cost a lot in fares—'

'Never mind that. Now that we know you're taking on the job, Papa has arranged for a contract to be delivered to your office in Geneva tomorrow. There's a monetary advance to pay for initial expenses, and Papa said to tell you that if you find the contractual terms of your engagement objectionable in any way, just let him know and he'll tell the legal boys to change them. OK? Is that all right?'

'I must say it's a very unusual and more than generous way of—'

'Yes, yes, the main thing is to get the ball rolling. I want us to be meeting and getting to know each other by the beginning of November, you know. We need to play together, catch each other's pulse, if you see what I mean. Get Clifford – he's important, he's got this sweet clean sound and I want him to be my shadow while I play clarinet. I need to learn how he thinks and feels. The pianist is important too. I'm not expecting you to get me an Art Tatum, but it's got to be somebody who has the lightest of touch, you understand, so as not to beat out the rhythm too hard although he's got to do that to some extent because we're not having drums, only double bass, as I expect you noticed.'

Still babbling, he accompanied Greg to his car and waved him off. 'Stay on message,' he was urging as the car moved away. 'Let me know if any of them are no-show, I'll suggest replacements . . .' The sound of his voice died. Grego waved out of the open window as he took the first turn in the long drive. The entry gates opened magically as he approached. The moon was bright on the country road. He felt cheerful and even enthusiastic. The madcap scheme would at least give him the chance to see Liz.

She gave a cry of delight when he telephoned to tell her his plans. 'Splendid, brilliant! When will you be here?'

'I'm going to ring this Clifford guy now. It's late but I imagine a jazz player would be up and about at midnight, wouldn't he?'

'He might be on stage, or wherever he plays.'

18

'Well, I've got his mobile number so I may get him during a break. I'll let you know. If he agrees, I plan to see him the day after tomorrow.'

'Lovely. A trip to Bristol. I'll look at the dress shops while you interview the jazz boy.'

Liz was a fashion consultant and designer for some well-known chain stores. She was one of those unprincipled persons who, managing to wheedle a ticket to a fashion launch, would ensure that copies of the best designs would be in High Street shop windows within a couple of weeks. She worked very hard, travelled a great deal, so that it was often difficult for the two of them to get together.

Moreover, the ex-Queen Mother disapproved of her absolutely. They had never met, and never would, if Nicoletta had her way. Nor must her grandson ever marry such a person. This was the great anxiety of Nicoletta's life, that darling Grego would be inveigled into going before a minister or a priest with that awful girl.

Darling Grego drove home so that he could make his long-distance telephone call. He might have tried to do it on his mobile while on his way, but the transmission could be dodgy in mountainous country. He found the old farmhouse silent, his father and grandmother both probably sound asleep. He went into his father's office, which was a little apart from the main house. He consulted the sheet of names and addresses and contact numbers supplied by Gilles Guidon, then rang Bristol in England.

The phone rang the other end some ten or eleven times. He was about to give up when a sleepy voice said: ''Lo?'

'Is that Wally Clifford?'

'Yes, 'tis. Who's this?'

'My name is Mr Crowne, I'm an agent in the music business.' Quite true, but not the branch of the business Clifford might expect. 'I thought I'd ring, Mr Clifford, to see if you could be free for a project I'm putting together.'

'You what?'

'A jazz group, to play in and around Geneva—'

'Geneva, Switzerland?'

'Yes, over the winter season, and then—'

'Is this some kind of a joke?'

'No, no, Mr Clifford—'

'What kind of an agent calls me Mr Clifford? Who're you?'

'I mentioned my name, I'm Gregory Crowne.' This was the name he used in English-speaking countries, so as to disguise the troublesome fact that he was an ex-royal. In French-speaking areas he used the name Couronne, in Germany he was Herr Krone, in Italy Signor Corona, and so on wherever it proved convenient. But Mr Crowne was the name he used most, because English was the most generally accepted language.

'Well, I never heard of you. You just setting up?'

'Er . . . yes . . . And I've got this proposition for a new group.'

'If this is one of Brunie Revelston's gags, it's not funny. I was sound asleep.'

'I'm sorry if I woke you, Mr Clifford, and it's not a gag.' He was going to say he didn't even know who Brunie Revelston was, but thought it might emphasize the fact that he knew nothing about the jazz world. 'Could I come and see you, to explain it properly?'

'Come and see me? Where're you at this moment?'

'I'm . . . er . . . in Geneva, but I'll be in London tomorrow and next day I could—'

'That's Thursday you mean? You'll be here Thursday?'

'If that would be convenient?'

'Must be important,' said Wally Clifford. 'OK, I'll be here, morning I mean, afternoon I'm rehearsing, evening I'll be at the club, what time you thinking of?'

'Let's say, about noon?'

'About noon. Just to be clear, you sure you're not somebody Brunie's talked into setting up a big take-in?'

'No, this is a genuine business scheme, Mr Clifford.'

'Oh, for Pete's sake, call me Wally, everybody does. So you'll be here about midday, yeah? You know how to get here? You driving?'

'No, I'll be coming by train. And I've got your address so I can take a taxi from the station.'

'Okey-doke, Mr Crowne, noon Thursday, I'm writin' that in my memo book, my memory isn't what it used to be.'

'That's a date. See you Thursday. Goodbye.'

As he replaced the receiver, Mr Crowne had several thoughts. The first was that Wally was not, as he'd imagined, an American. The voice was English, with some faint regional accent that he didn't know although he had an acute ear for such things. The second thought was that Wally was not young. He'd thought he'd be speaking to an eager, twenty-five-ish African-American. Instead he'd heard this fifty-ish, wary Englishman.

When he mentioned it next day to Liz, she shook her head. 'You just told me he played with Stan Getz. He couldn't be in his twenties, Greg.'

'You know the name Stan Getz?'

'Well, of course. "The Girl from Ipanema" – you know that, don't you?'

His Highness looked baffled.

'Oh, goodness, everybody knows that song. It's been around forever. And I'm pretty sure he wrote it – Getz, I mean. You hear it played for dancing, Latin American sort of thing, and I think he – Getz – was around in the Eighties or thereabouts.'

'So if Wally Clifford played in his band, say at twenty, and that was in the Eighties, that would make him—'

'Well, he's no teenager. Does it matter?'

'I've no idea,' said Greg, with a shrug and a sigh. 'Gilles asked me to hire him, and that's what I'm trying to do. What's that English saying about a pig in a bag?'

'A pig in a poke – yes. How many other pigs do you have to contact?'

'Well, I did some telephoning today before I left for the airport, and Amabelle's doing the rest. So far I've got appointments with five – the next one's in Cologne, I'll do that on my way home.'

'Cologne! Is there jazz in Cologne?'

'Seems so. There's another one in Germany, in Stuttgart.

21

I've contacted a pianist in Stockholm, but he's coming to
see me, not the other way round – it's like playing chess,
you've got to keep your eye on all the pieces.'

A very lucrative chess game. When he'd read the terms
of the contract from Auguste Guidon that morning he'd expe-
rienced something like euphoria. For a short moment he'd
felt envy about the jazz scene, on the supposition that agents
for jazz men always got terms like this. Then common sense
reasserted itself. This kind of money surely didn't come with
little groups of musicians playing in smoky late-night venues.
No, the money came from the Famille Guidon, and long
might it continue to do so.

Since it was growing late, he and Liz went out to eat. And
so to bed, as the great English diarist was fond of saying.

Bristol next day was shining in an autumn glow. Coming out
of Temple Meads Station, Greg was agreeably surprised. Liz,
in boot-cut jeans and a sweater that matched her brownish-
gold hair, was ready for a busy morning in the city she knew
well. She headed them off in a taxi towards the shopping
streets, then dropped a kiss on his head before getting out.
'So you'll get away from this Woolly—'

'Wally . . .'

'When? Let's say we meet around one o'clock. You don't
know your way about so head for the Theatre Royal. I know
a nice little restaurant near there.'

'Yes, dear,' said His Highness in a tone of obedience.

She laughed and waved him away.

The taxi man headed out of the city centre towards what
became a refurbished area where industry had once flour-
ished. Wally's address proved to be a renovated factory. There
was an immediate response when he pressed the button on
the entry-phone, then Wally came down himself to greet him.
'I'm top floor. Practice, you know – the sound drifts away
over the roofs without getting anybody in a fret.' They
entered a lift, he pressed buttons, and they glided upwards.
'So. You're from Switzerland, right?'

'Yes. Geneva.'

'I played once at the Montreux Festival. I didn't much like

it then but I think I've slowed down a lot now. Appreciate the quiet things more. Here we are.'

His flat was essentially one huge room. The developer had ensured there was a sleeping area on a little gallery, and the necessary cooking and bathing facilities in a block in one corner. Wally had done almost nothing by way of interior decoration except to hang up some posters and a collection of rather battered musical instruments. On a cabinet along one wall were those that presumably he used now – saxophones of various types, which Greg took to be tenor, alto, perhaps bass.

'I've got coffee going. Want some? Or I've got whisky or the local brew—'

'No, no thanks, I'm meeting someone for lunch by and by. Let me explain why I'm here.' He gave a short account of Gilles Guidon's ambition, acknowledged that he was only the business agent, and waited for a reaction. Wally Clifford didn't exclaim, 'My God, Guidon the banker?' In fact, he seemed never to have heard of him, and fell into deep thought.

Then he said, 'I've got to be straight with you. That's part of the treatment. It's like this, Mr Crowne. I'm an alcoholic.' He waited for a reaction and when the Prince merely nodded for him to go on he said, 'Well, that usually puts folk right off. So we're doing good so far. I been sober now two years. Never ventured too far from home in that time 'cos I get nervous, you know? But this guy you're fronting for, he's got a good idea there. I'd like to be part of it. What do I have to do next?'

'Well, Gilles wants to have a gathering at his home, he's got a big apartment where he can make as much noise as he likes so he's planning to have a session or two there, see who would fit and who wouldn't. Do you think you'd like to make the trip, try it out?'

'How much would it cost?'

'Oh, all expenses paid, Wally.'

There followed exclamations of surprise, and then pleasure at the thought of having decent financial terms for once. Wally agreed he would make the trip to Geneva. 'Let's say

23

next Monday morning. I'm playing at the Swannee Club Friday, Saturday and Sunday, but I can take a plane straight from the club, get a real early-morning start. No problem about the Swannee getting a replacement, they're queuing up to play there. Can you arrange for somebody to meet me at the airport? I don't speak the lingo, you know.'

Greg forbore to say that almost anyone at the airport would be able to speak English, and agreed to meet him. When he met Liz for lunch he was able to report that he'd scored on the first attempt.

Eight days of strenuous negotiation and travel found nine musicians installed as guests in a wing of the Chateau Guidon. Greg withdrew to let them come to terms with each other. For his part, he went to Montreux to see what kind of venues he could hire for next July. This proved tricky, because so far the band didn't even have a name and most of the best places were already booked. Moreover, M. Guidon had absolutely forbidden Greg to use his name so there was no chance of using that influence to persuade anyone.

With some half-promises given, he went home for the weekend. He was invited to the chateau on the Sunday, to hear how matters were progressing. Gilles was jubilant. 'We played every day for seven days. Egar Lotski backed out first, said he didn't like my kind of sound. I asked Joe Trigg to go because his piano style turned out to have turned a bit strident these days. Then Seymour Emeritt said he didn't think he wanted to play cool jazz and I couldn't persuade him to change his mind so he left. Then—'

After a long catalogue of problems, it turned out that Gilles had engaged Wally Clifford as sax player, Nils Peters as pianist, Emilio Mavez as clarinet, and François Sesillon as string bass. 'Early days as yet but I really like the sound we make. I'll be interested to hear what you think of it when we get together again.'

'Get together again? They've gone?'

'Oh, certainly – they had things to do at home before they could commit themselves to spending the winter here. Not Wally so much, he didn't really care about going home

24

because I gather he's got no family or anything. But he decided to split, go and visit a few old pals in Paris. They'll all be back by next Friday.'

In this Gilles was proved wrong. Word came through on Tuesday that Wally Clifford had fallen under a train at the Gare du Nord and was dead.

Three

The news came to them in a roundabout way. The police had found Wally's passport with his home address, so tried to contact someone there. Receiving no reply, they had contacted the Bristol force, who sent a constable to ask the neighbours. The constable learned that Wally kept himself pretty much to himself but played at a jazz club. There were only a few places in Bristol to try. Brunie Revelston, club owner, told him that Wally had gone abroad on some project and gave the name of the contact: the Hirtenstein Agency, Geneva.

'I always knew there was something fishy about that offer,' growled Brunie.

The constable relayed this remark to his sergeant, so that it eventually reached Geneva. The *inspecteur* of the local force in Geneva was horrified at the opinion. 'Fishy? The Crown Prince? Never!' All the same it was strange that M. Couronne should be having anything to do with a jazz-band player.

He went personally to M. Couronne's office to relay the news. He was surprised when it turned out to be true that the Prince was somehow involved. Being a very discreet officer, he kept his thoughts to himself.

Greg telephoned Gilles, who groaned and asked him to the Banque Guidon for a discussion. Greg found the entrance hall very impressive, walled with an amber-toned marble and furnished with an elderly receptionist in black jacket and striped trousers. 'Yes, Monsieur,' he said, 'M. Gilles is waiting for you in the small salon.'

The small salon was on the first floor and panelled in mahogany. Leather armchairs were dotted about with little tables at hand. A decanter of what looked like Madeira and glasses stood on an ornate buffet. An assistant arrived immediately with a silver stand holding cake and elaborate biscuits. Gilles came hurrying after him, his pale round face flushed with emotion.

His first words demonstrated the way he was feeling, and the order of his priorities. 'It means I'll have to find someone else . . .' Then, perhaps shocked at his own callousness, he asked, 'How did it happen?'

'The Paris police say he was dead drunk.'

'Drunk? But he was on the wagon. Had been for a couple of years, or so I heard. Otherwise I wouldn't have put him on my list.'

'You said he'd gone to Paris to meet with some old friends – people he'd played with in the past, I imagine?'

'Yes, he told me he wanted to spend a couple of days and then go home by Eurostar.'

'Do you know any of their names? Perhaps we could find out how he came to be drinking, if we contacted them.'

Gilles scribbled down a short list of four names on a pad in a silver case on one of the tables. He didn't have addresses but made a guess at the names of their agents. They spent half an hour while he lamented the problem that now faced him. 'We'd just begun to play ourselves in,' he explained. 'Now we'll have to start all over again – that's if we can find a replacement. I'll have to think about it. I'll let you have some ideas in a day or so—'

'Gilles, the man is still lying in a police mortuary. We have to do something about that.'

'Oh! Oh, yes of course – well, those names I gave you – get one of them to see about a funeral, OK?

But none of them wanted to take on the task. When he asked them what had started Wally drinking again, they declared themselves to be mystified. 'Sure, yes, we had a long talk, he was thrilled to bits at getting a start with a new band.' Everyone denied that he'd been drinking.

In the end Greg got in touch with Brunie Revelston, who agreed to see to a decent burial in Wally's home town. 'All the boys will turn up for it, I'll see to that,' he said mournfully. 'Poor old Wal . . .'

The news of the death made a small item in the arts and entertainment section of the Paris weekend papers. On Sunday morning when Gregory called up the phone messages from his office, he found one from a stranger, Lou Ferigiano. The name suggested an Italian but the message was in English and the voice was American – Philadelphia, thought Greg, who was fairly good at guessing such things.

'Say, Mr Crowne, I checked with Brunie in Bristol after I saw that bit in the press about Wally. That's really rotten, isn't it? Wally was here with me for a bit, said he was off to the Gare du Nord. Call me, will you? I might be able to straighten out a few things.' A number for somewhere in the 13th arrondissement followed.

Greg rang back at once. After a slight delay, a woman's voice answered. ''Lo?'

'This is Gregory Crowne here. I'm ringing back for Lou Ferigiano?'

'Oh. Sure. Just a minute.' Then, off the receiver: 'Louie! Louie, that guy in Geneva.' Then to Gregory, 'He's coming.'

Her voice too was American. So this was probably Mr and Mrs Ferigiano from Philadelphia. After a pause, Lou himself spoke. 'Mr Crowne? Say, that was a quick comeback. Listen, Mr Crowne, I read the bit about Wally . . . Brunie said you're the guy at the agency that hired him – is that right?'

'Yes, on behalf of a client. You knew him well?'

'Oh, can't exactly say well.' There was a pause while he considered the point. 'See, he gave me some good pointers when we were playing for Pierre Vernon in Marseilles coupla years back. Called me to ask how I was doing, you get me? Wanted to know how his old pupil was getting along. So I asked him to drop by. A good guy, old Wal.'

'I only knew him slightly,' the Prince acknowledged. 'You say he was with you just before he set out for the station?'

'Yeah, sat for a bit, had a drink or two – when I got in touch with Brunie earlier this morning, he said he'd been dry for more than two years but I'd no idea about that.'

'When he left, he was drunk?'

'He was pretty much afloat when he got here. Didn't seem out of line to me cos he was drunk a lot in Marseilles. I poured him into a taxi and felt sure he'd sober up on the train to London. I'm sorry about that now.'

Gregory sighed. 'Not your fault,' he murmured. 'But when I spoke to him he was so . . . so firm and honest about his drinking, and I gather that while he was here with Gilles – that's the band-leader – he was fine.'

'Well, you know . . .'

'What?'

'It happens. Guys fall off the wagon sometimes when they come to a big challenge. And this was a big challenge for Wally, being away from his home in a foreign country, playing with a new band . . .'

'But he seemed so completely at ease with everything.'

'Yeah, yeah, what do I know – amateur psychologist. He just seemed to have the jitters about it. But say, Mr Crowne . . .'

'Yes?'

'This guy that's heading up the combo – Gilles?'

'Gilles Guidon.'

'Right. He's short of a sax player now. Right?'

Good heavens, thought Greg. One thing I'm learning about jazz men – they think about playing jazz before anything else. 'Yes, Gilles was asking me to think about finding a replacement.'

'Well . . . How about putting me in there? I'm pretty good, play tenor and alto and can do soprano if he needs that. And it so happens I don't have anything lined up at the moment – I'm booked for a gig in Lisbon in the spring but I could call that off if your guy is planning something permanent. Would you ask him?'

'Of course.' No harm in that, although Ferigiano's name hadn't figured on the original list. 'I'll let you know in a day or so.'

'Thanks a lot, Mr Crowne. Nice to talk to you.'

It seemed best to let Gilles know about this offer, so he rang him at the chateau. Gilles gave a cry of delight at hearing his voice. 'Oh, I was just going to ring you! Listen, Grego, can you come here at once?'

'What?'

'Come to lunch. We have a sort of family thing on a Sunday, very informal. Please come – there's a crisis here.'

'What sort of crisis?'

'Well, the women-folk have ganged up and are making life difficult and Papa is dithering and I'm not doing very well on my own and really it would be such a godsend if you could come and talk sense to them all—'

'Talk sense about what?'

'About going on with the festival plan.'

'Your parents want to cancel?'

'No, Papa is still in favour but he's being worn down. Listen I've got three men staying in the north wing who're expecting to play at Montreux next year, and how am I to face telling them that it's all going down the drain?'

Never mind Gilles and his reluctance to face them. Greg knew from experience how hard life could be for musicians. Some of the artists he engaged for his classical concerts and recitals were earning hardly more than a pittance. To have raised the hopes of these men and then to dash them would be cruel. He felt responsible for them because having found them and brought them together, they were now his clients.

'Right you are, I'll be there in about an hour,' he said.

He changed hastily from his working clothes – he'd been helping his father in the stables. Within fifteen minutes he was on the road. The November day was not welcoming, the mountains indistinct as ghosts in a light mist. There had been some snow earlier but it was melting: strange weather these days, snow was inconstant as a young lover and was breaking the hearts of the winter sports providers.

When he reached Chateau Guidon he found Gilles outside in a mouflon jacket, pacing nervously. 'I thought you'd be here ages ago,' he complained. 'Come along, we're in the morning room, let me take your coat, just leave the car, Roger will park it in the garage yard, it's sheltered there if it should snow, come along, they're waiting.'

Breathless and flustered, he urged his guest into the hall.

This was quite baronial in its appearance – chequered tiles on the floor, a chandelier overhead with many false candle-lights. Heavy dark bureaux and tables were arranged around the granite walls, most of them bearing pieces of china that the ex-Queen Mother Nicoletta would have loved to get her hands on. She generally had to use replicas for her more grandiose interior design schemes but these were clearly genuine.

Gilles led on through a drawing room with a great deal of ormolu and enough mirrors to cause eye-strain, round a turn in a corridor lined with family portraits, and into a large room with tremendously large windows and dotted about with tropical plants on wrought-iron stands.

Though he had described the gathering as 'a family thing, very informal', the Guidon idea of informality was somewhat glossy. There were five people in the room, taking their ease on rattan chairs and sipping aperitifs. Gilles ushered Greg forward for introductions. First, of course, came Mama, Mme Rosanne Guidon, clad in peach-velvet leisurewear but decked with a double row of pearls and earrings to match. She was a tiny figure, her face glowing with good cosmetic care, her blonde hair artfully careless.

Next came Mme Armonet, Auguste Guidon's widowed sister, in a dark green wool dress and black stockings, a rather sombre figure but impressive in her plump dignity. Last of the ladies was Nounou, former nurse to Auguste Guidon and then to Gilles, clad in black trousers and fine cashmere sweater lightened by a handsome gold brooch.

Auguste Guidon was already known to Greg. The other man in the room was introduced as 'Mama's private secretary, Sasha'. He shook hands gravely. A slight, dry-looking character, his age was difficult to guess but he was no longer exactly young. It became clear that Sasha's role was to act as barman. Greg opted for Campari, took a seat, went through the necessary small-talk about his drive to the chateau and weather conditions.

Everyone was determined to be easy and assured, yet there was an underlying tension. Greg soon identified the source. Gilles had said the 'women-folk' were ganging up, which he'd taken to mean Mme Guidon and her relatives. But it was Nounou who led the attack.

'This man who died, the Englishman,' she said. 'The police said he was drunk, no?'

'Yes, and I heard from one of his friends this morning that he was very much the worse for drink when he set off for the station that day.'

'Ha!' She gave a triumphant glare towards Gilles. 'And here they behave just the same, do you deny it, Gilles?'

'They like to relax after a hard session of practice—'

'My angel, they have no manners! Thank God we don't let them come into the rest of the house! Their clothes are dreadful, they ask for food at all hours of the day and night, they drive off to Montreux to drink themselves silly and they make such a terrible noise!'

It emerged that Nounou's apartment was in the north wing, her windows facing the old stable block. There was excellent soundproofing in Gilles's hideaway, but the rooms above, where the grooms used to live, were not proofed. Musicians practising alone in their rooms – the clarinettist, the bass-player, the tenor sax – undoubtedly made a sound that could reach Nounou. And of course, as might easily happen, they played late at night, at what she considered an unseemly hour.

She stated her objections forcibly. Mme Guidon supported her, though on less personal grounds. 'This man who fell on the railway line – you told us he was a recovered alcoholic, darling. But he lied to you, you see?'

'It's an omen!' cried Nounou. 'His death is a warning! The whole idea was wrong from the outset.'

'Excuse me, Nounou dear,' Auguste put in. 'You know I thought at the time that it was a good idea.' It was strange to hear this powerful man speaking so weakly to his old nurse.

'Yes and I told you, Augie, it would never work. My poor darling boy thinks he should be a public performer, and we have nothing against that, do we? An occasional appearance for charity – that would be fine. But these people – to acknowledge them as equals is disgraceful.'

'Nounou, they're fine musicians – aren't they, Greg?'

Greg was taken aback. 'I don't know,' he said, ashamed that he couldn't be more supportive. 'I've never heard them play except on your recordings. This man who telephoned this morning – I've never heard him at all.'

'Who telephoned this morning?' Gilles demanded.

'A saxophonist called Ferigiano – Lou Ferigiano. He rang to say he was probably the last person to see Wally Clifford the morning of the accident and that he was already drunk then.'

'He plays sax?' Gilles said eagerly.

'Yes, tenor and alto, and says he can play soprano if asked. Do you know him?'

'Can't say I do. I could look him up on the Internet—'

'Now, Gilles darling, there's no need to do that because we're deciding to drop the whole thing, now aren't we?'

'No, we're not, Nounou! Papa, don't let her seize control of this just because she doesn't like modern musicians!'

'Musicians? You call them musicians? They're just like those two you picked up last year in Interlaken – they're sponging off you, and you're letting them because they make you feel a big man.'

'Nounou,' said Auguste, 'you're going too far. They're not sponging off Gilles. I authorized the expenditure, and I'm sure M. Couronne here has taken care of all the business side in a very efficient manner—'

'And talking of that,' Gilles burst in, 'you can't just throw out a group of musicians like that as if they were empty bottles! They were told they'd get contracts – weren't they, Grego?'

'Yes, of course, and the contracts are in my office at this moment waiting to be signed,' Greg agreed. He felt he must stand up for his clients. He had been asked to find these players, had made them promises that he thought would be fulfilled, and he wasn't about to let them be dismissed just because a cranky old lady didn't like them. The contracts would have been signed on Friday, but everything had been thrown into confusion by the death of Wally Clifford.

'Contracts,' sighed Auguste. 'But unsigned . . .'

'There could be a case of bad faith,' said Greg at once. He wasn't about to let him wriggle out on grounds like that. 'I'm sure you wouldn't want your name connected with anything so damaging, Auguste.'

Auguste's face clouded at the words. Bad faith was not a term that any Swiss banker liked to hear.

At that moment a little team of servants came in, bearing covered dishes which they placed on a long side table. Lunch was served. Business discussion was for the moment suspended.

Once they had chosen what they wanted, the group settled down around a large circular table already laid with cutlery and glasses. One of the servants hovered to pour wine or mineral water but disappeared at a wave of the hand from Mme Guidon. Conversation became polite again, as required by good manners – no spoiling good food with serious business discussion. They chatted about the lack of snow this year, then last night's television programmes.

Gilles ate quickly then rose. 'I'll go and see if I can find a Web page for Ferigiano,' he said.

'My darling boy, why bother, since the whole thing is going to be dropped?' Nounou objected.

'Oh, really, Nounou,' Gilles exclaimed, 'just because you feel they're a nuisance—'

'Please, no raised voices,' said his mother. She glanced at the old nursemaid. 'Let him find out what he can about this new man, dear. There's no harm in that.'

'Mph,' sniffed Nounou.

Gilles hurried out. The others finished their meal, the conversation dying away as anxious glances were cast towards Auguste. It seemed to Greg that they were wondering if he would stand up to the old termagant. Those remaining around the lunch table seemed mostly hoping to bid a fond farewell to the jazz band.

'Perhaps you'd like to see my cars?' Auguste suggested. 'I believe I told you – I've got some quite interesting specimens. This way.'

Greg rose, understanding that they were now about to have a chat free from the interruptions of Nounou. He suppressed a smile. What would the financial world think if they knew that M. Guidon, President of the Banque Guidon, took pains not to annoy his old nurse? And that, moreover, she addressed him as Augie?

They went along a corridor and eventually down a stone staircase to the outside. The vintage cars were housed in a part of the new garage, with a plate-glass wall allowing them to be viewed from the main division where about half a dozen expensive modern cars were kept. Auguste pressed a button that caused small spotlights to illuminate the vehicles.

'That's my favourite,' he said, pointing to a red Peugeot Bebe. 'The Lanchester is new, I bought it at auction last year.' But he wasn't really interested in the cars. He paused then went on, 'You can't really mean you would accuse me of bad faith in the contracts for the musicians?'

'Certainly,' the Prince said in a non-aggressive tone.

'Good heavens, boy, don't you think we bankers have enough problems these days without silly accusations like that? What with the American crime-prevention procedures and the reparations we had to make to World War II clients ... You surely know the American Drug Enforcement Agency insists we notify any large movements in the accounts of private clients – it causes endless trouble – and then there are the takeover bids!'

The head of the Banque Guidon stopped, a little red in the face and ashamed of himself. 'I'm sorry,' he muttered. 'You're not to blame for the world's financial muddles.'

'I know there are problems,' said Greg. 'I read the financial columns. But all the same, I have to protect my clients' interests. Performing musicians have a very hard life, Auguste. You asked me to find and engage these men, and although the papers haven't been signed, there is an oral contract between myself and those three. I'd feel obliged to honour it. And the only way I could do that is by calling on the contract you made with me, promising to meet all fees and expenses.'

'But if I met all the financial terms—'

'There's still the matter of damage to their reputation, engagements lost through coming to the chateau to get the band started, disappointment over losing the chance to play at Montreux—'

'Hm,' interrupted Auguste. 'You're a stiffer opponent than I quite imagined . . .' He took a few paces along the glass wall, head bent, deep in thought. 'What do you think about the idea of a replacement for M. Clifford? I had thought that his death would put an end to the whole scheme.'

This was what Greg had been waiting for. The antagonism of the women of the household weighed heavily on the banker. 'I quite understand that Mme Guidon is against the project. The other ladies too.'

'Oh, you've no idea . . . I could perhaps win over Rosanne, and my sister always follows where Rosanne leads. But Nounou . . .'

'A very forceful old lady.'

'You've no idea! My dear boy, I owe my life to Nounou,' murmured Auguste. 'You might not think so to look at me now, but I was a very delicate child. Nounou was my nurse. She was assistant nursemaid in my father's boyhood when the household was much larger – my grandfather had relatives living here, cousins with young children – you're perhaps aware how it used to be in Swiss households.'

The Prince nodded. He realized that Guidon had forgotten he didn't come from some old Swiss family, that his origins were in a little kingdom now changed into a republic.

'Nounou came to the chateau at sixteen to do the menial tasks of the nursery under the command of an English nanny. And by and by, when the cousins and nieces and nephews dispersed and the English nanny had gone home, she was kept on because my grandmother had taken a fancy to her. Then when my father married, Nounou was already there, so I was put into her charge.'

He tilted his head to look at Greg and smiled in apology. 'Old family tales, huh? But they're important. It seems I nearly died of pneumonia one dreadful winter, and she sat up with me night and day. The fact that I'm still here is all thanks to her. So I could never . . . you know . . .' He tailed off, his thoughts far back in his past.

'But although she dislikes the presence of the musicians, she agreed in the first place to have them here, surely?' queried Greg.

'Oh yes. Even with some enthusiasm. She adores Gilles, you see, and she thought my scheme to bring him to his senses was excellent. It's just that I don't think she'd realized what a difference it would make to our circumstances – to her circumstances.'

'So what does she suggest as an alternative if you were to cancel the whole thing now? How would she deal with Gilles's reaction?'

'How do you mean?'

'Gilles would be devastated.'

'Oh yes. Yes, I don't want to think about that.' It was clear Guidon hadn't thought that far in this master-plan of his.

'Would Nounou be happy to see Gilles so unhappy?'

'Oh, dear Heaven,' cried Auguste, clutching his forehead. 'I don't know what he might do! I promised him this chance.'

'So don't you think it makes more sense to go on if that's possible, and do what you can to mollify Nounou?'

'Mollify Nounou . . . It's the noise that upsets her.' He thought about it. 'I could offer to move her to another apartment, perhaps . . . She's been in those two rooms for the last ten years or so, but she's always rather fancied one of the guest sets, the one that has a view of the Col de Chaude.'

Greg said nothing, letting the idea settle itself into the banker's mind. After a pause, Auguste said, 'If he's suitable, this new fellow . . . you recommend that we go on with the plan?'

'If you're asking me whether he'd help to form a good jazz band, I told you at the outset that I knew nothing about that, nor about the outlook for the band's success.'

'You must know that I don't want it to succeed,' groaned Auguste. 'I hoped that the news of Clifford's death would put an end to Gilles's foolish notions. Now there is this Ferigiano . . . And you know nothing about him?'

'He was a friend of Clifford's. He played with him in . . . I think he said Marseilles. That's all I know, except that his name wasn't on the list that Gilles gave me at first.'

'Which means what?'

'That Ferigiano wouldn't have been a first choice. It all depends on what might come from looking him up on the Net.'

Auguste sighed deeply. 'Let's go back upstairs—'

But before they could do so Gilles burst into the garage waving some sheets of paper. 'He's there, I've got a résumé of his career, he was with the Phillie Fantastics a couple of years ago, he's been playing at le Jalon in Paris recently, there's a picture of him with some of the boys, he's quite young, not more than thirty, seems to be me he could be an asset, what do you think?'

'My dear boy,' his father objected, 'you wouldn't think of engaging him just on his looks?'

'No, no, of course not, Papa, that would be stupid, of course I'll audition him but the Web page says he's based in Philadelphia. You've got a telephone number for him in Paris, Grego?'

'Yes, I've got it here.' He felt in his pocket. Gilles grabbed the slip of paper as if it were a lifeline.

'I'll go and ring him this very minute, set it up for tomorrow, you said he was free to take up a gig, didn't you, Grego?' Then with a glance at his father, 'Tomorrow evening, of course, after office hours – listen, Grego, can you meet him at the airport, bring him here? It would be better because of course I could be tied up at the bank, I hope you don't mind me asking you, and you could explain to him about the money side, that would be important to him and I want to get things going, no silly arguments about terms or anything like that, is that OK?'

Greg agreed to it without demur. If the project were to go ahead, he wanted his musicians – he thought of them as his protégés, his clients – to have proper financial terms, suitable contracts. The contracts were in fact already in existence.

He left after Gilles had made contact with Lou Ferigiano. It was arranged that Greg would meet his plane at Cornavin next day. He drove home through a murky twilight wondering if tomorrow the band members – which might then include the new man – would actually be signed up.

Next day he spent at his office in Geneva. At mid-afternoon he drove to the airport. By the time the flight landed and the passengers had passed through the formalities the November evening was closing in. There had been a little more snow, touching trees and roofs with a chilly gleam. He stood in the arrivals hall holding up a placard produced by the office printer, giving his name in large letters.

A tall young man in jeans and a bomber jacket hesitated then raised a hand in greeting.

'Monsieur Ferigiano?'

'Yes, glad to meet you. And this is my sister Morena.'

Behind him came a girl in a form-fitting coat of dusky pink suede. Beneath it emerged long legs in black lace tights. Her feet were in little ankle boots that came from the belle époque. Her black hair was swept back in a ponytail held by a gold clasp. But any notes on her fashion statement were forgotten when Greg saw her face. She was one of the most beautiful women he'd ever seen, her face like something painted by Giotto.

They all shook hands, then Greg gave instructions to the porter to take out the luggage – several instrument cases and two very large suitcases. Morena Ferigiano paused, perhaps in dismay at the sight of snow out on the car park, but perhaps at the elderly Mercedes. She shivered.

'Gee, it's cold!'

'I'm afraid so. I hope you've packed some sweaters.'

'I told you, Sis! People come here for winter sports, you know!'

He got them settled, the brother at his side and the sister in the comfort of the back with a travel rug for her lacily clad legs. 'Is it far, this castle?'

'About an hour away. Don't worry, it's got central heating everywhere and it's not one of those dungeons-and-dragons places. How was your flight?'

They chatted as they made their way up into the high ground where the snow was more visible and extensive. Lou

Ferigiano wanted to know about the other players in the group, how much had they rehearsed, what were their show-pieces. The girl said less. The Prince was longing to ask what on earth she was doing there in the first place, but felt this wasn't the time.

Gilles was dancing about with impatience on the forecourt as they drove up. 'Hello, hello, welcome to Chateau Guidon, how are you, did you eat on the plane, I've got some food ready to bring in if you're hungry, I'm Gilles Guidon of course, your host, so this is who? – your sister? Well, I must say . . .'

He took Morena's hand in both of his as a gesture of welcome then stared at her in wonder. He had to look up ever so slightly, because she was a few centimetres taller. The light from the chateau's wide doorway shone on her face. It shone on her lustrous hair, lit up her wide smiling lips.

'This is an unexpected pleasure,' Gilles said.

And from the shortness of the sentence and the tone of his voice, Greg understood that the son of the house was ready to fall in love with Morena Ferigiano.

Four

It seemed that the rest of the band was equally likely to fall in love. They greeted the newcomers with enthusiasm, although rushing to help Morena off with her coat rather than carrying in Lou's instrument cases.

Morena was revealed in a black jersey dress, long-sleeved, high-necked, and quite loose. Yet somehow it hinted at a rich and supple body inside. Lou by contrast was very workaday, almost like a trucker or a boxer in his jeans and polo-necked sweater.

Gilles offered food again but Lou shook his head. 'You gonna ask me to play, right? I'd rather eat after, if you don't mind, I never like to eat just before a session.'

'Right, of course, just as you say,' burbled Gilles. 'So would you like to warm up? How about it, boys?'

The other players looked willing, drifted towards instruments propped on chairs. Lou went to the cases left by the door. 'What d'ya want to hear? Tenor? Alto?'

'Let's hear you on tenor,' suggested Nils Peters, the group's pianist. 'Wally played tenor mostly.'

There was a moment's silence at the mention of the dead man's name, then they all seemed to shrug and decide to get on with things. Lou snapped open the case of his tenor saxophone. The men settled on chairs. They were loosely gathered, not using the platform at the end of the room as if performing.

Nils, fingers on the piano keyboard, seemed to be leader for the moment. 'What's it to be?'

'I thought – how about "Night Stick" – you know it?'

They all nodded. That's to say, except the Prince, who'd never heard of this near-classic by the great Duke Ellington.

41

Morena, sitting nearby in one of the armchairs, came to his aid. 'Louie likes these oldies. Started with a group back home that specialized in Ellington and Basie and those guys.' She fell silent as Nils played a few introductory notes and her brother began to play.

He started softly, with a quick run of notes like a rivulet. But soon his tone increased, and though the room was large the sound seemed to fill it. Greg began to have a certain sympathy with Nounou.

He couldn't claim to love the saxophone in the first place – there were very few items featuring the instrument in the classical music repertoire that was his natural domain. And although the player was clearly expert, he seemed to enjoy what Greg felt were meaningless runs and decorations.

But then he was here to demonstrate what an expert he was, and he was succeeding. One by one the other players joined in, making a firm melodic and rhythmic background for the soloist in a way that could only rouse Greg's admiration. When they sensed that Lou was coming to his finale, they joined in with a triumphant final discord that was their sign of approval.

'Not bad,' said Gilles. 'Not bad for a first run. Let's play something really slow . . . We were trying out an arrangement for "Blues in the Night", Lou – do you know it?'

'Sure.'

'I'll take the front with this. Can you shadow me in a pick-up like a sort of duet?'

'Can try. You're the main solo, then?'

'Yes, but you can feature in the second chorus.'

'Oka-ay . . .'

Nils played a few opening chords in the key of A flat, then began the melody with Gilles. It proved to be a moody, slow tune that Greg was able to pick out for almost six bars before it vanished in the ornamentation of Gilles's clarinet. Then Lou joined in, a soft shadow in the same key but playing out of step with Gilles's rhythm.

It was clever, no doubt of that. And Greg could feel only admiration for the ability of the players – to be so quickly at one with each other in doing what was completely new to one of them. When Lou came to his solo, he went off in a mournful commentary of the original tune and quite lost Greg, but once again he was prepared to agree it was excellent playing.

'Right, right, good, what do you say, guys?' Gilles asked when the piece ended.

'Not bad, the child's got the message.' This was François Sesillon, the string bass player. He spoke idiomatic English with a very strong French accent. ' You played with Vernon in Marseilles?'

'Yeah, d'you know him?'

François shrugged. 'Never been to Marseilles, I don't like the south. I hear he's good, though.'

'Oh yeah, I learned a lot there. Starting the way I did – with a combo that was looking back to the oldies – it was called the Phillie Fantastics, can you imagine? – I needed someone to sort of kick me into the new scene. That's my aim now, to go forward more, not look back to the greats, although of course they're . . . well . . . great, of course.'

It struck the Prince that this prospective member of the band wasn't perhaps a great brain. He seemed to have difficulty putting thoughts into words, and then when he did the thoughts weren't exactly interesting. The other instrumentalists seemed to think he played well, and Gilles was making approving noises. He asked if Lou could join them at once.

'Oh, sure, we were hoping for that, weren't we, Sis? Sure, delighted to have a part in things here. So can you recommend some decent hotel?'

'Oh, you'll be staying here. They all do, don't you, boys?' The others laughed and agreed. 'It's OK here, I think you'll find, Lou. Greg will tell you the conditions are pretty good, and you won't disagree with the money arrangement either. So is that all right for you, you'll be staying at the chateau?'

'Well, yeah . . .' Lou seemed to have a problem with the idea. After a moment he said in a very plaintive tone, 'But what about Morena?'

It was clear Gilles was about to ask, 'What about her?' but pulled himself up. He was quicker on the uptake than his new instrumentalist. 'She isn't going back to Paris?'

'Well, no . . . See, the owner of le Jalon was practically stalking her – I had to bust him on the nose, which is why I was out of a job. She can't go back there. Besides, we gave up the apartment . . .' He gazed at Gilles like a puppy asking for a bone.

Gilles was at a loss. The others, however, immediately had a good idea. 'She could stay here, Gilles!' 'Why not let her stay with us?' 'There's one of those dinky rooms right next to me, she's welcome there!'

Gilles's face lit up, and then went murky. He pulled up his shoulders in a protective shrug. Greg guessed at once that he was thinking about Nounou. 'I . . . er . . . my family . . . you know, one girl among so many men . . .'

'Ah, it's the delightful old family retainer,' said Nils Peters in his perfect English. 'She would cause a fuss, is that it?'

'No, of course not, it's nothing to do with—'

'She's a bad-tempered old witch,' Nils rejoined. 'But if we all confront her as a group, she'll have to give in.'

'Yes, all for one and one for all,' contributed François, twirling his hand in the air like a musketeer about to bow.

'Call her on your magical communications system and tell her you want to speak to her.'

'Call her?'

'Yes, ask her to join us for a chat.'

His reluctance was almost visible, like a grey cloud resting on his forehead. But all the others were looking at him in expectation and so Gilles felt he had to make a show of dominance. He went to the telephone on a nearby desk. He pressed a sequence of buttons and after a slight pause said: 'Nounou, it's me. I wonder if you would come to the rag room for a few minutes?'

The reply must have been a surprised objection, because he went on, 'It's a matter of accommodation. We have an unexpected guest . . . No, a young lady . . .'

The response this time must have been unfriendly because he had the sense to switch to Romansch when he began again. Romansch is one of the four official languages of Switzerland but is seldom heard by visitors. The others were at a loss, but Greg listened with interest while Gilles tried to explain the situation and persuade Nounou to come.

'But she's here now . . . No, with her brother . . . We have plenty of room, Nounou! . . . Well, that's very unchristian . . .'

In the end, he prevailed. He replaced the receiver. 'She'll be here in a minute. She's very old, you know . . . set in her ways . . .'

No one challenged him as to why this old ex-servant should be so formidable to him. Morena said in a gentle murmur, 'Gee, I don't want to be any trouble,' but was hushed to silence by the others. François offered coffee, pouring it from the big thermos jug. Nils let his hands stray over the keys, producing a faint, comforting sound.

Nounou came surging in about five minutes later, frowning in disapproval. She was wearing outdoor boots and a padded jacket over a rather fine chenille dress. Her iron-grey hair seemed to bristle with the energy of battle.

'Nounou, this is Morena Ferigiano, and her brother Lou, who's going to be a member of the band. And Morena is going to stay—'

'That is quite out of the question! A young woman alone in this gang? Where is your moral sense, Gilles?'

'Madame, you misjudge us,' protested François Sesillon. 'She's the sister of a colleague.'

'Huh! When has that ever stopped a man from misbehaving? You must think I'm senile, young man!'

'But, Nounou, she has nowhere to go.'

'There are plenty of hotels in Montreux.'

'But that's a long way from her brother.'

'Well, she should have thought of that before she came.'

'But she had to come, Nounou – there was a man in Paris who was bothering her.'

'So isn't that just what I was saying? Men are like that.'

Emilio Mavez, the group's clarinettist, spoke for the first time. 'You are a very hard-hearted person,' he said with great solemnity. 'No woman in my family would ever turn away a guest with cruel words.'

Nounou glared at him. But then the colour in her rosy cheeks seemed to deepen. She blew out a breath. After a

45

moment she said: 'She can't stay among these men in the stable block. That's out of the question.'

'In the house, then, Nounou,' suggested Gilles, full of hope.

She hesitated then nodded. 'She can have my old rooms,' she said, adding with suppressed satisfaction, 'They face the stable block. I hope you don't mind being wakened in the dead of night by hideous noises!'

Morena uttered a muffled 'Thank you.' Nounou nodded at her then turned to the door.

'I'll see to it,' she said, and stamped out.

She probably heard the cheer that went up on her departure. Greg sighed inwardly. No wonder Gilles was so determined to try for a career that would take him away from Chateau Guidon. He must feel that he was fighting for his life against this bossy old woman.

Everyone crowded round Morena, patting her on the back or trying to shake hands. Gilles was pleased yet perplexed.

'You're going to find it terribly dull here, Morena. It's a long way from any activity – not like Paris at all, I'm afraid.'

'Well, say, listen,' said Lou. 'We were wondering, me and Morena . . . You got a vocalist?'

'What?'

'Anybody take the vocal if you play a song?'

'Well . . . no . . .'

'Morena sings.'

There was a little silence. Greg took it to mean that they'd never wanted a singer, that they had decided to offer only instrumental jazz.

'She and I used to do a coupla numbers at le Jalon – went down pretty good. We wondered if you could use her, eh?'

Gilles looked at his band. There was a hesitation, a moment when they tried to weigh up the consequence if they changed. Greg imagined that perhaps vocalists were a nuisance, or were apt to be vain, or some such objection.

But then Emilio said in his grave way, 'We could at least give a try-out, my friends, no?'

The others murmured agreement. Perhaps they felt that after being critical of Nounou's manners, they ought not to fall short themselves. Morena smiled and moved towards the piano. 'May I?' she asked, looking at Nils.

He was taken aback for a moment. The piano was his preserve. But she was waiting for his permission in a very charming way, so he bowed and waved her towards the piano stool.

She sat down, made herself comfortable by the usual twists of the knobs of the stool, tried a few chords on the keyboard, then began to play the introduction. Her brother stood by with his saxophone hanging round his neck untouched.

The song appeared to be a humorous dialogue between a boy and a girl. The girl kept saying she ought to leave, the boy kept telling her it was cold outside. Morena took the part of the girl, singing in a throaty, easy voice that – to Greg's ear – had had no training, her brother took the part of the boy in what was more or less a croak, but added to the humour.

When Morena started the second verse, her brother took the sax in his hands and instead of singing, began to play a little variation of the tune he'd sung for the response. It had a charm, a novelty that made a good impression. By and by the others, having picked up the melody, began to weave a gentle background to the duettists. When they finished they gave each other a little round of applause.

'What a talented family!' laughed François.

'Thank you.' She smiled and made a pretentious bow.

'Anything else?' asked Gilles eagerly. 'I mean, we couldn't make a programme with just one song, and of course you'd have to understand this is really an instrumental combo, we would never go big on the vocals, but a couple in a programme of, say, two sets wouldn't be bad, and it's different, we could play good variation while you sang pretty straight – what do you think, fellows?'

'I can do about ten or a dozen, most of them on my own but Louie can work up a jazz background if that's what you like. How about I play you one I do as a single. This is "Ain't We Got Fun?" – do you know it?'

Only her brother nodded. The others hung around the piano to listen. She played a tune in four-four time, then began to

47

sing. At the chorus words, 'Ain't we got fun?' the others began to join in.

The Prince didn't join in. He stood back, observing. In a way Nounou was right. The men were flattering the girl, wanting her to stay, wanting her to be a part of their life for the moment – and viewed dispassionately, she didn't really fit in.

Greg had heard this kind of singing in many a late-night session, when he relaxed after a concert or a recital with one of his clients. Cocktail-lounge music, to be found particularly in American cities, intended to be a pleasant background to end-of-the-day conversation and a quiet drink. He was no expert, but he was pretty sure that she wasn't a jazz singer. She'd need a mike, he thought. A nice enough voice, but not strong.

But she was lovely to look at, her style was full of charm, and they all liked her. So she was going to be hired, and tomorrow when he brought the contracts, he'd probably be bringing one for Morena Ferigiano.

Gilles and his band were milling about, clapping each other on the back and making suggestions on how to include the newcomers in their programme. It was still only mid-evening; if he left now, Greg thought he could get some work done for some of his other clients. He moved towards the door, waving a farewell to Gilles, who held up a hand, signalling, 'Wait.'

'Listen, guys,' he said, 'I'll call up for some food to be sent over, yes? And we can sit around and have a long talk. What shall I order? And listen, Morena, I'll arrange for your luggage to be taken into the house.' There was a hubbub of suggestions. After a few minutes Gilles picked up the phone to give instructions. Then he joined Greg at the door and went out with him.

'I think that pair will be a really excellent addition, don't you? So lucky, to find them just when we need them, and of course I'm sad we lost Wally but here was somebody almost on our doorstep, you might say. It's a marvellous bit of luck, don't you think?'

'Don't ask me,' said Greg. 'But I thought he seemed very expert?'

'Oh, quite – filigree fingers! He's no Coltrane, I suppose, and it's a pity he's not black . . . But he is American, which is the jazz homeland, and I wanted to include as many nationalities as possible and he's OK, yes, he's fine. And Morena is really something, isn't she? You know, there are critics who say that jazz is too masculine. I think it's a good idea, to have a girl in the band . . . well, we'll weave her in, it'll be interesting.'

'So shall I draw up a contract for her to bring with the others tomorrow?'

'Yes, why not.'

'But on what terms? She's not going to get the same as the instrumentalists, is she?'

'Ah . . . Well . . . Of course the others might say she's only going to do two numbers, three at most I suppose . . . What do you think? No, right, why am I asking you, you don't have any experience in this kind of thing. Well, right, OK, I'll have a chat with her about it, so if you leave the space blank on her contract then we can fill it in when we meet. And listen, Grego, I've had a really nice thought! It's so great to have found that pair and we're probably going to work hard at running in with the new sax tomorrow, so why don't we have a party?'

'If you like, Gilles.'

'I mean, not here, not in the rag room, but some less spartan locale, let's say for instance the Merveille, what do you think, we could sign the contracts there and have a proper meal together and a glass of champagne, eh? I'm sure my guys would like that, they go off on their own sometimes just to get a break, and it's true, what Nounou says, they tend to drink a bit too much if they do that, so this would be good, I think, more civilized. I'll set it up.'

The businesslike ending to this ramble told Greg that Gilles was determined to do it. He himself had no objection. It saved him a trip to the chateau, for the Merveille was a fashionable restaurant in Geneva. They agreed to foregather there at eight o'clock the next evening.

They had reached the Mercedes. He found that a servant was already wheeling the Ferigianos' luggage away. He allowed himself a moment to wonder how Morena would enjoy being in the bosom of the Guidon family but decided it wasn't any of his business. He drove off, his mind already dealing with the problem of a violinist in Bruges who needed an urgent repair to his instrument so that he could perform at the weekend.

When he got home, he used his father's office to do some telephoning on behalf of the damaged violin, then let its agonized owner know where and when the urgent repair could be carried out. He was about to dial the next business call when his mobile rang. Praying that it wouldn't be Gilles with yet more good ideas, he was delighted to find Liz Blair on the line.

'How are things on the Phillie Fantastic front?' she enquired after she'd greeted him with her usual mixture of love and mockery. 'Did the sax player measure up all right?'

'I gather he wants it forgotten that he ever played with a band called the Phillie Fantastics.'

'Well, that shows he's got sense, at least.'

'Mm . . . He doesn't seem too bright to me, but Gilles is absolutely delighted with him. And even more so with his sister.'

'His sister?' She was as astonished at this as he had been on first seeing her.

'He brought his sister with him. Morena – she plays the piano.'

'Just a minute, I thought you already had a pianist?'

'Yes, Nils, I rather think he's good although I don't know anything about how to play like that. But it's all right, Morena doesn't play jazz piano—'

'Oh, I see, she's not part of the band – just on a visit.'

'No, she's not on a visit, she's going to be the vocalist.'

'What? Just like that?'

'Seems so.'

'I didn't think he was going to have a vocalist, from what you said? A quintet, I thought it was to be.'

'Ah, there you are!' said Greg, with some amusement. 'Luckily Gilles hadn't decided on a name for the group, which I believe was going to be the Something-or-Other Quintet. I think it's going to have to be a sextet now.'

'Good gracious,' Liz said in a tone of moderate interest. 'She must be an awfully good singer to make him change his plans like that.'

'Well . . . no . . . Actually, she isn't,' he said. He could hear her voice now, replaying in his head. In his time he'd had to listen to many a singer, so that he was a judge not biased by good looks or a feeling of sympathy. He said: 'She accompanies herself on the piano and she puts me in mind of that kind of performer you get in the bar of a big hotel, late at night – pleasant, undemanding, a sort of background music.'

'Oh, yes, I know what you mean. How does that fit in with your pal's ideas?'

'I wish I knew. I thought he was going for a serious, clear-pitched line – relying on woodwind to a great extent—'

Liz made a tut-tut sound. 'You're not making sense, Greg. I got the idea from what you told me that Gilles was all out to be the reincarnation of the Quintet du Hot Club or whatever it was called – and surely that was ultra-jazz, wasn't it – I don't know because I'm not into that sort of thing. How does this soft background-type music fit in?'

'I'm as puzzled as you are – more so, in fact. It all happened in a matter of minutes, really. She did a number, with her brother giving her a bit of backing, and then one on her own – I'm afraid I can't tell you what they were, I never heard them before. But all the men were tremendously taken with her and that was that – she was voted in.'

'What d'you mean, all the men were tremendously taken with her,' she said sharply. 'She's pretty, is she?'

'More than pretty, Liz. She's a knockout.'

'Hm,' said Liz.

'I can see why they fell for her. I was a bit staggered myself when I met the pair of them at Cornavin.'

'Hm,' said Liz again. Then, after a moment, 'You know, I think I might fly over and spend a few days. I've got a couple of things to clear up here, but what about if I catch a flight tomorrow lunchtime—'

'To Geneva?' said Greg. He was thinking that his grand-mother was often in Geneva. It would not be a good thing if they ever met.

'If you're thinking the Dragon Lady might destroy me with her fiery breath, forget it. How's she going to recognize me unless I wear a label?' she demanded.

That was true. Liz knew what the ex-Queen Mother Nicoletta looked like because she'd seen her photograph in society magazines. But Nicoletta had no way of recognizing Liz.

'Well,' said Greg after a moment, 'it would be nice to see you. And as a matter of fact, Gilles is giving a party tomorrow evening at one of Geneva's smartest restaurants. You'd like that, wouldn't you?'

'A party?' Liz always liked parties. She liked to look at women in party frocks. Fashion was one of her main interests in life.

'It's for the signing of the contracts and so on. To give the band a bit of a – what do you call it – a spree?'

'So they'll all be there?'

'Of course.'

'Including the knockout?'

'Ah!' Then he said, 'Oh, Liz, you're impossible.'

'I'm vigilant.' She sounded proprietorial. 'I like to look after my belongings. So book me a hotel room and be there to meet my plane – I'll let you know my flight.'

He was laughing as he agreed to it all. Whatever had prompted her to come, the idea of seeing her so unexpectedly was delightful.

Five

Gilles had hired a room on the first floor of the Merveille. He was already there when Greg and Liz arrived. He was hopping from one foot to the other in anxiety as he chatted with his mother and father, watching over their shoulders for new arrivals.

He darted forward to lead them to Auguste and Rosanne. 'Delighted you could come, Ms Blair. Maman, may I introduce Ms Blair, the friend of M. Couronne, and this is my father, Ms Blair, so nice to meet you, Grego's told me so much about you.'

This was untrue. Greg had only mentioned her when asking if he could bring her to the party. But he let it pass as polite babble. 'Where are the others?' he enquired.

'They're on their way. Roger is driving them.' In one of the many modern cars Greg had seen in the everyday part of the garage, presumably. 'Did you have a good flight, Ms Blair? You find it a big change from London, I suppose. I saw on one of the bank's screens that the temperature there is forty-eight. We came straight from the bank, Papa and I. Maman came in from the chateau, she says she thinks the others were still getting ready when she left. Now what would you like to drink?' He beckoned a waiter hovering with a tray of glasses.

They made their choice, remaining by the side of the parents and making small talk. The arrival of the jazz contingent could be heard before they were visible, as they surged towards the door of the room from the lift. It struck Greg that they might have had a sip or two in preparation for the party. They drew up sharply when they saw Maman and Papa Guidon. Clearly this was unexpected.

'Hello, hello, so there you are! Come along, let me introduce you all, Morena first of course, here she is, Mama, this is Moreno Ferigiano, our latest addition, and this is her brother Lou . . .' And so on through what amounted to a reception line.

The band had clearly paid attention to the word 'party' and had made an effort. Gone were the somewhat grungy clothes of the rehearsal room. Nils was in a sky-blue sweater of very fine wool, Emilio was wearing a frilled shirt that might have been a uniform from some Latin American band, François had black jeans and a dress shirt with a tie. Lou was clad in blue jeans and a black silk jacket with letters in white, which might have been those of an American football team.

But it was his sister who drew all eyes. She was wearing a dress of filmy yellow voile above which her black hair, unbound, was like an ebony cloud. The dress was almost demure, with a high neckline, little cap sleeves, and not showing too much leg.

It seemed to Greg that Rosanne Guidon held on to Morena's hand a little longer than anyone else's. It might have been so as to study her for a moment. But the group were soon well into the room, looking towards the waiter. The waiter, however, had set aside his tray, clearly awaiting instructions from the host. So they milled about uncertainly.

Greg produced the contracts from his document case. There was a little side table, where he laid them ready with his pen. 'This way,' he commanded. Gilles came to his side eagerly, the others followed. Gilles asked for Morena's contract and wrote a figure in the blank space left for her terms of engagement. Greg had no time to examine, for the next moment the others ushered her forward to sign.

The rest signed their contracts after her. The waiter, at a signal from Gilles, ceremoniously poured champagne.

When they all held glasses, Auguste Guidon offered a toast. 'To the future and the great things that are waiting there,' he said. It was a neat avoidance of saying 'Good luck to the band,' but no one seemed to notice.

They broke up into two or three little groups. Gilles and

François stood with Morena in a corner, Nils and Emilio decided to get to know Liz. Greg took the opportunity to chat with the Guidons, for he'd noticed the dinner table was set for only eight. That seemed to mean the Guidons weren't dining with them.

It proved to be so. 'We shan't stay long,' murmured Auguste. 'I just felt I'd like to take a look at them all.'

It was a fact that he probably hadn't seen them properly until now. The family were in the house, the musicians were in the stable block, and never the twain should meet if Nounou and the other ladies could help it.

Mme Guidon leaned towards Greg so as to speak in an even lower tone. 'I wanted to see the girl,' she confided. 'Auguste and I were out last night, so Nounou had to use her own judgement when she agreed to let her stay. But you know she was so disapproving that I was very worried.'

'But you saw her at breakfast, surely?' Greg asked.

'Not at all. She didn't get up until nearly midday and then she went straight across to Gilles's "rag room".' She uttered the term with distaste. 'They like to be over there together, it's almost like a little tribe . . .'

'But the girl seems quite ladylike, *ma chère*,' said Auguste.

'That's true. I'm quite relieved. I thought she might be a . . .' She sought about for a word but decided against it. 'You brought her from the airport,' she went on. 'What was your impression?'

'She said very little. Lou did most of the talking.'

'He seems . . . very American.' This was uttered in a neutral tone.

'Yes, I think he is. He seems to be a good musician.'

'And she?'

'Well . . .' He couldn't in honesty say he thought she played well. Average, he'd have judged her – product of lessons taken at home with a decent tutor, but the voice never trained at all. 'She's a very attractive performer,' he said in the end.

Mme Guidon was satisfied. Her husband, thinking perhaps of the money Morena was costing him, gave a shrug. 'I rely on you, Greg, to keep an eye on things.'

Greg was irritated but didn't let it show. 'I can only handle the business side,' he said. If the parents were worried about a moral aspect, they would have to deal with it themselves.

The Guidons made the rounds of the guests, saying farewells and being polite. They made their escape by eight thirty. The waiter then appeared announcing that dinner was served so they took their places at table.

Liz was expertly manoeuvred to a seat between Emilio and Nils. Greg found himself on one side of Morena, with Gilles on her other side. François and Lou somehow lost out on the arrangement but everyone seemed happy. The champagne had been replaced by a very good white Côtes du Jura.

For the first course Gilles commandeered the attention of Morena. But when the veal *demi-deul* was served, she turned – as good manners perhaps dictated – to the man on her other side. Quite ladylike, as M. Guidon had said.

'This is a really nice place,' she said in her soft, throaty voice. 'Is this a local speciality we're eating?'

'Oh, Switzerland doesn't have much in the way of specialities except perhaps fondue and raclette and rösti.'

'And they're – what?'

'One cheese and bread dish, one cheese and potato dish, and a kind of roast potato,' he laughed.

'Oh, not very original.'

'But wholesome. Switzerland is a very wholesome place.' This produced a faint smile. He wanted to draw her out if he could. It was true her brother had done most of the talking, so far as he could recall. 'You have an Italian name – do you prefer Italian dishes?'

She shrugged. 'At home we used to eat mostly American. Mama never liked being in the kitchen so she left it to the cook – last time I looked, that was a black lady.'

'You don't go home much?'

She paused to let the waiter refill her wine glass. 'Papa washed his hands of us three or four years ago,' she said with a sigh. 'We're kind of vagabonds. Papa thinks the musical world begins and ends with Puccini. Mama used to sing at the Met, you see. Only in the chorus, you know, but it was a bi-ig disappointment when I proved to have almost no voice.'

'You sing very nicely,' he said politely.

'Yeah, yeah!' She dismissed the compliment. 'I get by. But it was Louie who turned out the worst. He couldn't sing either, so he had to take first piano, then the oboe. Very poetic, the oboe,' she said with an ironic tone to the words. 'When Louie threw it in and turned to the sax, I thought Papa would lose his mind.'

Greg was pleased at getting her to talk. He was about to make some encouraging sounds but to his surprise, she went on unprompted. 'Louie went off with the Fantastics ... let me see ... it'll be about five years ago. I went after him about six months later, because Mama was trying to marry me off to one of Papa's business associates – Papa's in textiles. So here we are now in the marvellous Merveille and staying at the Chateau Guidon. Never know where we'll be next.'

'How do you like it chez Guidon?'

'Hard to say – I only really paid attention to it this evening when I went over to change for the party. Very ...' she sought for the word '... opulent. Comfortable, though – I thought it might be draughty yet it's not. But it's got its chilly side – ice is supplied by the housekeeping lady.'

'Nounou.'

'Yeah. What is that, she's his old nurse?' She shrugged. 'We passed each other a couple times today – if looks could kill!'

'You have to understand that Nounou is decidedly not in favour of jazz men. And I don't think she ever imagined there were any jazz women.'

He waited for her to deny that she was a jazz woman, that her style belonged to another category, but she didn't. Perhaps it was important to her to keep the job. The next course came and she turned to Gilles again so that Greg found himself chatting with her brother, who was next to him on his left.

'You perhaps know my main interest is really classical music,' he began. 'Your sister tells me your mother sang at the Met?'

'Oh yeah,' said Lou. 'Big deal. In the chorus. But she "gave up her career" when she and Pa got married.

57

Philadelphia . . . woulda been kind of hard to keep up with a chorus job in New York.'

'Of course.'

'Did Sis tell you we don't see much of the old folks at home?' He waited for Greg to nod before continuing. 'We've been out on our own quite a while now. What I'm hoping,' he said with great earnestness, 'is that this thing with Gilles turns out permanent. I get the idea Switzerland is kind of a good place to settle. We'd be travelling, of course, I understand that, but home base would be, say, Geneva? Or Montreux?'

'That's still to be settled,' said Greg. 'And that reminds me, I'll need your passports and so on to apply for your permits.'

'Oh yeah . . . Permits . . .' There was a hesitation. 'I hear the red-tape-worms are pretty active here?'

He looked a little anxious about it. Greg wondered if there was something in his past – a drugs conviction, perhaps – that he feared might weigh against him.

'I'm not expecting any trouble,' he reassured. 'It'll take a few weeks, but that's always the case.' Indeed, he thought it might be dealt with more promptly – the Guidon name, and to a lesser extent his own, might have some influence on the bureaucrats. 'If you can let me have your documents tomorrow, I'll get things in motion. It's the same for the others,' he added. 'You all have to have B permits, I think. I'm going to be up to my eyes in it for the next day or two while I get the applications sorted out.'

'Tough,' murmured Lou without much sympathy.

Soon after the dessert course Liz signified that she'd be quite happy to go back to her hotel. The others clearly wanted to stay, drink yet another excellent wine that had come with the crème bavaroise, and talk about their repertoire. She and Greg quietly left them to it. They had better things to do.

He parted from her in the darkness before dawn. When he came to breakfast next morning his grandmother said in a disapproving tone, 'So you and your pop-music friends made a night of it, eh?'

'Grossmutti, it isn't pop music. It's a much more serious style.'

'Oh, very well, it's too early in the day to start a musical argument. As long as you're getting paid for it, I suppose one mustn't mind. What's your programme today?'

'First I'm going to the office, and then to the chateau to collect their passports and so on. After that I suppose I'll have do some telephoning.'

'If you're going into Geneva, you can take me.'

'Whereabouts in Geneva?'

'Oh, Mövenpick, somewhere like that.'

'Right you are.' Luckily the department store was nowhere near the hotel where Liz was staying.

When he called to collect Liz later, she was clad in outdoor clothes. 'I feel a desperate need for some fresh air and exercise,' she declared.

Liz was the kind of person who went running around parks in the early morning. Certainly she'd had no chance to do anything like that in the last few days.

'Right,' said the Prince, 'we'll drive to the grounds of the chateau and then walk up to it. There are quite a lot of paths and tracks, I think – but it's uphill, are you OK with uphill?'

'Of course I am.' She was indignant. But honesty compelled her to add, 'I might not run uphill.'

He grinned. 'Just let me ring Gilles to make sure it's OK,' he said, remembering the security gates at the estate.

Gilles was quite agreeable, telling him to ask Roger where to park. Roger was the chauffeur and keeper of the gate. 'We'll expect you – when?'

'Let's say sometime after twelve.'

'That would be good.' He was a little apologetic as he went on: 'We kept the party going until pretty late and when we got home I'm afraid we were a bit the worse for wear and disturbed Nounou. She's been giving me a hard time this morning, moaning about her "quality of life" and threatening all sorts of reprisals if I don't keep everybody in order, but you know they're grown-ups, I can't order them about like school children. I haven't been over to the rag room because I don't suppose they've surfaced yet, but I might try

59

to have a little chat with them just to keep Nounou quiet – what do you think I should say?'

Greg declined to offer any suggestions.

At the gates, the scratchy voice now identified as belonging to Roger the chauffeur advised him where to park. 'I'll cycle down in a minute, Monsieur, and bring your car up to the house, if you'll just leave the keys in the ignition.'

Splendid. That relieved him of the necessity of carrying with him the portfolio of forms that must be filled in today.

It was a good day for a walk. It was cold, but not freezing. The sun was well up in the sky, golden above the mountains so that the shadows in the valleys weren't so deep. One of the disadvantages of living among mountains is that the light dies when the sun goes behind the peaks, even in the daytime. He left the car inside the electronic gates of the estate then led the way on foot along the drive until Liz espied an attractive path leading off to the west.

The path led through an extensive shrubbery of hebes, dwarf pines and cypress, then through a copse of mixed woodland until they reached a stream. Here the path branched, but Greg turned off to the left without a pause. 'How d'you know which way to go?' Liz demanded, shaking her head at the trees that masked the view.

'Good Lord, if we want to get to the chateau we have to go upstream.'

'Oh yes.' She trotted to catch up with him. They kept alongside the stream for some time then took a rocky path uphill. After that came a steep rise with a more open aspect. 'Slow down,' she said.

'I thought you wanted some exercise?'

'It's not fair. You've got such long legs! For every two steps you take, I have to take three.' Puff. 'Is it much farther?'

'About a quarter of a mile as the crow flies, I think, perhaps a little more.'

'I'm beginning' – puff – 'to wish I was a crow.'

They topped the rise and began a shallow descent, but only towards the next slope. Over the top of that a little figure appeared, trudging sturdily towards them. Bulked out in a padded jacket and shapeless trousers, it was still recognizable to Greg as Nounou.

She paused abruptly on seeing them. For a moment it looked as if she would turn back. But the Prince raised a hand in salute as they approached, and she moved forward.

'Oh, it's you, sir! I thought it might be that American pair,' she said in Romansch. She was well prepared for her outing, in lace-up mountain boots and with a little tartan backpack. It was clear she wasn't at all out of breath after coming up the farther slope.

'Good morning, Nounou. This is my friend Ms Blair from London.'

'Good morning,' Nounou said, switching immediately to English. 'You are one of the musicians?'

'Oh no! Fashion's my job. Lovely morning, isn't it?'

Nounou was surveying Liz's outfit – knitted scarf and hat in lightning-stripe design, ski jacket of metallic blue, grey trousers tucked into bright blue trainers. She gave a wintry smile. 'Fashion must be very interesting. You're here on holiday, then?'

'For just a few days.'

'Where are you off to, Nounou?' Greg asked, to prevent any more acid comments about fashion.

'Oh, I've been to visit my waterfall. I go up there often, just for the pleasure of seeing it sparkle in the sun. And today I feel it was particularly healing . . .'

'Are you feeling unwell?' the Prince asked at once, intending to offer her any help she might need.

'Unwell . . . Not physically . . . You were at that party last night, Monsieur. I would have thought you would exert some influence on them. Their behaviour is positively barbaric when they're drunk.'

Liz took a step closer so as to put a comforting hand on her arm. 'We left quite early,' she said. 'I'm sorry if they bothered you, but they had a particular reason for celebrating, you see.'

'Ha! They need no particular reason! They'll drive me to my grave, and then Gilles will be sorry – when it's too late.'

'Now, now, madame,' said Greg, 'you mustn't talk like

61

that. I think Gilles is going to try to have a little word with them.'

'I don't have to put up with it,' she announced in a haughty tone. 'I don't have to stay here, you know, to be made a target of their bad manners. And who would run the house then, just answer me that? Who knows the household as I do? Oh, yes, if they make me suffer I can make them suffer!'

She was full of rancour. Liz stood back from her, having understood that kind words and a soft touch were going to do no good.

Nounou seemed to recover her manners. 'You should visit my little waterfall, Monsieur, the view from there is very fine. Take the left-hand fork if you wish to go there. Good morning, I must get forward, there are deliveries due at the house and I must be there.' She gave a stiff little nod of farewell and went on past them towards yet another upward slope.

'My word, what a little gorgon!' muttered Liz as she marched away. Then added with a sigh, 'But she's fit! She wasn't even perspiring after coming over that crest.'

'Do you think you'll be able to do that at her age, my darling little jogger?' He tucked away some strands of blonde hair into the sides of her knitted cap. 'And perspiration is very becoming on your pink little nose.'

'How old is she?' she asked, disregarding the taunt. 'Sixty? Seventy?'

'I think Gilles told me she was a little over eighty. And very set in her ways. She disapproves of almost everyone and everything, as you've just heard.'

'All the same, she makes me ashamed of myself. OK, then, onward and upward!'

They continued on their way but Liz voted to leave the waterfall for another time. Greg took pity on her. He directed their steps towards the chateau, where he found Roger the chauffeur waiting by his car.

'Your keys, Monsieur.'

'Thank you.' He opened up and got the leather case with the forms. They walked past the garages, through the arch to the old stables, and as they opened the door of the big studio room, the sound of a clarinet greeted them.

Emilio was playing alone, and to Greg's ears it wasn't jazz, more like a simple waltz. Morena was sitting next to the player, singing softly: 'The future's not ours to see . . .'

'That seems a familiar tune,' Greg murmured to Liz.

'I think it was a hit for Doris Day or someone.'

'Doris Day? The lady in the old films?' This didn't seem to have very much to do with cool European jazz.

Gilles, now on official leave from the bank, came to meet them in sweatshirt and jeans. 'Just trying out a couple of things,' he said. 'Good morning, nice to see you again, Liz, you and I didn't have a chance to get to know each other last night but it's really nice to meet you, I hope you enjoyed the meal and everything.'

'Yes. Thank you. What a great place you have here.'

'Oh yes, Papa did it all for my graduation party, I really love it, gives me – gives all of us the chance to try things out, make a noise if we have to, but we haven't got far this morning, I'm afraid we took a long time to get together because we . . . well . . . Come along, have a seat, can I offer you a drink or anything, let me take your coat.'

Greg had hung his jacket over a chair, and was already approaching the musicians to explain what he needed. Emilio gave a little groan of annoyance. He'd forgotten to bring documents from his room. He hurried out to fetch them, rattling up the outer staircase to the living quarters. François, accustomed to the bureaucracy of his homeland, had his in his jacket pocket.

Lou Ferigiano had his own passport and that of his sister. 'This is a loada hogwash, all this stuff. I thought you guys in Europe had done away with all of that entry permit and border-control stuff?'

'That's the European Union, Lou. Switzerland doesn't belong.'

'No?' He seemed taken aback. 'Didn't I see something on television about everybody belonging?'

'Never mind, Louie,' soothed his sister. 'Let Greg get on with his thing.'

He took a seat at the desk where the telephone was housed,

and started on the task of getting them to fill in the necessary forms. It took a long time. Swiss bureaucracy is complicated, and only François was familiar with the need to be compliant.

When they were finished, it was early afternoon. Gilles offered them lunch in the rag room but Liz had had enough of its stuffy atmosphere and Greg was tired of its occupants. They excused themselves and made their escape.

'Will they all get approval for their permits?' Liz asked as they sped down the drive.

'Oh, I think so, after the normal amount of objections.' He allowed himself a faint sigh. 'They're an odd assortment,' he said. 'Gilles is all joviality, like a bouncy castle, Emilio seems almost sombre, François seems to me to feel he's superior to all the others, and Nils is so self-contained he's like a diplomat.'

'And what about Lou and his sister the Knockout?'

'Well, she is very beautiful – don't you think?'

'And talented?'

'Ah . . . Well . . . You heard her, when we first arrived . . . What did you think?'

'Quaite naice,' said Liz, in the accents of an elderly Englishwoman giving modified praise.

'I beg your pardon?'

'I mean she's about the level of someone who can shine a bit at karaoke—'

'Oh, that's rather harsh. She plays quite well.'

'But you had to take her on because otherwise you didn't get Lou, was that it?'

'No, we took her on – Gilles took her on – because he's . . . wait, what's the word. Smitten?'

'Oh, very good. Yes, he's smitten, I could see that. While you were dealing with those chaps milling around you, I was sort of having a conversation with him. But his attention was really on Morena.' She looked at the road ahead. 'Where are we going?'

'To have lunch. There's a chalet restaurant a bit further along. Do you like raclette?'

'Love it.' Liz was constantly trying to be a vegetarian, but often falling short, and to be offered a dish that was substantial without using meat was a pleasure. She knew also, from last night's meal at the Merveille, that there might be very delightful desserts.

When they were settled in the restaurant and had ordered a pre-lunch drink, she returned to the topic of the band members.

'Lou doesn't seem very bright.'

'No, his sister seems to have the brains of the family.' He considered them for a moment. 'Seems to me the family must have given more attention to Morena than to her brother. He's the elder of the two, I saw from their passports.'

'Really? Well, I suppose that happens. You have a son and he turns out to be not very good-looking and a bit of a thickie, and then you have a little girl that's an absolute beauty. And papas are always inclined to love their daughters more than their sons, aren't they?'

'If you believe some of the things psychologists tell us.'

'So they lavish their attention on Morena, perhaps – buy her party frocks, give her piano lessons, that kind of thing.'

'I suppose so.'

Their first course arrived. Liz hungrily attacked her melon then, when she'd eaten about half, paused to ask: 'Do jazz players earn a lot of money?'

He grinned. 'Well, those that are clients of mine do quite well. Since Papa Guidon is paying for it all, I made sure Gilles's group got very good terms.'

'But generally speaking?'

'I don't imagine so.' He gave a little shrug. 'Why do you ask?'

'I was just thinking . . . That dress Morena was wearing last night at the party . . .'

'What about it?'

'I thought it had a certain look . . . Sort of Madeleine Vionnet.'

'Is she someone well known?' he asked, being an ignoramus about fashion design despite the names his beloved was often quoting.

'She was, she's been dead for quite a while. But Morena's

65

dress had something of that style. And there's a young designer in New York now who's making clothes very like that.'

'So what are you saying, *mon ange*?'

'Well, you don't buy things like that at Wal-Mart.'

Their plates were exchanged for the raclette. They ate for a while in enjoyment. Then Greg said: 'Well, if your theory about her being Daddy's girl is right, it may mean she's getting an allowance from him.'

'Uh-huh.'

'She told me he was in textiles. I don't know what that means – whether he makes them or imports them or what. He could have a lot of money . . .' He paused. 'But she told me he'd washed his hands of them, of her and the brother.'

Liz giggled. 'Maybe she has a sugar daddy.'

He shook his head at her. 'Just because she was wearing a pretty frock! Maybe she bought it in . . . what do you call it? A charity shop.'

'That's possible. I'll have to ask her which charity shop, I wouldn't mind being a customer there.' She gave herself up to the crunching of little onions for a moment or two then said, 'What are we doing for the rest of the day?'

'I have to look over those applications to make sure we've ticked all the boxes. Then I have to get them to Quellen-weg—'

'Which is where? Can we drop them off on our way back to town?'

'No, it's in Bern, but I would like to deliver them personally so I think I'll go there tomorrow. Would you like to go to Bern? Nice shops there.'

'That's tomorrow. What about the rest of today? Can you for instance read through those confounded forms at my hotel?'

'Well, I really need my computer and my address book.'

'Nonsense,' she said. 'As the Beatles used to say, "All You Need Is Love".'

He smiled. 'Not quite. But it helps.'

The forms were eventually checked and the visit to Bern next day was achieved – a much more successful excursion

66

than the Prince had feared, because he'd always connected Bern with stern business matters. He sent Liz shopping while he had a short conversation with an official at the Federal Office for Foreign Workers, left the documents, then took her up a funicular to a mountain restaurant for lunch.

The following day, Friday, was the day when Liz had a flight booked for early evening. She had to go back to London because of business commitments. She packed in the morning, so as to take her luggage with her when Greg drove them to Chateau Guidon. Greg wanted to report on the processing of the permits, and Liz had been invited to take part in a discussion.

Gilles was still trying to choose a name for the band. 'He has to get on with it,' Greg explained. 'I need a name because I have to start booking them into venues over the Christmas and New Year season – so that they can see how their repertoire goes down with the club-going public.'

'The Guidon Gang,' she suggested.

'Heaven forbid! Auguste doesn't want the family name used.'

'Gilles's Gems – how about that? I like alliteration.'

'Only works in English. In French it would be les Bijoux de Gilles. Besides, it's a bit . . . frilly.'

'Oh, you don't appreciate me. I've helped suggest advertising slogans for clothes that have appeared in chain stores all over Britain.'

'These fellows aren't going to wear dresses, Liz. Be serious.'

Her suggestions became more outrageous as they drove towards the chateau. They arrived there in a state of merriment.

But that was quelled immediately by the news that Gilles was waiting to give them.

'Nounou's gone missing,' he wailed.

Six

Both Greg and Liz were astounded at his words.
'Missing? What does that mean?'

'She's gone! She and Maman have English tea together most afternoons and this afternoon Nounou didn't appear so Maman rang through to her room – she's taken up new quarters, well, of course, you don't care about that but she wasn't there so Maman tried her old room, the one Morena has now, and she wasn't there either so Maman rang the staff room and they said she wasn't there and they hadn't seen her since before lunch and so Maman rang Papa at the bank and he's here now and he's so upset!'

Gilles was clasping and unclasping his hands in misery. Liz took them in hers and said, 'She's gone to see some friends, I expect.'

'No, we've been in touch with them, there aren't many – Papa is nearly out of his mind with worry – and he's talking about abandoning all our plans, Grego, you must come and talk to him, it's a frightful prospect.'

He urged them before him into the house. There a flustered maid took their coats before they were ushered along the hall and into a very elegant little sitting room. Mme Guidon was huddled on a couch, with her sister-in-law Marie Armonet holding her hand. In the other was a sodden handkerchief. Sasha the secretary was hovering in the background with a notepad and a pen.

The master of the house was pacing about behind the couch. He had clearly hurried home from the bank in Geneva in the full splendour of his business suit, but now he had abandoned the jacket and the tie, and the fine poplin shirt was unbuttoned at the neck. His usually neat hair looked as if it had been clutched many times by anxious hands.

'Monsieur Couronne!' he cried as they came in. 'What a dreadful business this is! Gilles has told you?'

'I understand that Nounou—'

'Yes, yes, and I'm so afraid! It's really quite dark already and you know the night temperatures . . . If she's out there . . . Oh God!'

'You're thinking she's had an accident in the grounds?' asked Greg.

'Well, we searched with no results, but what other explanation? We have tried her acquaintances – those we know of – she doesn't have many friends outside of the estate, you see.'

'Monsieur Guidon,' soothed Sasha, 'you know she's played this kind of trick before. Depend upon it, she's going to telephone from somewhere any minute now and say she's in the Hilton Hotel for the night.'

'She's gone missing before?' Greg repeated.

'Frequently.'

'Now, Sasha,' reproved Rosanne Guidon tearfully, 'only twice. No, perhaps three times.'

'Madame, she uses it as a weapon to punish Monsieur when she can't get her own way.'

'That's enough!' cried Auguste. 'We're speaking here of a fine old lady who has devoted her life to this family.'

Liz murmured: 'She did say something to that effect when we met her on the footpath – do you remember, Greg?'

'To what effect? What do you mean, Mademoiselle?'

'Well, I seem to recall she said . . .' She paused, her memory bringing up the words clear and distinct. She didn't want to utter them.

'Please, Mademoiselle, tell me – I need every little clue I can find because she's been so upset these last few days. Please, I beg you!'

'She said . . . she said that if you made her suffer, she would make you suffer.'

Sasha muttered something in French that sounded uncomplimentary. Auguste rounded on him. A tirade of angry criticism poured out, to which Sasha responded by shrugging and saying very emphatically, '*Vous vous en trompez toujours! Elle n'est pas une sainte, pas de tout!*'

This verdict on Nounou's lack of saintly attributes served only to make Auguste even angrier. His wife struggled out of the encompassing embrace of the couch to go to him and comfort him.

Liz whispered to Greg, 'I shouldn't have told him.'

'But it's what she said. And perhaps that's what's happening – she's making him suffer.'

'But if so, she's – they're all in such a state about it.'

'I'm sorry, Liz, I shouldn't have let you get involved.'

'How could you help it?' she groaned. 'We were practically roped into it by your pal Gilles.' She broke off to think for a moment then said: 'Listen, love, I don't think I'm any use here and besides if they're going to quarrel in French I don't even understand what they're saying. I think I ought to push off.'

'Of course. I'll just explain to Gilles that we've got to get to the airport.'

'No, no, you stay. You're needed here. I'll just get the secretary-bird to telephone for a taxi.'

'No, of course not, I'll drive you.'

In the end, having broken into the quarrel between Auguste and Sasha and the soothings of Rosanne to ask permission, Greg arranged that the chauffeur Roger would drive Liz in Greg's car to the airport and accompany her with her luggage to the departure desk.

He went out to see her off. Gilles trailed him to the outer door but had the good sense to stay in the house while they exchanged farewell kisses.

'I'll be back home by some time after ten. Ring me if you can,' she urged.

'Sweetheart, I'm sorry about all this. Your little visit hasn't been much fun.'

'Oh, I've had quite a lot of satisfaction out of it. At least I've been able to make sure you're not the least bit attracted to the Knockout.'

'You're impossible!'

'I'm reassured!'

70

He kissed her on the nose. She giggled and got into the car. In a few seconds the lights of the car had disappeared round a turn in the drive.

Greg went back indoors. He had mixed feelings. He'd of course expected to part from Liz this evening but he'd thought they'd have time together at the airport. Now she'd gone and there was a strange gap at his side.

But no – the gap was filled at once by Gilles, dithering in the hall to snatch at his sleeve when he went indoors.

'Did she really say that?' he asked. 'Nounou – about making us suffer?'

Greg sighed. 'I seem to remember something like that.'

'Oh, she's such a tiresome old nuisance!' cried Gilles. 'No, I don't mean that, of course she's wonderful, she's been a pillar of strength in our family all my life and as for Papa, he wouldn't even be here if Nounou hadn't nursed him, but all the same she does sort of blackmail us all, particularly Papa, and now he's saying it's our fault she's taken off, and we ought to disband the group and let her have some peace and quiet . . .' He faltered into silence as they entered the sitting room.

There had been a slight alteration in the battle lines. Rosanne was now scolding Sasha for his attitude while Auguste was apologizing for calling Sasha callous. Mme Armonet was comforting herself with a glass of something deep red and smelling of spice – mulled wine.

'Ah, Greg, you've come back to us. I apologize for dragging your sweetheart into such a dismal scene, and I thank you for changing your plans. But we do in fact have more than one reason for wishing you to stay with us, at least for the moment.' Auguste waved him to a chair. 'But first, please, tell me what it was that you heard from Nounou yesterday.'

Greg cleared his throat. 'Liz and I were walking to the house. We'd taken a path that led eventually to an incline just beyond the copse above the stream. We met Nounou coming down the path. She told us she'd been to her water-fall, which she—'

'Ah yes, she loves it there.' He groaned. 'We've searched there, Roger and some of the other men went up and along

71

the banks.' He made little urging movements with his hands. 'Go on, about making us suffer.'

'Mmm . . . She said she found the waterfall particularly comforting . . . healing, perhaps she said . . . Then she made some criticism of the musicians and their behaviour after the party.'

'You see!' cried Auguste, with a glare at his son. 'We've been so dreadfully inconsiderate!'

'But, Papa—'

'Go on, Greg, please, what else.'

'I . . . er . . . you must understand I didn't pay any particular attention. I think she said she didn't have to stay here to be a victim of their bad manners, or something like that. And I'm pretty sure she said you'd be sorry, and that stuck in my mind because it's so—' He broke off, because he'd been going to say, 'So childish.'

'Now you must admit, Monsieur Guidon,' said Sasha, 'that here you have a typical example of Nounou's tactics. She loves to make you feel guilty.'

'But I am guilty! I never gave a single thought to how she would be affected by having a graceless band of ruffians—'

'Papa, that's not fair! They're perfectly reasonable, normal—'

'If we could just keep to the point,' Greg intervened. 'If Nounou is really "punishing" you, and has done this before, what usually happens?'

'She telephones, and we go and collect her and bring her home,' sighed Rosanne. 'And we make much of her for the next few days and it all gets forgotten.'

'And this time it's different. In what way?'

'She hasn't telephoned.'

'But there's still time for her to—'

Gilles was shaking his head in doubt. 'She likes to go to bed early. If she were going to come home, she'd have let us know by now and she'd be tucked up by ten, ten thirty.'

'I see.'

'Of course, this time she's much more upset,' sighed Auguste.

'Humph,' said his sister Marie into her glass of wine.

72

'She is, she's deeply wounded, and I blame myself! So, Monsieur Couronne, Greg, I'm afraid I must say . . .'

'Yes?'

'I must say that I'm putting an end to all this foolishness of Gilles and the Montreux Festival. I was wrong ever to have let the thing get started.'

'But you thought it was a marvellous idea, Papa! And Nounou agreed, now didn't she! And you can't just go back on your word like this! You made me a promise and you know you've always prided yourself on—'

'But the comfort and well-being of our dearest old friend depends on being at ease here, where she's lived for longer than you or I, my boy. I can't let her suffer. I'm going to put an end to the whole foolish scheme.' He turned to the Prince. 'I want you to tell them that I'm withdrawing. Make what financial settlements you can so long as you keep it a private matter.'

'Excuse me, Auguste,' Greg said, 'but how will that help? I mean, in the immediate circumstances?'

'Well,' said Auguste, as if the matter were self-explanatory, 'when Nounou hears, she'll come home.'

'Perhaps. But how will she know?'

'I beg your pardon?'

'She's gone. You've no idea where she is. How will you let her know that the musicians are banished?'

The banker stared at him. A long silence ensued. Sasha said under his breath, 'There speaks the voice of logic at last.'

Auguste was silent for almost a minute. Then he said with authority, 'We'll find her, and then I'll explain—'

'You've telephoned her friends, her relations?'

'Nounou has no real friends,' said Marie Armonet in an acid tone. 'And as for relations, she's outlived them all.'

'The hotels where she's stayed on previous occasions?'

'I tried them,' said Sasha. 'No luck.'

'What about her car? Is it a noticeable model?'

'Oh, Nounou doesn't drive. She had to give up because her eyesight isn't too good and she began to get flustered out in heavy traffic.'

'So then Roger would take her if she wanted to go? But then not today, otherwise he'd have told you where he took her,' reasoned Greg. 'What then, she calls a taxi?'

'That would never be necessary,' Auguste said with some indignation. 'We would always provide her with transport if she wished to use it. But Nounou is a very independent old lady. Quite often she walks out.' He reported this with some pride.

'I beg your pardon? Walks? All down that long drive and then where?'

'She doesn't have to go by the drive. There are half a dozen ways out of the estate,' he explained. 'Gates and stiles, you know – it's always been our family's policy to allow access to walkers, hikers. It reflects well on the bank, of course – we support the local community. And then when Nounou leaves the estate she can take the post bus, or there are one or two funiculars not far off.'

Greg was silent, taking this in. Sasha said, 'If you're going to ask about the hospitals, I've tried those.'

'Where might she be heading if she was on foot?' Greg asked.

'Oh . . . Who knows. She likes to make the trip into Geneva to go to the department stores sometimes – to see what's new in cleaning equipment, that sort of thing. She likes to go to the tulip festival in Morges – that's spring, of course, but at any time of the year, in fine weather she likes to sit on a bench and watch the mothers and children.'

'But we've enquired in Morges,' put in Marie, 'and she hasn't been seen. And believe me, they'd have noticed, the mothers – she gives them little lectures about how to bring up their kiddies.'

Greg could tell there was no love lost between Auguste's old nurse and his sister. She caught his puzzled glance and went on: 'Don't imagine I'm as devoted to her as Auguste. Nounou never had time for me as a child – she only really likes boy children. I was brought up by a succession of nursery-maids – none of them stayed long because she was so beastly to them, but at least they were quite kind to me. But Nounou – from her, hardly ever a kind word.'

'Oh, Marie!' protested her brother.

This piece of history caused some muted disapproval from the Guidons – not so much because of its criticism of Nounou but because it showed their family life in a bad light. When they'd stopped murmuring against it, Greg said, 'So in fact until she chooses to get in touch or come back of her own accord, there's no way to let her know you're winding up the jazz band. So why not put that into cold storage for the time being?'

'And what good would that do? They've got to go!'

'It would allow you to defer the arguments and legal challenges that come with breaking their contracts.'

This quiet statement caused the banker to hesitate. Gilles burst into the interval: 'Yes, Papa, you see it's not so easy as you thought, to please Nounou! Although I'm willing to work out some compromise – Grego will help with that, won't you, Grego? After all, these are free men you're talking about, Papa, they're not slaves you can sell down the river when it takes your fancy. And of course not forgetting Morena – she's a stranger in our country, you can't treat a young woman like that, it's . . . it's . . .' He sought about for a telling phrase and remembered Emilio's word. 'It's unchristian.'

'My dear,' Auguste's wife said to him gently, 'I do think you must not be hasty over this. We would not wish it said of us that we turned the young woman away. Nounou will telephone, you'll go to fetch her home and we'll all be nice to her. Some arrangement can be made, I'm sure.'

Auguste bowed his head in acknowledgement of her rebuke about Morena. His wife had met her and judged her 'ladylike'. He suggested in calmer tones, 'Perhaps we could get them a place to stay elsewhere. In Montreux, for instance.'

Gilles brightened at the idea. The atmosphere became less tense. Greg took the moment to suggest, 'Could we go across to the rag room, Gilles? The band must have heard what's happened? They're probably wondering . . .'

'Oh, of course, we were searching everywhere, we looked there, unlikely though it seemed—'

'Then I dare say they're in a bit of bewilderment – perhaps they're even a bit anxious?'

'Oh. Yes. Of course, I should have thought of that, only you know we're been totally taken up with trying to find her and it just didn't occur to me to think what they'd be feeling but I do see what you mean, so perhaps we ought to trot over there and just put them in the picture – would it be OK, Maman, if I did that?'

She nodded approval; they went out. Gilles was chattering all the way, but Greg tuned him out.

The rag room was stuffy and smelt of cigarettes and drink. A small table and the desk that housed the telephone were cluttered with empty beer cans and half-empty wine bottles. Ashtrays full of squashed cigarettes littered shelves and the top of the piano.

Nils was at the piano, playing a rhythmic progression in accompaniment to the bass-player, who was taking the lead and making a big show of his skill. Morena was nearby, listening, but hurried away to greet Gilles at the door. She threw her arms around him and hugged him.

'Poor, poor Gillie,' she murmured. 'I've been so worried for you! Have they found the old lady yet?'

He shook his head, his hair catching in the wool of her white sweater. He said something that was muffled against the comfort of her breast.

Nils and François gave up their music to join them. Lou was already in a chair in the main part of the room, staring up at the ceiling. The others sat down, Morena perching beside Gilles on the side of his armchair.

'So what gives?' Lou asked. 'She come back?'

'There's no word so far,' Greg said. 'There doesn't seem much more to be done for the moment.'

'You had your guys poking in every hole and corner. She's not on the property?' Lou persisted.

'Well, Roger cycled round first of all, taking all the paths she liked to walk, but no, she'd not had a fall or anything like that, so he took some of the other men out while there was still enough daylight and searched everywhere he could think of on the grounds and then they looked in all the out-buildings, including here—'

'Out-buildings,' François repeated. 'That means places

76

where you keep the cattle and the pigs, eh? They rooted around in here. Is that what we are, livestock?'

'Ssh,' said Emilio. 'Go on, Gilles.'

'The only conclusion is that she's gone away, perhaps overnight, we think she'll get in touch, it's not as if this is new to us, so we're not too worried – well, we're worried, of course, but we think she'll come back when she's ready.'

'One of the guys that came in here said she'd never come back while we were still around,' persisted François.

'Well . . . you mustn't pay too much attention to that. It's true Papa thinks she left because she couldn't stand it any more—'

'Couldn't stand it! And we had nothing to put up with?' Nils enquired, in a cooler tone than François and yet with some rancour. 'Of course I wish the old lady no harm, but doesn't it seem to you that she's rather mean? Because of course, what she is doing is emotional blackmail.'

'Well . . . yes . . . she's always been good at that. But you see she's been such a strong force in Papa's life—'

'Let's get down to the nitty-gritty,' François broke in, acting the tough guy in pseudo-American mode. 'Is she going to win out? Are we going to get the brush-off?'

'No, no, of course not – Greg, tell them . . .'

Greg took over. He was sorry for them, but was a little taken aback at the veiled aggression he could feel. 'I think by and by the band will have to move out if Nounou's to come back. And it's clearly imperative that she does come back.'

'Of course,' murmured Emilio. 'We couldn't be responsible for keeping on old lady out of her home.'

'Exactly. But that's for the future. At present M. Guidon is really too distracted to think about altering the terms of your agreement. That agreement made it a condition that you all stayed here – perhaps it was so he could keep an eye on you, Gilles – but when it comes to the point I think we can move you out en bloc.'

Gilles broke in in mournful tones: 'What it means is that Nounou is more important than me, in the end.'

Greg said nothing. It seemed to him Gilles might have just

77

stated a truth, but only a temporary truth. Morena leaned over to put an arm around his shoulders and drop a kiss on the top of his head. 'Never mind, we love you, Gillie,' she murmured.

'Let's not get mushy,' François groused. 'I'd like everything out on the square. Are we going on, because if not, there's a six-week gig in Brussels I can have just for the asking.'

'François, please, don't say things like that. We've got a lot of work invested already—'

'Yeah, but what kind of work, that's what I'd like to clear up! Yesterday you had Morena and Emilio working on a waltz – a waltz, for God's sake! What next? The polka? An American march by Souza?'

Nils made a sound that might have been agreement. Morena gave a little laugh and said quite lightly: 'OK, don't get your hair in a pigtail, I won't ask for anything if it's going to cause this sort of hassle. I only thought—'

'Don't put it all on Morena,' Gilles protested. 'I know very well that you've got your own ideas for making a change in the group. You want a bigger rhythm section—'

'I never said that!'

'So what was all that about having a Roland drum kit? We agreed from the outset that the emphasis should be on—'

'But that was when we started,' François returned. 'Now all of a sudden we've changed to a sextet, so why not seven by adding a drummer and—'

'Please, everybody,' Greg cried, trying not to be irritated by the argument, 'let's have an intermission! Squabbling isn't going to help.'

François said something very uncomplimentary in French, which Greg shrugged off. The man was in a very bad mood, had had perhaps a good deal to drink, and perhaps it was time to have some food. Food, the Prince had found, was a good way to calm people down. He asked Gilles if something could be sent over from the house.

Gilles unwound himself from Morena's embrace to telephone the kitchen. Everyone seemed to relax. Greg took up the objections that François had been making. 'The contract you signed specifies you're part of a six-piece ensemble, the name to be confirmed before your first engagement. You can't become a seven-piece nor should you dwindle away to a five-piece – not without altering the contract and that could mean a lot of fuss. Is that understood? And speaking of naming the band, I'd like that as soon as possible so I can start telephoning a few clubs for Christmas and New Year.'

This appeal to their business sense had its effect. The tension in the air went away, they looked about for half-finished drinks and sprawled more at ease while they began to ponder on names. None of their ideas seemed particularly good.

The food came, hamburgers and pizza, the kind of thing that musicians eat in short rehearsal breaks. The difference here was that everything had been made in the kitchens of the chateau. Greg glanced at his watch and said that he ought to go soon. He had an hour's drive along dark mountain roads before him.

'Oh, please don't leave!' begged Gilles. 'Papa thinks a lot of you and you know you talked such good sense to him when he was losing his head over Nounou, and it makes me feel better if you're here to help me deal with him because I know he's blaming me and it makes me feel—'

'But it's getting late, Gilles.'

'We can put you up here – no problem.'

'Oh, sure!' agreed François. 'You can have that dinky little room next to me. Bed down with the underlings, kept out in the stables because we're not fit to hobnob with the aristos!'

Gilles went red with embarrassment. François of course had no idea that M. Couronne, his agent, was more than a mere aristocrat, but was in fact a royal. He made flapping movements at François and said, 'Oh, for Pete's sake, François, drop the communard attitude! Don't you think things are hard enough without sneering at everything?'

'And why are they hard, explain that to me? Because that bad-tempered old crone leads your family around by the nose, that's why! A bunch of rich idiots, that what you are.' But the words died away in something of a mumble. François was really quite drunk and unfocused, though still aggressive.

The Prince thought it best to stay, simply to avoid them coming to blows. Gilles telephoned to the house for a servant to prepare a room upstairs in the stable block. After a long unfruitful session about names, Gilles showed him up to it. It was one of six that had formerly been used by grooms and coachmen. As they reached its door, Papa Guidon appeared crossing the stable yard with a manservant in tow.

'My dear Greg, Gilles let us know you are staying. Philippe here has brought a selection of items you might need – dressing-gown, you see, and toilet articles, and if there is anything else you want, please use the room telephone to call for it. This is so good of you!'

'Not at all,' murmured the Prince, wishing he would go away so he could get to bed.

'Maman and I are going to retire now, and so should you, Gilles, but Sasha is going to stay up in case there is news of any kind. My dear sir, I can't thank you enough for being so thoughtful of us. Perhaps in the morning, if there has been no . . . no improvement, perhaps you and I could have a chat about what to do for the best. Goodnight, goodnight – Philippe, just check and see that Suzette has prepared the room properly.'

Father and son departed, chanting farewells and words of gratitude. The manservant ushered Greg into the room. It might once have been used by the stablemen, but was in a much more civilized state than when horses lived below. It was furnished with a studio bed, a dressing-table, a comfortable armchair, toilet facilities in a glassed-off corner, a bureau with a small television set and a telephone.

The servant set his tray on the bureau and catalogued the contents as he laid them out. 'Nightwear, toothbrush, razor . . . Suzette stocked the little refrigerator with brandy and mixers but if there's some other drink you would prefer, please dial six on the phone.'

'Thank you.'

The man hesitated. 'Do you think something bad's happened to the old girl, sir?'

Greg sighed. 'There's no way of knowing. But this is unusual, isn't it? She usually lets you know where she is?'

'Last time, she'd taken the train to Zurich and was in the Dolder-Grand. Monsieur went himself to bring her back next day.' He muttered under his breath as he headed for the door. 'Wicked old crow ... Well, goodnight, sir.'

Greg sat down at the telephone to let his family know what was happening. 'I shan't be back tonight, Grossmutti, I'm staying over at the chateau.'

'What, can't bear to leave your music-makers?'

'No, it's more than that. You remember I told you about the authoritarian old nurse?'

'I do seem to remember something rather amusing along those lines.'

'It's not so amusing now. She's caused a bit of trouble.'

'And why are you required to stay because the nurse is causing trouble?' she challenged in a rallying tone.

'Oh, perhaps they think I've got experience in handling troublesome old ladies.'

'*Unartiger!* I'll make you pay for that!' She laughed. 'Well, I shall see you some time in the morning, yes?'

Next he rang Liz. She had clearly been fast asleep. She answered with a mumble.

'How was your flight?' he asked, to give her time to wake up.

'Fine, fine ... Wha' time is it?'

'Pretty late. I'm sorry I woke you.'

'That's all right.' She was trying to think what had happened during the day. 'Did you ... ah ... .work out a name for the band?'

'Not at all. We had a long try at it and their ideas were no better than yours.' He considered. 'There's a lot of tension there. François in particular. He's spoiling for a fight.'

'And François is ...?' But although the question tailed off, she was more in touch with what he was saying.

'He plays the bass fiddle. I think he's getting touchy at the way Morena's behaving.'

'How is she behaving?'

'Well, she's ... what's that English thing you say, about people who're affectionate ... something about ... a *tour-tourelle*?'

'A turtle? I talk about turtles?'

'No, no, *tourtourelle*, that's – let me see – a dove. You say people are like a dove when they cling and kiss.'

'Oh, you mean lovey-dovey? Morena's lovey-dovey? Who with?'

'Gilles.'

'Good heavens.' Now she was wide awake. 'Why Gilles? He's no pin-up.'

'But he's rich.'

'Oh yes,' she agreed. 'Now I should have thought of that.' She paused a moment then said, 'But listen, I was forgetting, what about the Nounou situation?'

'Not good. It's getting very late and we haven't heard a word. Gilles keeps saying that when she's done this before, Nounou's always telephoned to let them know, so they'll come hurrying to bring her home. But not this time.'

'Oh dear. What are you thinking? An accident seems likely?'

'It could be. They've tried the hospitals but nothing's been reported.'

'I still think she could have slipped and fallen somewhere in the grounds. We saw her up there among all those fearsome rocks.'

'They've done a thorough search. No sign of her.'

They discussed other possibilities, then Liz sighed, 'Ah, poor love. What are you doing, holding everybody's hand and being sweet to them?'

'I'm staying overnight. Auguste seems to be thinking he must take some action in the morning and wants me to help decide what comes next.'

'And what are you going to say to him?'

'Call the police,' he said.

Seven

Auguste Guidon begged the police to be discreet. The commissaire didn't reply, as he might have done, that discretion was the watchword of the entire Swiss nation.

He summoned up a team, who began by interrogating the servants. No one had seen Nounou after about eleven thirty on Friday morning. The sergeant in charge then asked to speak to the musicians. At a glance from Auguste, Greg undertook to escort him to the rag room. As it was now almost midday, the musicians had surfaced after their late night. They stood and sat about in the room, which during their absence had been swept and dusted and cleared of the debris of the night before.

Greg thought it was almost comical to be asking them about Nounou. The sergeant, a bulky man in his late thirties, took it all very seriously, addressing them in textbook English.

'So, at eleven thirty yesterday, where were you, mademoiselle?' he asked Morena.

'Getting dressed.'

'And your room is in the chateau, is that correct? So did you see Mlle Bartelet?'

'Who?'

'That's Nounou's name,' Greg supplied. 'She's Josephine Bartelet.'

Everyone stared. No one had ever thought of her as having an identity other than the shrewish old nurse. Emilio shook his head and said sadly, 'Her saint's day is the same as my sister's.'

'You were in your room, mademoiselle, and when you left it to come to this . . . er . . . studio, did you perhaps see Mlle

Bartelet, perhaps in the passage? I gather that your room is not far from hers.'

Morena shrugged. 'It's round a corner, as far as I can gather. I never spend much time over there, Sergeant. We're usually here, getting things together.'

'What things?' asked the sergeant, to give himself time to think.

'It just means discussing what they would do next, Sergeant,' Greg prompted.

'I see. So all the others were already here?'

'Well, no,' Morena said, with a smile and a nod towards her brother. 'Louie came over to ask if I wanted to make a trip to Montreux in the evening. We were beginning to have an attack of cabin fever.'

Sergeant Duchene avoided asking about cabin fever, instead sticking like a bulldog to his assemblage of facts. 'So M. Ferigiano was also in the house. Did you see Mlle Bartelet, monsieur?'

Lou shook his head. 'I'd have a run a mile if I did,' he grunted. 'No, me and Morena just decided about what to do after rehearsal. I said I'd call up a taxi round about eight, and that was it. We came out of the house and across to the rag room. No sign of the old biddy.'

'Thank you. And you, Monsieur Mavez?'

'I got up about noon,' said Emilio. 'I just had a few cups of coffee and then I came down to the rehearsal. We were all working together until the men from the chateau came in asking if we'd seen the poor old lady and looked around a little – there's a closet over there.' He nodded to the far side of the platform. 'It's where brooms and things are kept. She wasn't in it.' He stopped abruptly, aware how silly it sounded, and his olive skin coloured up. 'I mean she might have got in there accidentally . . . Well, anyway, we hadn't seen her, I'm sorry to say.'

The others nodded agreement. Nils and François said they had come down from their rooms above the stable block, had started work after a few minutes' discussion, and no one had seen anyone except each other until the search for Nounou began.

'Thank you,' said Sergeant Duchene, closing his notebook. 'I think that is all.'

'What happens now?' Greg asked as he went out with him.

'We've already started enquiring if she was seen on any of the buses or the funiculars. I gather she's quite well known on the various routes, she uses them quite frequently. And also we're asking at railway stations, and in the department stores that she liked to visit. We'll find her,' he said firmly.

Greg could see that the matter was now being taken care of without the emotional tension caused by Auguste. He felt he could make his escape. Gilles, hovering around in the sitting room at the chateau, was at first unwilling to let him go but gave in when Greg pleaded business to attend to.

He looked in on his office. Since it was Saturday, Amabelle was there, her two children sitting patiently waiting for their mother to finish a morning's work so that they could lunch at Migros. He had a short discussion about a choral perform-ance in which one of his clients was to sing, signed some cheques, then drove home.

His father was in Hungary for a few days, at a horse fair advising a rich competition rider on the purchase of a cross-bred colt. His grandmother was in her atelier – a barn given over to her rolls of furnishing material, samples of wallpaper, boxes of swags, silk rope, door handles and other accessories to fine décor.

'So here you are,' she greeted him. 'Almost lunchtime. I waited breakfast until almost ten.'

'I'm sorry. I should have rung to tell you I couldn't get away.'

'More trouble with the awkward nurse?'

'You might say that. She's vanished, Grossmutti.'

'Vanished? Meaning what?'

'Almost literally – vanished. She hasn't been seen since before lunch yesterday.'

'Good gracious.'

He gave her an outline of the situation.

'She's eighty? Well, heavens above, she's not likely to have run away with a lover. What are you thinking?'

'I don't know. I never had much contact with her but she's got a reputation for being a tyrant. I just wondered if . . .'

'What?'

'She'd annoyed someone so much that they . . .'

'Hit her on the head?'

'Well . . . Perhaps not. She might have had a brainstorm and wandered off . . . The police will find her.'

His grandmother gave him a comforting pat on the hand, and resorted to some comforting words from her Austrian childhood. *'Mein Kind, sei nicht drum besorgt. Es geht dich nichts dran.'*

He nodded in agreement, but inwardly wondered if it was true that it had nothing to do with him. Logic told him that he'd never even heard of Nounou when he undertook to find musicians for Gilles. Nevertheless, those musicians had perhaps driven the old lady to do something drastic. He felt somehow guilty.

In the afternoon, when he judged owners and managers of nightclubs might be awake and aware, he did some telephoning. He got one or two nibbles; a bierkeller in Zurich had a vacancy of a few nights during the Easter break, and a ski centre in the Vaud Alps were willing to replace their disc jockey and his dubious jokes with live entertainment for St Valentine's Day.

Next day the two Hirtensteins, like good Lutherans, went to church. Afterwards, the prince took himself off with his dog for a long scramble on the slopes above the house. Rousseau, his red setter, was delighted. He pranced along while still on the lead while they walked to the upper regions, then when he was set free ranged about scaring jackdaws and snow-finches. His master joined in this exercise at first but after a while slowed down to allow himself to think about the Guidons.

What a family they had proved to be. Everyone imagined that bankers were steady, reliable people, yet here was Auguste acting like a wounded child because his nanny had gone away. And no one else in the family seemed to like her; Rosanne Guidon clearly saw her as a rival, her sister-

86

in-law Marie Armonet still resented her childhood treatment, to Gilles she was a hindrance and a burden, Sasha the secretary despised her.

'But no one would actually harm a tiresome old lady,' he muttered to himself.

Rousseau came to his side at the sound of his voice.

'What do you think, Rousseau?'

The dog put his nose into the curve of his hand. Clearly something was troubling Master, and he must offer comfort.

Liz too offered comfort when he telephoned later. 'No news is good news,' she insisted. 'Bet your life she's in some comfy pension somewhere, eating chestnut mousse and drinking good coffee.'

'Of course. But why hasn't she let the Guidons know where she is?'

'Because she's a tough old terrier, that's why. What do you say – she's let them have the weekend to worry themselves to death and tomorrow she's going to turn up full of spice and sizzle.'

He could only hope she was right.

In the morning he went to the chateau to report on the possible engagements he'd been offered. It was a little too early when he arrived so instead of going to the rag room, he rang the bell at the massive front door of the house. He felt honour bound to pay his respects.

He could tell by the demeanour of the maid who answered the bell that things hadn't improved. 'No news?'

'No, sir, and Monsieur is almost ill with worry. Just be kind enough to wait a moment, I'll tell him you're here.'

'M. Guidon is at home?'

'Oh, yes, sir, and I feel sure he'll be glad to see you.'

So Auguste hadn't gone into the bank this morning? Was he going to stay at home until Nounou returned? Greg didn't know how the work at a bank was carried on, but he'd heard Auguste bemoaning the fact that things were difficult these days. He'd have thought he wouldn't absent himself any longer than necessary.

The maid came back to usher him into the morning room.

Auguste was there with a youngish man in a business suit, who was putting documents into a briefcase. 'Thank you, sir,' he was saying. His manner told Greg that this was a minion from the bank, taking back signed papers and instructions. He left the room as Greg was shown in. Auguste rose to shake hands as if he were clutching at a lifeline.

'My dear Greg, how kind of you to come again to our unhappy home. Come in, let me offer you coffee. Suzette, fresh coffee.'

They sat down on a sofa that gave them a view of the mountains. Greg said, 'How are things, Auguste? The maid told me there's no news.'

'Ah,' sighed Auguste, 'that's not strictly true. But the news isn't very enlightening. The police have been industrious, of course, and it's more or less established that no one has seen Nounou on any of the transport routes that we think she habitually used. Her credit card hasn't been used. One of the women officers searched her room with the help of one of the maids, and something . . . perhaps useful . . . I don't know, but something emerged from that.'

He studied the distant peaks, shaking his head.

'So what did they learn?'

'We know more or less what Nounou was wearing. She was dressed in a tweed skirt and a maroon padded jacket, and had her little backpack that she usually takes . . . she carries her purse and a handkerchief and a bar of chocolate in it . . . you know the kind of thing.'

'Yes.'

'But strangely enough, two pairs of shoes are missing.'

'Two pairs of shoes?'

'So it seems. My wife's maid, who assisted the police officer, looks after Nounou's things when she has time, and is a very reliable person. When she says the shoes are not in the wardrobe, that must be correct.' He shrugged. 'I don't know what it means, if anything.'

'I suppose Nounou didn't leave any message – a note, perhaps? Or mention anything about her possible destination?'

'No, no, we've been over all that dozens of times. Nounou

doesn't confide in people, she just does what she wishes to do, and of course why shouldn't she? She has a perfect right to be independent.'

'Quite true. So what are the police advising?'

'They say there is nothing for it but to wait. Thousands of adults go missing every year, they tell me. Many of them come back perfectly all right, in their own good time. In the case of teenagers, they say it's often because they feel conditions have become impossible for them at home. Then often when they experience the difficulties of life on their own, they return.' The banker looked with hope at Greg. 'Perhaps that will be the case with Nounou.'

It might well be so. Certainly Nounou was unlikely to meet the same respect and consideration elsewhere as she knew at the chateau. He said what he could to reassure Auguste, then went across to the stables.

His news about the offers of employment was greeted with little enthusiasm. 'Good Lord, Grego, a bierkeller isn't the sort of place to play our kind of jazz!'

'But Zurich? That would be good exposure, surely?'

'No, no, we can't perform in a place where they're going to request the Lorelei song—'

'We could explain to the manager that you wouldn't—'

'Greg, you don't explain things to the manager when you're starting out,' François said with scorn. 'You have to—'

'So what about the ski place? How does that sound?'

'I bet it's a big dance floor. Disc jockey – that usually means amplified music, heavy beat—'

'They're not going to like cool jazz—'

'But you wouldn't b e expected to play for dancing—'

'So who'd be taking care of that? You mean split billing—'

'No way!'

So yesterday's phone calls had been a waste of time.

'Look here,' he said, 'it would help a lot if I had a name to give to them. When I say you're a "new jazz combo", they've no idea what it means. You could be playing Dixieland, for all they know.' A little investigation and the loan of a few discs from friends had taught the Prince that there were many varieties of jazz.

89

'Well, that's true. Listen, guys, we really gotta work out a name,' said Lou.

So they sat down with coffee and fruit juice and pastries to consider the problem. Morena and Gilles sat side by side, sharing a croissant and giggling at the crumbs with which they decked themselves. François snappishly called them to order. Morena made a little face at him, but they obeyed.

The group bickered and ridiculed each other's suggestions. It seemed to Greg that Gilles played very little part in this, but instead followed Morena's lead, shaking his head when she disagreed, nodding when she seemed in favour.

'We ought to let them know there's a vocalist with the group,' she suggested.

'What, you want us to call ourselves The Fabulous Five with Morena?' This was François, ready to pick a fight.

'She didn't say that, François,' Lou protested.

'It's what she meant! I'll tell you this for nothing – I'm pretty tired of the way your sister wants to star in this out-fit—'

'Quit racing your motor, Frankie,' Morena said with a shrug. 'It was just a thought.'

François muttered something to the effect that her thoughts were as stupid as the songs she sang, but everybody decided not to hear.

By midday they'd come to a reluctant agreement. They were going to call themselves The Sophisticates.

Greg didn't know whether it was a good name or not. The public took to certain notions and slogans, for reasons that he couldn't understand, and rejected others. All he could do was try out this label and see how it worked.

He said his farewells. The rest of the day was spent alone at his office, returning phone calls from concert artists and the managers of venues, and then catching up with emails. At last he went home to a rather good meal made by his grandmother, who in her girlhood in Austria as a minor member of the Habsburgs had been taught six good dishes in the repertoire of haute cuisine. Exile and the necessity to be an economical housekeeper had taught her how to adapt these recipes. She was a quite notable cook.

She asked him about Nounou. When she heard there was still no news, she frowned. 'I'm an old lady too, Gregoire. I don't think I'd like to be adrift in the big world without money—'

'But she has money. She's got a credit card.'

'But didn't you say she hadn't used it?'

'Ah . . . yes . . . that was what Auguste told me.'

They looked at each other. 'She must be staying with friends,' said Grossmutti. 'There's no other explanation.'

He didn't reply that he'd been told repeatedly that Nounou had no friends. To change the subject, he gave her a sketch of the rumpus over choosing a name.

'The Sophisticates? Is that a good name?' she wondered.

'We'll find out soon enough. I'm going to start again in the morning, telephoning around and sending out some emails.'

'Will you do it from your office? If so, take me into Geneva with you. I want to collect some paint cards from Friederberg's.'

'I thought I'd do it in Papa's office, since he's away. But if you want to go into town, I'll—'

'No, no, it's not urgent.' She refilled her wine glass, staring at it for a moment in thought. 'What you told me about Gilles Guidon and that girl—'

'Morena.'

'That sounds rather serious. And it sounds as if François is jealous.'

'Ye-es. Perhaps.'

'I imagine your friend Auguste didn't imagine his son was going to fall in love with a cabaret girl.'

'Cabaret? Oh, come on, Grossmutti, she doesn't do anything flamboyant. She just plays the piano in a muted sort of way and sings.'

'And is very pretty.'

'Yes, more than pretty. Really beautiful.'

'My darling boy, you aren't beginning to have tender feelings for her?' she said in alarm. She was always terrified that he would fall for someone even more unsuitable than the dreadful English girl, and be involved in a scandal.

'Not at all, not at all. I regard her as a beautiful work of pictorial art.'

She laughed. 'Nicely put. And Gilles – how does he regard her? Is he going to bed with her?'

'*Chère madame, c'est une question sans savoir-faire.*'

'Well, I would like to know. It's intriguing.'

Her question was answered next day. Greg was busy at the family computer in his father's office, with Rousseau for company, when he was startled by the ring of the telephone. Rousseau sat up, staring at the phone as if it were a hare he should chase.

'Greg, please come!' begged Auguste Guidon in a voice of misery. 'We don't know what to do.'

'What's happened? Has Nounou come back?'

'No, no, it's nothing to do with Nounou. Gilles and Morena have eloped!'

Eight

Greg was out of the door at once, Rousseau racing along beside him in excitement. When his grandmother saw him from the window she hurried to the door, to call as he was closing the car: 'Where are you going?'

'To Chateau Guidon! I'll explain later.'

As he put the car in gear, he felt Rousseau's moist nose against the side of his neck. The dog had jumped in while he turned to speak to Grossmutti and, as always required, had taken up position on the back seat. Well, he wasn't going to stop to send him back to the house. 'Sit back, Rousseau,' he commanded.

The dog obeyed. Lovely. A car outing. Nothing the setter enjoyed more than an outing like that. It usually involved a good romp en route in some big open space.

At the chateau, Roger opened the gates for him instantly and was waiting for him in the courtyard by the front door. 'I'll take your car round to the garage, sir, if you don't mind. The police may be here later, they take up a lot of room.'

'OK. You don't mind my dog being in the car?'

'Not at all. In fact, Monsieur Couronne, it's likely you'll be here quite a while. Madame doesn't allow animals in the house but why don't I let him out and have him by me in the garage? I might even find him a biscuit.'

Rousseau gave a little bark of appreciation at the word. 'He's your friend for life,' Greg said.

The maid led him straight to what he thought must be Auguste's study. A big room, its stone walls furnished with framed photographs of Guidons of the past, and degrees and diplomas belonging to the present master of the house. A decanter of Madeira and a plate of biscuits stood at the ready.

Even in times of crisis, one must always provide for the nourishment of guests.

'You can imagine what a state we're in,' groaned the banker. 'Rosanne is prostrate! To think our son would behave so rashly! And she quite liked the girl, you know – a cut above what we expected when we knew Gilles had given her a contract.'

'So what has happened? How do you know she and Gilles—'

'Because he left us a note!' wailed Auguste. 'Here – see for yourself.'

The note was on paper headed with the chateau's emblem. Dated the previous day, the message was: 'Morena and I need some time to ourselves to find out how we feel. The pressures in the house, what with Nounou's silly behaviour and the quarrelling in the band, make it impossible for us to sort ourselves out. I'll be in touch in a few days. Please tell Greg to get the guys to hang together until I get back.'

'When did you find this?'

'It was here on my desk this morning. His car is gone. He of course opened the gates from the house before driving off, and he closed them behind him by using the keypad under the gate telephone. So we noticed nothing amiss. He didn't appear for breakfast, but of course, since he began rehearsing with the musicians' – here Auguste shuddered in disapproval – 'he's been getting up very late.' He hesitated then added: 'And of course, since we've had this worry about Nounou, I haven't been sleeping too well, so I didn't come in here until about ten thirty.'

'So how long do you think they've been gone?'

'Well, this is dated as if it was written yesterday, but that might have been any time in the middle of the night. But generally, the band seems to stop making a noise between one and two in the morning, I gather. So if he wrote this about two a.m., they've been gone about ten hours by now.'

Ten hours in a first-class car on Swiss motor routes meant they might be in another country by now. Greg said nothing.

'Now, my dear sir,' said Auguste, 'I wanted you here because you know this girl better than I do. In your opinion, what are her feelings towards my son?'

'I . . . er . . .' A difficult question. 'Only yesterday I was thinking that perhaps she was showing a great deal of affection for Gilles.'

'And he was . . . responding?'

'Oh yes.' He thought about it and added, 'He's been attracted to her from the moment she arrived.'

'But this!' protested Auguste. 'Gilles has made a fool of himself over one or two women in the past, but . . . but . . . not to the extent of taking off in the middle of the night!'

Greg was surprised by it too. Gilles had more or less fallen under Morena's spell from the word go, yet to leave the band, to endanger the great plan for a career in jazz – that was very unexpected. He thought it likely that Gilles and Morena had perhaps slept together a couple of times, but the commitment implied by their leaving was deeper than a passing affair.

Auguste had something he wanted to pursue. 'My good friend, what do you advise now? My wife is begging me to inform the police. But Marie thinks that's a foolish idea, and also that conceited secretary of hers says we have no grounds for calling in the police. What do you think?'

'Sasha's right. It isn't a crime for a grown man and a woman to go off together.'

'No. And in any case, I feel we'd look ridiculous . . . it's wrong of me to think about appearances, I know . . . yet I can't bear the thought of other people hearing about this.'

No doubt the idea that the Guidon household was losing members as fast as falling leaves would amuse a great many people. The banker, of course, had enemies, rivals, who would glory in his discomfiture. His old nurse can't stand the place any more and walks out, his son runs away with some floozie . . . What a lovely item it would make for the gossip columns.

The Prince was wishing himself almost anywhere else in the world at this moment. It was painful to witness Auguste's misery. The fleshy cheeks had fallen in, the rosy skin was pale and wan, there was a frown line between the bushy brows.

'Morena's brother Lou may have been in their confidence,' he suggested.

'Ah! Of course! Let's go and speak to him.' He grasped Greg's sleeve in his eagerness.

'But he may still be in bed—'

The banker made a sound something between a groan and a laugh. He went to his desk, picked up the telephone, and after keying in a number said: 'Please find Mr Ferigiano and ask him to come to the chateau.'

That done, he poured himself a full glass of Madeira and only afterwards thought to offer any to his guest. Greg shook his head. He detested sweet wines.

They stood waiting in the study for some minutes. Then Auguste exclaimed, 'Not in here! I don't want that man in here!' It was clear this was his retreat, his den to which he could retire for peace in troubled times.

They went along the corridor and into the hall. Here he hesitated, but before he could decide which room to select, a maid came to open the door to Lou.

Lou looked as if he'd been up for some little while. At least he was shaved and properly clad. He gave them an indignant stare. 'What's up,' he demanded, 'sending for me like a bellhop!'

'Did you know?' cried Auguste, rushing up to him and almost seizing him by the front of his sweater. 'Did you know they were going?'

Lou pulled back against the angry features thrust into his. He let a moment go by. Then he said, to Greg's eye somewhat uneasily, 'They've done it, then?'

'You knew! My God, how could you let them do this?'

'Say, how could I prevent them?' Lou countered, edging away. 'Morena's over twenty-one and in her right mind. What d'you think, I can give her orders about what she does?'

'Where have they gone?'

'No idea.' 'And I wouldn't tell you if I knew' was somehow implicit in his tone.

'But Morena told you she was going to go away with Gilles?' Greg asked, just to get the situation clear.

'We-ell . . . Not in so many words. Sis doesn't tell me everything, you know. But they were so gone on each other, and he was so miserable about the way things were heading here at the White House what with all the fuss over the old hag, that it don't surprise me that they've taken off.'

'Surely you tried to prevent her from taking such a foolish action?' Auguste demanded in a voice of despair.

'Foolish? What's so all-fired foolish about it? He's keen on her and she's keen on him and they wanted to get away from the dungeons-and-dragons atmosphere. Good luck to 'em, is what I say.'

'But it's impossible!'

'What d'you mean, impossible? Sis can give him a lot of love and sympathy.'

'Love and sympathy! And when the newspapers get hold of it, we'll look absurd.'

'Absurd? Say, you mind your mouth! My sister's not the kind to look absurd! She's got a lot of class! Anybody that knows her can tell you she wows 'em in the downtown joints, let alone in backwater shacks in a nowhere country like this—'

'Lou, have you any idea where they've gone?' Greg broke in, to deflect the tirade.

'No, and if I had I'm not gonna tell you and this pin-striped idiot here.'

'This is just the kind of behaviour I should have expected!' cried Auguste. 'And to think my poor wife imagined the girl was a something like a lady.'

'Hey!' shouted Lou, lunging at him.

Greg caught him by the arm. 'Calm down—'

'Calm down nothing! Who the hell does he think he is? Stupid stuffed shirt!'

'Out!' It was a roar of rage. 'Out of my house! Pack up and leave!'

'Great, the best thing I've heard since I got here.'

'Lou, for the love of Heaven calm down.'

'Oh, shut up, you pigeon-brained sap! I should never have let you talk me into this gig!' He turned back to Auguste with a snicker of amusement. 'Set you down a peg or two, right? Your little lamb's fallen for a singer in a band!'

'I want you to leave,' yelled Auguste. 'If you're not gone in ten minutes I'll have you thrown off my property!'

'Don't try it! I'm off, and glad to go!'

He marched to the door, swung it open, and went out closing it with a bang that echoed through the hall and onward.

Greg's first instinct was to dash after him, for Lou might still have information about his sister's thoughts and intentions. But Auguste was staggering and gasping, reaching towards one of the big oak chairs that stood against the wall.

Greg helped him to sit. 'What's the matter?' he asked, really scared by the man's appearance.

Auguste waved a hand in front of his face, panting, uttering a few incoherent words. The maid who had opened the door to Greg ran into the hall, having heard it bang shut in such an unaccustomed fashion.

'Quick, fetch Madame,' Greg commanded.

She went at once to a telephone on a dark wood table and pressed a button. When she heard a reply, she offered the receiver to Greg. 'This is M. Couronne,' he said. 'Is that Madame?'

'This is Arlette, in Madame's room.'

'Is she there? May I speak to her?'

'I think she's with Mme Armonet, sir.'

'Go and fetch her at once. Ask her to come down to the hall at once.'

'Yes, sir.' The response sounded scared. The whole household had apparently begun to expect the worst at every moment.

'A glass of water,' he said to the housemaid, who was dithering at his side.

'Yes, sir.'

Auguste was still gasping and bending over to catch his breath as if after a hard race. 'Your wife is coming,' Greg said.

Auguste nodded. A moment later came the sound of machinery. A lift of whose existence Greg had been unaware glided to a stop round a curve of the hall. Rosanne Guidon appeared at the run, her sister-in-law a couple of steps behind her.

'Auguste! Auguste, my angel, my darling, this has all been too much for you! Marie, take his other arm. Dearest, try to stand up. There, just lean on us—'

But Marie had edged away, so Greg took the other arm and between them they helped Auguste to the lift. At the press of a button it ascended to the first floor. With increasing strength Auguste held himself erect and was ushered into his bedroom by his wife. She nodded thanks to Greg but clearly let him know he wasn't needed any longer.

He took the stairs down. Marie Armonet was still there, sitting now in the chair that her brother had occupied and sipping the water the maid had brought.

'Are you all right?' Greg asked in alarm. Not another heart attack!

'Yes, quite all right, just a bit scared.' She handed the glass to the maid and nodded dismissal. 'Let's go into the sitting room.' She led the way. They sat on either side of the welcoming wood fire crackling in the grate. 'He's got a slight problem with blood pressure,' she explained. 'Nothing serious, you know, and the doctor prescribed medication, but ever since that confounded old harridan decamped, he's been forgetting to take it, and so now this!'

'I'm sorry. I know he's been very worried about Nounou—'

'Not only that, things haven't been going too well at the bank, as far as I can gather. You know, government interference, demands from the United States about money-laundering, that sort of rubbish. Nothing that won't pass over, as all those things do in the end, but he's always had a tendency to take things too much to heart.' She shook her head in irritation. 'I mean, look at the idiotic way he goes on about the old girl. She saved his life, yes, I suppose she did, but that was fifty years ago. Good God, hasn't he repaid her enough by now? Does she have to make him pay over and over again?'

He offered no opinion on that. He let a moment go by then said, 'Does Gilles have any places he likes to go in particular? Holidays – where does he go on holiday?'

'Oh, Lord, the Bahamas? New Orleans for the jazz? Anyway, don't bother about it. He'll be back in a few days, he says so in that ridiculous note. My opinion is they'll come back when the girl's got a ring on her finger.'

'Is that what you think? That she's . . . what do they call it, a gold-digger?'

'What else? Don't tell me she's fallen in love with Gilles, nothing would make me believe that. The boy's a fool, of course. She's not the first one he's imagined to be his true love, and Auguste has had to buy them off. He'll buy off this one.'

It seemed only too possible. He rose. 'If you don't mind, I'd like to get over to the rag room.'

'Oh, of course. Tell them the days of wine and roses are over, and they should pack up and go.'

'But Gilles asks in his note that they should be kept together.'

'I tell you, the boy's a fool. What, you think my brother will let this go on? Nounou's run off because of them, Gilles makes a fool of himself over the girl, and you think Auguste will permit it any longer? No, no, my dear Monsieur Couronne, tell them the money bags will close up and the dream of an easy life is ended.'

He smiled as if in agreement and went out. He couldn't say he thought that living in little rooms above the stables was exactly wine and roses, but it was true they had very good financial terms with the Guidons. He found the maid still hovering and asked for a quick way to the stable block, because he wanted to speak to Lou, to persuade him not to leave. She showed him to a side door.

Too late. As he went across the garage yard, he heard a car drive off. He ran round the stables and to the front of the chateau. Lou was just being driven away in a taxi.

'Wait!' he shouted.

Useless. With a few inward words of frustration he went back towards the rag room.

The door was open and the musicians were just straggling in again, after waving goodbye to Lou Ferigiano. Three of them, looking very depressed. No one bothered to greet the Prince.

'Did he say where he was going?' he enquired.

They shook their heads. 'There wasn't any talking to him. He was red hot with anger at the way he'd been treated,' said François, with some schadenfreude.

'After all,' Nils pointed out, 'it is not his fault if his sister falls in love with Gilles.'

'Ha!' snorted François. 'Love? As the tennis player used to say, you must be joking.'

'Well, Gilles fell in love with her,' amended Nils.

'So now you have to say it's not Lou's fault if his sister gets talked into a dumb stunt with Gilles. Is that what you're saying? Because, if you want my take on it, Morena ain't the girl to be talked into anything she don't wanna do,' François said, taking comfort in his idea of Americanism.

No one disagreed with that. Emilio sighed. 'I was very surprised at what Lou told us. Of course I could see that Gilles and Morena were . . . getting very attached—'

'Attached? He couldn't keep his hands off her!'

'François, please don't be so cruel. He had deep feelings for her, that was clear, but still I did not think they would do anything so rash as to elope. In my family, a thing like that would bring disgrace.'

'I bet it's brought something pretty much like disgrace to the Guidons. I bet they're miffed, to say the least. What's the situation back at the ranch, Greg? They crying into their Napoleon brandy?'

'They're not happy, François. And it's no laughing matter even from your point of view. At least one member of the household would like to see you all packed up and gone.'

'This is a house of trouble,' said Emilio. 'I think we must agree that we are not welcome. We never were, but now it seems we must make their hearts ache just by being here. I think we should leave.'

'Right! I can go to Brussels tomorrow if we break up—'

'But is it right that we do so?' Niles asked. 'We signed contracts, after all.'

'I bet you Papa wouldn't bother about the contracts if we told him we're splitting.' François looked at Greg in challenge. 'Am I right or am I right?'

'But Gilles wants you to stay,' he answered. 'In his note he specifically asked—'

'His note? He left a note?' François burst out laughing. 'My God, he's been reading Red Rose Romances!'

101

'He specifically asked,' persisted Greg, 'that you stay together until he gets back.'

'Oh yeah! That's going to be fun then, isn't it? Trying to get a new combo to work together when two of them have behaved like a pair of star-struck teenagers. I never thought much of our glorious leader in the first place, but now I've had it up to here with him.'

François couldn't prevent his tone of jealousy. Nils shook his head at him. 'Let's keep personalities out of it. And also, let's not do anything in haste. I don't know how the rest of you are feeling, but the situation is still absolutely new to me. Less than half an hour ago Lou came rushing in saying that M. Guidon had insulted him, and now he's gone.'

'Naturally M. Guidon would be upset that his son had run away with Morena. That is not the right way to start out in married life.'

'Emilio, you don't really think Gilles and Morena are going to get married, do you!'

'Of course.' To the Latin outlook of the clarinettist, no honourable man would run off with a young woman unless he intended matrimony.

'What Gilles and Morena decide to do is not our business,' said Nils, trying once again to be businesslike. 'Greg tells us that Gilles wants us to stay together until he gets back. He wants the band to continue. We signed contracts stating we would stay until at least the Montreux Festival. It seems to me we ought to—'

'We ought to think of ourselves and for ourselves, same as Gilles and his lady-love—'

'You're keen to break up because you have a gig waiting for you in Brussels. What about you, Emilio?'

'No, I have no plans,' Emilio said. 'But, Nils, I do think we are unwelcome here.'

'What do you say, Greg?' Nils asked. 'What is your opinion about the contracts, if we were to go?'

'I think François was right when he said M. Guidon would take no action,' Greg admitted. 'All the same, I can't see any reason to dash off in the next ten minutes. Gilles will be back. If I remember rightly, he said he'd be back in a few days. Why not wait and talk it out with him?'

'Because he's a great big baby who doesn't know a thing about the real world—'

'François, François, for the love of Heaven, shut up! I know you're angry with him, and if I tell the truth I'm not too pleased with him myself. But let's wait and see what he says. You know, we were beginning to make a very good sound together.'

Emilio nodded agreement with Nils's verdict, although with some reluctance. 'We were making something that had a feel to it . . . If we were to stay, we could always keep out of the way of the family. We could do some work on that E minor thing . . . "Shadow Falls". It needs a lot of thought, the way the tempo changes. And when we go into town we could be a little more quiet when we get back, eh? Make ourselves less of a problem. What do you say, François?'

'I say I want to go to Brussels—'

'Brussels won't disappear if you leave it for a few days,' Greg broke in. 'If it's a genuine offer, that is.'

'Of course it's a genuine offer,' cried François, indignant. 'Starting the week before Christmas.'

'Well, that's almost five weeks yet.'

'But I have to let them know.'

'Leave it a week, François,' urged Nils. 'That will still give them plenty of time to find a replacement if you can't make it.'

François looked from one to the other. He gave a groan. 'So . . . I'm outvoted. OK. I'll wait a week, or until Gilles and Morena turn up if that's less than a week. Then we sort it out, one way or the other, no holds barred. Agreed?'

After they nodded and muttered assent, Greg left. He went to fetch Rousseau from the chauffeur's lair in the garage. Roger gave the dog a friendly rub with both hands before letting him go.

'He's a great fellow, isn't he, sir? He asked to go walkies' – Rousseau wagged his tail at the word – 'so I took him all round the lawns and up the drive a bit and he's done it, you know, so that's seen to. I used a bit of string for a leash, you know, because dogs aren't allowed off the lead close to the house although walkers can give them a run on the rocky terrain higher up.'

'Thank you,' said Greg. 'Well, Rousseau, say goodbye to your new friend.'

The setter obediently held up a forepaw to be shaken.

'He's a lad, isn't he?' laughed the chauffeur, shaking it. Then he became serious. 'How're things over at the house, sir? I was expecting the police to be called but nothing's come of that, and then I was told to be ready to open the gates for the doctor but that order's been changed now.'

'M. Guidon had a bit of a turn, that's all. Scared his wife for a moment, perhaps. But he's probably all right now.'

Roger shook his head. 'That American gentleman that went off in a taxi – was it something to do with him?'

'It's all taken care of, Roger,' the Prince said. And, unable to get any useful gossip, Roger let him take his leave with his dog.

It was now mid-afternoon and he was hungry. He stopped en route at a little restaurant, leaving Rousseau in the car. In great need of comfort, he called Liz Blair on her mobile although at this time of day she was almost certainly out on business.

When she spoke, she sounded harassed. 'Oh, it's you, sweetness. Listen, I'm in the middle of something, so be quick.'

'I'm sorry. I just wanted to be in touch. You're busy, though.'

'What's the matter?' she asked at once. 'You sound . . . peculiar.'

'Oh, thank you.' He couldn't help being a little offended. 'So you're not at liberty to chat?'

'Just a minute.' He heard various sounds, one of them the closing of a door. Then she said, 'I was at a planning meeting for spring fashions, but I'm in the corridor now. What on earth's the matter with you, Greg? You sound absolutely miserable.'

'Oh, never mind.'

She made a little sound of irritation. 'Come on, laddo, tell me what's up! Has the Dragon Lady been at you again?'

'No, it's nothing like that. And for you this is a bad time—'

'And getting worse from how you're behaving!' She let a little moment go by then said in a coaxing tone. 'I'm sorry I've been ratty with you. It doesn't matter about the meeting – spring is months away, if I remember rightly. So come on, forgive me and tell me what's happened. Is it something to do with the jazz band?'

'Gilles has eloped with Morena.'

'What?'

'In the middle of last night. Auguste has had something like a heart attack, François is threatening to pack up and go to Brussels, and I feel as if I'm in the middle of *Elektra*.'

'Where's *Elektra*?'

Despite everything, it made him laugh. 'It's an opera by Richard Strauss, all about family problems. Listen, *carina*, I'm sorry I bothered you. I just felt the need to hear your voice.'

'Good Lord! It's as bad as that, is it?'

'No, of course not. But seeing Auguste in a state of near collapse was scary.'

'Of course it was. And so with Gilles having gone on an unexpected honeymoon the band is going to disband, eh?'

'Well, that's another problem. Gilles has asked me to keep them together until he gets back.'

'Hmm . . . He's been in touch, then?'

'No, it was in the note he left.'

'You're kidding! He swans off with the lady in the Gatsby dress, and leaves you to take care of the resulting mess?'

'What's a Gatsby dress?'

'Oh, just my way of describing it – what Morena was wearing when I met her – never mind that. Listen, precious, what about if I come to Geneva for a few days?'

'Could you? I thought you were busy.'

'Oh, nuts to that. I'll finish up here and then to tell the truth, everything will quieten down until we start the office Christmas-party season. So would you like me to come?'

'In my Latin classes that was always described as a question that expects the answer yes. So what flight will you take?'

'Not sure. I'll tell you what, book me into that little hotel again and I'll give you a call on your mobile – somewhere around nine, I imagine. How about that?'

'Sounds marvellous. You're sure you can give up the time?'

'Anything to make things better for my special person. I'll soothe your troubles away in my own particular fashion.'

When they disconnected, he already felt a hundred per cent better. He knew she couldn't quite soothe his troubles away, but somehow having her there would ensure that things didn't get worse.

A foolish notion.

Nine

It was fully dark by the time Greg was winding his way out of Geneva towards the old farmhouse at Bredoux. Rousseau knew they were almost home. As soon as Greg drew up, he escaped from the car to run to the house door, where he leapt up towards the handle barking eagerly. Footsteps in the passage told Greg that his father had returned from his horse-buying trip.

Rousseau leapt up to greet the wanderer. Ex-King Anton submitted to being licked once or twice before the dog was quelled by the voice of the mistress of the house. 'Behave, Rousseau!' Like the owners of Chateau Guidon, Grossmutti wasn't in favour of dogs in the living quarters – they shed hairs on sofas and left paw marks on carpets.

Greg gave his father a hug then took the setter to his night-time place in the stables. When he got back, Anton was still recounting his negotiations in Hungary. The ex-Queen Mother was dying for him to finish to that she could hear the news from the chateau.

'So you think it was a fair price and you'll be taking a look at the foal in the spring,' she intervened. 'Excellent, excellent. So, Gregoire, what was happening at the chateau? Did the cross old lady come back?'

'What cross old lady?' Although Anton had been kept up to date to some extent by telephone chats, he knew only that his son had been gathering musicians for the son of the rich Guidons.

His mother gave him a rapid résumé of what had happened thus far. 'And so this old nurse has walked out and poor M. Guidon is very upset, She's been demanding that the band should be dismissed from the chateau. That's right, isn't it? So is she still making the same fuss about it?'

'She hasn't come back. It wasn't about Nounou. You remember Morena—'

'Oh, yes, the American beauty.'

'She and Gilles have run off together.'

That was enough to astound even Nicoletta, who in her time had been a witness to many scandals, royal and diplomatic. After a moment she said: 'Oh-ho! Well, that certainly wasn't what M. Guidon was hoping for in his efforts to cure his son of his jazz mania. Go on, tell us the rest.'

He gave them a short account of the situation. His father shook his head in sympathy. 'Poor souls,' he said in his gentle way. 'They don't seem a happy family, do they?'

Nicoletta had had a moment to think. 'I'm sorry in a way that I encouraged you to get involved, Gregoire. What do you say? In a few days he'll be thinking it's all your fault for bringing the girl to the chateau in the first place!'

'That could be. Excuse me, Grossmutti, I'd better feed Rousseau, because I'll be going out later.'

'Back to the Guidons?'

He chose not to hear this question but instead went out to see to the dog. Then he settled down in his father's little office alongside the stables to use its telephone, calling up any messages from his office. As always, there were a few from his clients in various parts of the world, only one or two of which required action. That done, it was around the right time for his rendezvous with Liz.

She was in the little bar of the hotel, looking rather tired but still to his mind the most beautiful sight in Geneva. She was wearing city clothes, a business suit with an unexpectedly bright scarlet shirt that sent faint tones of russet into her honey-coloured hair.

'How was your flight?'

'Crowded. Ski season, of course. How're you? Still downcast?'

'Not now that you're here.' They kissed, and the barman allowed them a moment before he came to take Greg's order.

'Any further happenings?' she asked.

108

'Not at Chateau Guidon, thank heavens. At home, Papa's back from Hungary.' The barman brought his drink and asked if they'd like a menu. 'Are we going to eat here?' Greg enquired.

'Oh, why not.' They put their heads together over the menu, but Liz wasn't really interested in food. It was the Guidon family that held her attention. 'So did you say the brother, Lou, didn't know anything?'

'That's what he said. But I never really had a chance to talk to him about it – he stormed out in a huff and was gone before I could get to him.' He paused, thinking about it. 'He must have packed in a devil of a hurry, when I recall all the luggage they came with.'

'Meaning what? That he dashed off because he didn't want to be asked if he was in on it?'

He shrugged. 'No, I've no real reason to think so. No, he surely wouldn't have wanted Morena to cause trouble, because that might put paid to his chance of playing at the Festival.'

'Oh, come on,' she countered, 'if his sister's going to tie up with the rich Guidon family, what does he care about a job in a jazz band?' She gave him a pat on the arm. 'Good job you didn't let her know you're a Highness. She might have preferred royalty to riches!'

He was shaking his head at her when his phone rang. He looked his apology then got it out. It was, of all people, Nils Peters. 'Sorry to trouble you at this time of the evening, Greg, but we're in a bit of a dilemma here. Could you come and sort things out?

He stifled a groan. 'What's happened now?'

'A secretary person came here to the rag room and ordered us out.'

'A secretary? Sasha?'

'He didn't give his name. He just said he was the secretary to Mme Guidon and Mme Armonet and that we were to be packed up and gone by midday tomorrow.'

'Oh, for Heaven's sake!'

'We tried ringing the master of the house, you know, M. Guidon, but they won't put us through to him, they say

109

he's not too well. In fact, nobody will speak to us. François was all for going up to the house and having a showdown but Emilio and I talked him out of that. He's agreed to wait and see what you can do. You told us this afternoon that Gilles expected us to stay. It's a bit of a problem.'

'All right, I'll be there in about an hour.' He disconnected as he turned in apology to Liz. 'I've got to go to the Guidons.'

'More trouble at t'mill?'

'Oh, that's your peculiar English saying. Yes, I think you could say the mill is in big trouble. I'm sorry, *mi amor*.'

'Can I come with you?'

'You'd like to?'

'Oh, absolutely. I've never been in a chateau where somebody is actually living, they've all been museums.' She got up. 'I'll just fetch my coat.'

He paid for the drinks and told the barman they wouldn't be eating in the hotel after all. Liz reappeared with a thick wool coat. They set off out of the lights of the city and into mountain country.

She gave a little cry of delight when Roger opened the gates of the estate for them. 'My word, this is really posh!' But the chateau itself disappointed her. 'Why, it's quite small. I expected something with at least twenty turrets.'

He drove to the forecourt of the house, where Nils was waiting for him. 'I thought it would be a good idea if I came out to give you the picture. François is quite drunk now and really aggressive.' In the light from the porch he looked at Liz with pleasure, and shook hands. 'I believe Greg has mentioned you. How do you do. Listen, Greg, the sooner we clear this up the better. Emilio is quite depressed about it and you know . . . François . . .' He ended with a shrug.

'Let's see if I can get a word with Auguste.' He hesitated. 'Do you want to come in with me?'

'I don't know. I think the servants might have been told not to let us in.'

'Oh, really, what a way to behave!' the Prince exclaimed. 'OK, then, I'll take it from here.' He paused. 'Are you coming with me, Liz? Or would you rather go to the rag room with Nils?'

'Doesn't sound much fun there,' she observed, smothering a grin. 'One of them is depressed and the other's blotto. I think I'll stick with you.'

They went to the door and rang the bell. After a delay, during which they were aware they were being examined through the little window at the side of the great door, it opened. It was the housemaid who'd been on duty that morning. 'Good evening, sir.' She sounded weary.

'Good evening. Would you inform M. Guidon that I would like to speak to him, and that I'm bringing with me Mlle Blair, whom he met at the Merveille last week.'

'Er . . . M. Guidon . . . isn't very well . . .'

'I know that,' said the Prince in a quiet tone. 'If you remember, I was here when he had his setback.'

'Yes, sir.'

'Please tell him it's important.'

She sighed. 'Very well, sir. If you'll just wait here, I'll tell monsieur.' She let them into the hall and offered them a seat.

'The hall's not bad,' Liz murmured, gazing around. 'Quite in chateau mode.'

He smiled. She took his hand. He was glad to see that she was wearing a ring he'd given her earlier in the year. Not on her engagement finger, but that was only to be expected. Liz always said she wanted to keep their relationship on a sensible basis, and sense told them both that if he ever talked about marriage, his grandmother would throw him into Lake Geneva – and Liz after him.

The maid returned. 'This way, please.' She ushered him into the room that he now identified as the small sitting room. It seemed to be a favourite sanctum, cosy for the winter weather. Auguste was there with his wife, Auguste in a velvet quilted jacket and slippers, his wife in an after-six dress and a perfect hairdo.

'My dear friend,' said Auguste, getting up from his armchair to take Greg by both hands. 'Now please come to the fire, sit down, let us be comfortable. And your friend, Ms Blair.' He spoke English, in deference to Liz. 'May I offer you something? Glühwein? Hot chocolate? Something stronger?'

111

'Nothing, thank you. We shan't be staying long, I hope, and I apologize for spoiling your evening.'

'No, no, my dear Greg, we are always delighted to see you.'

'Yes, indeed, after you were so good and kind to Auguste this morning, my dear Greg, you will always find a welcome with us.'

Greg demurred, they insisted on thanking him, and in the end he got to the point he had come to discuss. 'It seems that you've ordered the band to pack up and go?'

'I beg your pardon?'

'The musicians. They tell me they've had instructions that they must be gone by tomorrow midday.'

Auguste raised bushy eyebrows. 'Where did you get that idea, my boy?'

'Your wife's secretary came to the rag room with a message to that effect, earlier this evening.'

'*Oh, que le diable l'importe!* That's Marie, taking things upon herself again!'

'*Auguste, mon cher, ne te dérange pas!*' cried Rosanne. 'Please be calm, be calm.'

'Did you know about this?' he demanded, shaking off her anxious touch on his arm.

'No, no, of course not. As if I would do anything without asking you first . . .'

Auguste sat down in his armchair. 'Really,' he said in tones of exhaustion, 'why can't she leave well alone? And why didn't Sasha check with me before doing such a thing? He must surely have known that it would go against my wishes . . .' He paused. 'Well, perhaps not. I've said some rather angry things about the band since Nounou went away.'

To give everyone a chance to calm down, Liz said, 'Is there any word from Nounou yet?'

'No, nothing. And time is going by . . . The police say her credit card hasn't been used at all, and yet, you know, she left with only the clothes she was wearing.'

'What was she wearing?' asked Liz.

Auguste glanced towards his wife for the reply. She said, 'Arlette – that's my maid, you know – she said it must be a brown tweed skirt and a maroon padded jacket.'

'Not very noticeable.'

'There was that strange matter of the two pairs of shoes,' Greg recalled.

'Two pairs?'

'Yes, Arlette supposes she was wearing one pair and the other must have been in the backpack she uses.'

Liz frowned. 'May I see?'

'See what?'

'Her wardrobe.'

Rosanne looked perplexed. Greg explained, 'Liz is something of an expert on clothes. It's her business, you see.'

'Oh, by all means, then, my dear. Dearest, just telephone for Arlette, will you?'

Auguste picked up the receiver from the table next his chair and spoke into it. He then turned back to Greg to say, 'Of course you must tell your musician friends that there is no question of their leaving. My son asked that you keep them here, and although he perhaps deserves no compliance from me, I think they should stay until he comes back.'

'Thank you, sir.'

A very smart woman in her early forties came in. 'Arlette, will you just take Mlle Blair to look at Nounou's clothes, to see if she can explain what's been taken. Greg, will you wait here or would you like to go with them?'

'I . . . er . . . I think I'll go with them, if you don't mind, madame. Liz and I would like to go on somewhere else by and by, so if I may take my leave now?'

'Certainly. You will want to speak to the musicians. Please tell them that they can disregard anything Sasha may have said. And once more, my thanks for your care and kindness to me. Good evening, Ms Blair. I shall be interested to hear if you can learn anything from what you see upstairs.'

Arlette escorted them to the lift, which Liz eyed with amusement. They went smoothly up to the first floor. Along a passage and then round a corner which, as far as Greg could tell, was just south-east of the stable block, they came to Nounou's room.

They filed in. The room was in perfect order, the bed turned down, the pillows plumped up, fresh flowers in a little vase on the bureau, the curtains drawn against the winter sky. Arlette opened a door of the double wardrobe.

There was quite an array of clothes. The maid pointed to the left-hand side. 'Outerwear, coats, raincoats, jackets . . . You see the empty hanger. That was where the dark red jacket would be. Dresses, skirts and trousers here.' She nodded at them. 'Then here – ' she opened the other door – 'handbags, hats, shoes, sandals . . .'

Liz studied them. After a moment she pointed to trousers folded over a hanger. 'She was wearing those when we saw her out on the grounds last week.'

'Yes, those are a favourite with her.'

'But she didn't choose them the day she went away. She was wearing a skirt.'

Arlette shrugged. 'Yes.'

Liz bent down to study the racks of shoes. There was a space on the lower one, which held trainers and walking shoes. 'What should be here?'

'Grey trainers with a stripe along the side.'

'And here?' She pointed to a space on the upper rack.

'Dark red court shoes.'

'Which would match the jacket?'

'Well . . . yes.'

Liz touched a raincoat. 'Aquascutum,' she murmured. 'Very good quality.'

'Oh yes. But she keeps everything too long.' She nodded at the trousers Liz had noticed. 'These are Jaeger. I have mended tears and put in new zips – I can't tell you how many times.' There was contempt in her voice, scarcely veiled. 'And there is no need for it. She has her salary, which is more generous than the rest of the staff, and also an allowance from Monsieur – really, she is something of a – a—' She glanced at Greg. '*Un avare*?'

'A miser.'

Liz gave a little laugh of understanding. 'Of course, good clothes never date,' she acknowledged. Then she added casually, 'Do you take care of the clothes of Mlle Ferigiano?'

Arlette was extremely indignant. 'Certainly not! I only look after the beloved Bartelet as a favour to Monsieur.'

114

'Oh, I'm sorry, it's just that . . . you remember there was a party at the Merveille in the city last week?'

'Of course. Madame wore her Chanel.'

'Did you happen to see Mlle Ferigiano that evening?'

'Not at all.'

'She was wearing a lovely dress – clothes are my business, you see, and I thought it might be an Anika Roth, but she's a very new designer – in New York – perhaps you wouldn't have recognized her clothes even if you saw Mademoiselle wearing them.'

Arlette hesitated. Greg could see that she was sorely tempted to uphold her reputation as a knowledgeable personal maid. She gave in to temptation and said at last: 'Well, I did happen to pick up a jacket Mademoiselle had left hanging on a chair in the passage by the side door, and took it into her room . . . The yellow dress is by Roth, and you know, she's got some very nice things, including a jersey frock by Donna Karan. Very nice indeed.'

'Oh, I'm glad to find I was right! I think Roth has a future, don't you?' Chatting, she led the way out. They parted outside in the corridor, where Liz set off for the stairs with Greg following. When they reached the hall, she turned to him and said, 'Nounou was going to meet someone in a town somewhere.'

'What?'

'She was wearing trainers for the walk to the side gate or the stile or wherever she left the estate. I suppose she took public transport to the town – what would it be?'

'No way of knowing. Go on.'

'She chose not to wear the comfortable old trousers. The court shoes were to wear in town. She was going to dress up a little. She was going to meet someone or see someone.'

He stood staring at her. 'My God,' he said.

'Are you going to go in and tell M. Guidon?'

He left that for the moment. 'Everybody says she doesn't have any friends! Who could she be going to see?'

She sighed. 'Poor old thing.' Then, after a moment, 'It couldn't be a man, could it?'

'Darling, she's eighty-four or something.' He thought

about it. 'Doctor? Dentist? I suppose she might have had an appointment of that kind. Or a woman friend – there might be someone the family don't know about – I know they've tried everyone in her address book.' He shook his head. 'What was all that about Morena's dress?'

'Oh that! That was vulgar curiosity, I'm afraid.'

'You said when you were talking about it before, that it cost a lot.'

'Yes, I'd imagine so.'

'And the other one – black jersey? I think she was wearing that when she arrived. That was a good designer?'

'First class.'

'Expensive?'

Liz shrugged and gave a pretended pout of annoyance. 'I can only afford copies.'

'But a designer might give clothes to women as a sort of advertisement.' He knew something about that because he himself was occasionally the recipient of first-rate products, but they were generally only on loan – cars, for instance, and once a racing yacht.

'My dear man, a designer might give a dress to Madonna or Nicole Kidman, although even that's a bit doubtful, because they've got pots of money and should have to pay. But who in their senses would give away expensive clothes to a girl who plays and sings in a cocktail bar?'

'Yes. Of course. So as we were saying before, she must have money of her own.' He considered. 'So Grossmutti and I are probably wrong. We were thinking she's a gold-digger. But perhaps she does really care for Gilles.'

'And pigs might take off and fly over Mont Blanc.'

'You don't think so?'

'Could anybody really fall for Gilles? I only met him that once, but he struck me as D minus in the heart-throb department.'

He stood looking baffled for a few seconds. Then he took a deep breath before tapping on the door of the sitting room. He went in immediately with Liz at his elbow. 'Auguste, Liz has a suggestion about Nounou.'

The banker rose from his chair to hurry to Liz. He took

116

her hand. 'My dear lady, please – please – tell me!'

'It's not much, really. Please don't think it's going to find her all at once. But it seems clear to me that Nounou was going to meet someone.' She explained her theory.

Auguste listened in silence but his wife gave an exclamation of agreement. 'Of course! Why didn't we think of that? Of course, she was carrying the town shoes in her backpack and she would change into them in the bus station or somewhere like that.'

'Yes, my love,' said Auguste, with muted anguish, 'but where does that take us? We have tried every name or address that we can think of.'

'The police could probably try some professional people – doctors, lawyers—' Greg began.

'Doctors? You think she might be ill? Oh, how like her, not to tell us if she was suffering, she never thinks of herself! I must telephone the police at once! My dear Ms Blair, I can't thank you enough.' He was dashing back to the telephone table as he spoke.

Rosanne thanked Liz again, though with less emotion, and escorted them to the front door. They made their escape. 'So that's what it's like, living in a chateau,' commented Liz as they got into the Mercedes.

'Just like living in a cottage, perhaps.'

'Only with more caviar.'

'And speaking of caviar, it's very late and I'm very hungry. Let's just tell the band that they're to ignore Sasha and his commands, and then we'll find a restaurant before they all close.'

As they walked round towards the stable block Liz slowed down to say: 'I hope I haven't started a wild-goose chase.'

'My angel, in the state that Auguste is in, any goose is better than none.'

'But he absolutely leapt on that mention of a doctor. "Suffering"! He's kidding himself. When we met her out on the estate, she was in better shape than I was!'

'But not so loveable.'

She laughed, but waved it away. 'She certainly wouldn't win any popularity contest, by the sound of it.' She hesitated and added, 'Did you catch that bit about Nounou and money?'

'Of course.'

'Well, could she have had money with her? Cash, I mean. You said she's not used her credit card but could she have . . . oh, I don't know . . . planned this so as to make every-body suffer and be paying for everything in cash?'

'Oh, Liz . . . That would make her utterly vindictive . . .'

'Or of course, if she had a lot of money in that backpack, she could have been mugged.'

'Don't say that,' he said.

Ten

Greg had brought together a group of local instrumentalists to play for a children's concert in Zurich on the following day. He wanted to attend the morning rehearsal, an idea that struck Liz with dismay. She brightened when he described the shopping in the Bahnhofstrasse and was convinced when he promised lunch in the bar of the Baur au Lac, one of the great hotels of Europe.

'OK,' she said, 'I'll settle for that.'

They made an early start and travelled by Intercity train. Though the weather was dreary, Zurich was bright with decorations put up early in November for the Fasnacht Carnival, and crowded with business people hurrying to offices. He was conducting Liz towards the crossing for the Bahnhofstrasse but she was enticed by Shopville near the station, so he left her with instructions where to find a taxi rank at lunchtime.

He made his way to one of the lesser halls in the Tonhalle, where his orchestra was tuning up. He was just about to switch off his mobile – so as not to disturb the rehearsal – when it rang. It was Rosanne Guidon, calling to invite him to English afternoon tea at the chateau.

'Auguste is back at his office today, and so I thought it would be pleasant just to have you as a guest and have a chat.'

'I'm so sorry, Rosanne. I'm in Zurich today, as a matter of fact. A musical event, you know.'

For a moment she seemed taken aback. 'Oh. Of course. One forgets that you have other things to think of besides the Guidons! Well, tomorrow, then? May I invite you to tea tomorrow?'

He had a feeling she needed someone to talk to. He hesitated. 'Mlle Blair is with me, you recall? May I bring her?' English afternoon tea at the chateau – it was just the kind of thing that Liz would love to experience.

'Of course, of course, I'd be delighted to see her again. Such a charming, kind-hearted young lady. By all means, Greg, please bring her if you think she would like it.'

At lunch when he conveyed this plan to Liz, she made a little face. 'I was going to ask if we could go somewhere and have a good long walk,' she muttered. ' I was in a meeting all day yesterday, cooped up in a plane in the evening, trotting around city streets and shops today ... I really should have gone for a run this morning only we started out so early ...'

'Well, I can ring Rosanne and cancel.'

'No, don't do that – what about that walk we did last week? We could go to the chateau and leave the car and maybe do a different route up the hillside and so on.'

'That would be rather good. We could collapse into chairs at the chateau afterwards and let Rosanne feed us cream cakes.'

'Cream cakes! You know I never eat cream cakes!'

He laughed. Liz was always trying to live like a good vegetarian and follow a healthy diet, but she had a weakness for Continental patisseries.

'No, wait,' she exclaimed, holding up a hand. 'I can't go to a posh tea in jeans and old trainers.'

He explained that the Swiss were very understanding about outdoor clothes but she wasn't reassured. 'All right,' he suggested. 'We'll carry your party shoes in a carrier bag in the car.'

She stared at him. 'There you are,' she said. 'That's just like Nounou.' The thought depressed her. But she cheered herself up by buying a good wool skirt to wear instead of jeans.

Next day he arrived at a reasonable hour to collect Liz for the walk. He himself wasn't an early riser; it was the one point on which he disagreed with his beloved. But on this occasion he was justified – it was no good walking in the mountains until the sun was ready to shine over the peaks.

As he was getting into the car, Rousseau appeared from behind the house, trotting up and looking expectant. He was going to tell him to go back, but conscience made him pause. The last time he'd taken the setter out for a good romp was Sunday. 'Hop in, Rousseau,' he said. He'd get Roger to give him a walk.

Liz had never met Rousseau although she'd heard mention of him. She knew, for instance, that he was a red setter and not the Genevois philosopher. She was delighted with him, especially when on command he held up a paw to be introduced.

'Oh, let's take him with us on the walk, Greg. He'd love it, I bet.'

'Yes, he would, but Roger told me dogs aren't allowed off the lead until outside the formal part of the garden.'

'Well, we're going up among the rocks, aren't we? Yes, Rousseau, my friend, we'll take you for an outing where you can have a good run.'

When Greg rang the chauffeur to ask for the gates to be opened, he enquired whether there was any objection to his taking the dog with them on a walk. 'Not at all, sir, so long as he stays on the leash until the first signpost. Leave the car where you did before, but take the second path off to the left, where you'll find a signpost pointing towards Herat, that's a little viewpoint where you can get a vista of the Jura. Beyond that signpost it's OK to let the dog loose.'

'Thanks a lot, Roger.'

Liz was wearing the new skirt, a muted check of green and brown from a Scandinavian firm that specialized in country wear. Her trainers didn't match in any way, but that didn't matter. Her soft light hair was tucked up under a brown wool cap with lappets to keep her ears warm. Greg thought she looked adorable.

They walked along the chosen path, among the bare twigs of decorative shrubs, Rousseau ranging ahead at the far end of his lead to investigate various promising scents.

When they reached the signpost, Greg let him loose. At once the dog was filled with flamboyant energy. He went haring off up the path, then off to one side, then to the other, his tail waving like a feathery flag.

'Told you he'd like it,' Liz said.

'At this point he expects me to run after him and find a stick to throw.'

'Off you go, then.'

He grinned. 'I know when I'm in good company, thank you.'

'Oh, you!' She gave his arm a squeeze.

The viewpoint at Herat proved to be a walled semicircle made smooth with gravel, containing a post with a plaque naming the main points in the vista and a bench made from blocks of rock. They sat in the misty sunlight to admire the view.

'What's that glistening off there in the distance?'

'That's the Jura mountains. They're part of the border between Switzerland and France.'

'Really? As close as that?'

'Oh yes. Geneva's a canton almost completely surrounded by France. You do realize, my child,' he said, raising a finger and looking schoolmasterly, 'that only one side of Lake Geneva is Swiss? The southern side is French.'

'No!'

'Yes!'

'Well, I never. So then . . . listen . . . Gilles and Morena only needed to drive a few miles and they'd be in France?'

'Well, yes. But so what?'

'Didn't you tell me they contacted you originally from Paris?'

'Yes, Lou rang from Paris. At least . . .' He paused. 'He said he was calling from Paris. Well, of course, he was . . .' He frowned. 'Damn it, I've no reason to think he was calling from anywhere else, but I never checked.'

'There was no reason to.'

'Probably not, but Gilles was in such a flurry about finding a replacement for poor Wally Clifford that we never checked anything or asked for a résumé.'

'But when they arrived, they arrived on a plane from Paris, so that's where they came from, yes?'

'Oh, so they did! Yes, right, why didn't I remember that?'

'Stop beating yourself up about it. You weren't to know that the lady was going to cast a spell on Gilles and carry him off to Elfland. Or more likely, Paris.'

'Mmm.' Was it likely they'd gone to Paris?

Rousseau returned from a foray among the higher reaches and came to sit neatly by Liz's feet. He put his nose on her knee, gazing up at her with what looked like adoration.

'Your dog has very good manners,' she said.

'It's the Irish in him, it gives him a lot of charm.' He paused, but she made no response. 'You're supposed to say, "Like his master".'

'Oh yes, of course, but listen, are you wearing cologne or something?'

'Not I.'

'Well, I can smell something rather nice.' She glanced about. He followed suit.

'Oh, it's probably that,' he suggested, pointing to a tangled bundle of brown stalks and narrow leaves at the foot of the stone wall.

'What's that, then?'

'I think it's a yellow campanula, grows in high summer. As far as I remember, it has a rather nice smell when the flower is out.'

'Campanula? You mean Canterbury bells?'

'Do I? That sounds like a non-botanical name. But you're probably right.'

'But Canterbury bells are blue, not yellow!'

'Well, all right. I don't know the correct name of every-thing, I'm sorry to say.' Yet in the course of serving his annual stints of military service, the Prince had scrambled and manoeuvred all over these mountains, and had learned quite a lot about the flora and fauna. He surveyed the little platform where they now sat.

Some former owner of Chateau Guidon had taken an inter-est in gardening. There were plants growing around the view-ing platform that weren't native to the terrain – withered leaves of something he thought was a saxifrage, and some very low-growing evergreen that looked like a berberis he'd seen in a Japanese garden.

123

When they resumed their walk, he noticed other signs of cultivation, tastefully done so as to enhance the view with a touch of green. For a time they were walking up a path parallel to a stream, on whose banks he could see an array of ferns, some tall and proud, some low-growing so as to shield the long stalks of the taller plants. There was even some ivy growing on the rock face here and there – ivy, he'd always thought, was rather too tender for mountain winters. It looked good, although in principle he wasn't in favour of 'dressing up' the scenery.

It was now almost noon, so they munched on raisin bars and drank from the bottle of mineral water Greg had brought. The next stint of the walk was on rockier ground. They could hear the sound of falling water some way off on their right although it died as they rounded a turn in the narrow path. Great boulders formed a sound barrier. Rousseau dashed off ahead to a band of greenery, which looked like a foreign import, tall Magellan fern perhaps.

'He's looking for a way to get into the stream,' Greg muttered. 'Just wait – he'll come back and shake the water off all over us.'

He called, but Rousseau refused to obey. 'Rousseau!' No response.

'Is this part of his Irish charm?' Liz teased.

'Well, you know the Irish can be wayward. Rousseau, *reviens*!'

There was a loud outburst of barking. 'He's having fun,' she protested. 'Let him be.'

'Ha! Wild creatures on these mountains are protected by law – if he's disturbed anything important he's going to be in trouble. Rousseau! *Alerte!*' But the dog was enjoying himself too much to listen.

With a shrug Greg set off after him. The track of the setter was clear through the fern, which grew thicker as he neared the water, showing that the landscape gardener had been at work even so high on the slopes.

The dog was barking persistently. 'If that's a marmot you're threatening, you're a villain. Come on, Rousseau—' He stepped on to the surface of a boulder to look for him. And was somewhat surprised by what he saw.

The dog was in the water up to his shoulders, standing with his eyes fixed on something ahead. Great boulders caused the water in the stream to dam up so that a pool was formed, partly shaded by the ivy that Greg had noticed elsewhere, cascading down the basalt slab at the stream's edge and scrambling over rocks to form something like a tent.

Unwillingly, Greg picked his way down from his lookout point and along the rocks to grab Rousseau's collar. To his master's dismay, the dog resisted. He pulled away from his hand, his gaze 'set' as his instinct required, on something to be noticed and gathered up as booty.

Greg edged closer. There was something shadowy wedged against the rocks. Rousseau was whining now, insistent that his master should do something about the target he was pointing out to him.

He let go of Rousseau's collar. He hunched down on the rock, leaning forward a little to see what was under the ivy.

The stream chuckled over it, ripples causing colours to appear and disappear. He caught a glimpse of red, faded by the action of the water. He put his hands on a stone further out, waited while the current curved and turned until he saw the thing again.

Red, and then perhaps green, in a pattern. Tartan, perhaps? A backpack? Further into the shadow of the ivy, a larger, darker bulk. He crouched where he was, studying it.

He drew back. Rousseau was shivering now, straining at his hold on the collar.

'No, Rousseau. Leave!'

The dog turned his head to stare at him as if in reproach.

'No, we mustn't touch. Come along, now. *Viens!*'

And Rousseau reluctantly allowed himself to be dragged back to the bank.

Greg attached his lead. He said gently, 'Come on, *mon ami*, you've done well, but we must go back to Liz.'

She was waiting on the narrow track. 'What was it, a water rat or something?'

He made no reply. She stared at him. 'What is it?'

He gave a half-shake of the head. 'I think Rousseau has found Nounou.'

125

'What? Where?' She glanced around as if expecting the old lady to walk up, then her gaze returned to Rousseau, wet, shivering, whimpering in anxiety. 'No . . .'

The setter leaned against his master's leg, seeking comfort. Something was badly wrong, he could tell.

She shivered. 'What are you going to do?' she asked.

He got out his mobile phone.

'Are you ringing Mme Guidon?'

He paused. 'This isn't something you can tell on the phone.' He had two numbers for the chateau, one for Auguste's private phone, one for that of Gilles. He knew that neither of these two was at home. After a moment's thought he rang the number for Gilles.

There was a wait. A voice answered. 'This is Château Guidon.'

'Sasha? Is that you? This is Gregoire Couronne here.'

'If it's about your car, I saw Roger take it round by the garage.'

'Oh. Thank you.' He didn't want to tell Sasha what he'd found. He'd always seemed to Greg an insubstantial figure, without importance except that he kept Mme Armonet's social and charity diary in order. But the chauffeur . . . Roger was a practical, organized kind of man. 'Is it possible to transfer this call to the garage?'

'Of course. Hold on, it will ring there in a moment.'

One or two clicks, and true enough, the ringing tone began. Roger's sturdy baritone replied. 'Garage?'

'Roger, this is M. Couronne. I want you to come here at once.'

'Here? Where do you mean, sir?'

'Here, up on the mountainside, above the waterfall, some distance along the stream.'

'You've had an accident?'

'No, but it's very urgent. Please come at once.'

Like a patriotic Swiss citizen, Roger too had done his national service every year until his age allowed him exemption. He recognized the voice of an officer. 'Yes, sir.'

Greg returned the phone to his pocket. 'You called Roger?' Liz said in surprise.

'We've got to have someone here to keep this area as undisturbed as possible. Although,' he added, 'I don't think she fell in anywhere near here. Probably upstream, and the current carried her down and she—'

But Liz had gone white, and he stopped abruptly. He put his arms round her. 'I'm sorry, sweetheart.'

They waited for almost fifteen minutes, scarcely speaking, until the sound of a low-powered motocyclette could be heard. Then Roger could be seen, carefully manoeuvring the little machine between the stones on the track. He parked it, came towards them frowning in anxiety.

'Yes, sir, what seems to be the trouble?'

'I'd better not stamp about among the ferns. I'll stay here and let dog show you. Rousseau, *va!*'

He handed the lead to Roger, who took it in perplexity. Rousseau led off at once, straining to get back to the object he'd found.

There was a lengthy pause before Roger came back looking grim. 'Looks bad, sir.'

'Indeed.'

'What now?'

'I want you to stay here while I go back to the house to speak to Madame. Then I imagine the police will be here as soon as possible.'

'Oh, poor Madame! And Monsieur – he's going to be devastated!'

'I'm afraid it's inevitable, Roger. But we can at least do what we can to keep things in good order until the authorities get here.'

'You think police will be involved, Monsieur?'

'Of course. Accidental death, they have to be notified.'

'Yes, that's true. I'll take care of the area, then, sir. Do you want to borrow my moto to get back to the house?'

'No, no, Mlle Blair will be going with me. Goodbye for the present, Roger.'

Unwillingly, and with an arm about each other, they headed towards the chateau to break the news.

127

Eleven

Auguste rushed home from the bank as soon as he heard the news.

There was then a long wait for the police, during which he became more and more agitated. 'You are sure it was Nounou?' he kept asking, like a child wanting to know if the Tooth Fairy would really bring a silver coin. He wanted to rush to the scene himself, but his wife and his sister clung to him, imploring him to remain in the house.

'It's better if you leave the coast clear for the police, Auguste,' Greg told him. 'You know officials prefer to be left alone to do their work.'

'But you really think it was Nounou? And Roger thought so too?'

'I'm afraid so.'

It was nearly dark when at last a uniformed inspector asked Auguste to come to the ambulance to identify the body. He rose from his chair in the sitting room, chalk white. Rosanne took his arm and went with him. At a glance from her, Greg fell in behind. And just as well, because when he stepped down from the ambulance doors, he was in a state of collapse.

Greg helped him indoors. Marie Armonet had lingered in the sitting room, and at the sight of her brother returning like a broken man went at once to the telephone to summon his doctor. Sister and wife hovered over him, murmuring and soothing, forgetting everything else in their anxiety to help him.

Throughout it all, Liz had stayed in the background. 'We should go,' she whispered to Greg.

'Yes. Just let me say a word to somebody before we go.' He found Sasha in the hall, pacing about, waiting for the

128

doctor. Sasha was nearly as pale as the master of the house, shivering with reaction, but summoned good manners enough to say goodbye.

'I'll telephone later, if I may, to see how things are going, Sasha.'

'Certainly, Monsieur. And I know Madame would wish me to thank you—' He broke off. He was trying to express gratitude, but in fact he seemed repelled by all that was going on.

Roger was standing patiently by Greg's car in the garage forecourt. He had Rousseau on his lead by his side. The dog sprang up to welcome his master with a bark of joy.

'Well, that's it, then,' the chauffeur observed as he handed over the car keys. 'The old girl's dead after all.'

Greg nodded.

'Probably has been dead all the time we've been accusing her of playing us one of her tricks . . .' He sighed. 'I'm sorry now, for the things I said.'

'You couldn't possibly know, Roger.'

'Poor old soul. We tried to tell her she was too old to be trudging about on her own up there. Still, in a way, it's probably where she'd have chosen to start playing her harp, she loved it up there by the stream.'

'Yes, so she told us the day we met her up there.'

'Lost her footing, I suppose. Easy enough to happen.'

'That must have been farther upstream. Then the current downhill carried her until she got caught in the ivy and was held captive by the rocks.'

'I suppose so. Though why she'd be on the bank of the stream that far up, I don't really understand. If she was going out on one of her little outings to town – which is what people seem to be saying now – well, I'd have thought she'd keep to the path. That goes east and stays well away from the verge. The waterfall, now . . . she liked to take the path to the waterfall and sit on the rocks . . . Well, we'll probably never know, will we?'

Greg was about to say goodbye but hesitated. 'I ought to go and have a word with the band before I leave, just to explain what's happening.'

'Oh, they're all out, monsieur. Sent for a taxi during the morning, said they were going to have lunch in Lausanne and then perhaps go on to Montreux for the evening. I don't think they've been rehearsing or playing much these days.' He made a grumbling sound. 'We know what that means. They'll have me up to open the gates to them again around three in the morning.'

'What a shame, Roger. Well, in that case, I'll call them some time tomorrow.'

'Shouldn't bother,' growled Roger. 'Everybody will be dying to tell them the bad news, you can be sure of that.'

Greg shook hands and drove off. Liz breathed a great sigh of relief, and Greg, glancing at her, was jolted by how pale and weary she looked. 'I'm sorry, angel. I never meant you to get involved in anything like this.'

She shrugged and was silent for a time. Then when they had turned on to the main road towards the city she said, 'I'm beginning to think there's a jinx on that family.'

'Jinx?'

'A hoodoo. An evil star.'

'Oh, *une porte-guigne* – a bad-luck wish.'

'Don't you think so? First the old lady goes missing, then Gilles takes off, then the old lady turns up dead ... And didn't you tell me that Lou Ferigiano was brought in to replace some poor elderly Brit who fell under a train after they'd engaged him?'

'Wally Clifford ... yes.'

'I'm glad I don't live at the chateau, and that's a fact! That secretary-type Sasha would be well advised to pack his trunk and go.'

He shook his head at her. 'You're tired and you're hungry, that's what's wrong. We'll find a nice quiet café and we'll have lots of hot coffee and a glass of wine and some food.'

She shrugged and but said nothing more. For the rest of the drive they were almost silent. Rousseau thrust his muzzle between them as if to ask whether something was wrong.

Because it was still early evening, the café they chose was relatively empty. On the outskirts of the city, it had adopted a rustic style, and offered a range of wholesome dishes. But first came the coffee, hot and strong and restorative.

Liz studied the menu. 'This dish that says it's au Bleu-de-something-something-Jura comes from those mountains we saw?' she asked.

'It's a cheese. The whole thing is a sort of omelette.'

'OK, I'll have that. And lots of vegetables. I'm starving, although it seems rotten to be thinking about food.'

They ordered. He looked at her with concern. 'You're really distressed about Nounou,' he said.

'Well . . . I didn't altogether expect anything like this when I came winging into Geneva.'

'No, of course not.'

'I think I'll go home, Greg. I'm not doing any good here, now am I?'

He was taken aback. 'But—'

'These people are in a lot of trouble and you're a bit involved with them, and all I am is a nuisance.'

'Of course not!'

'Oh, come on!' she said, her voice unusually sharp. 'You've got to think of me every time you want to do anything. You had to cart me along when you went to Zurich to a rehearsal. And then when you had to deal with . . . that business at the stream . . . you didn't know how to get me off the scene. Well, I think I'm just a botheration.'

'No, no.'

'Honestly, Greg. I feel terribly useless. And you know, I only intended to stay a few days anyway.' She was less contentious now; her tone was almost pleading.

'Yes, but—'

'I think I'll fly back tomorrow.'

He was unable to think of any good reason to stop her. If she stayed, there was no likelihood of enjoyment in the next day or two. There would be a police enquiry into the accident, and then a funeral – why should he beg her to stay for any of that?

After a long hesitation he said, 'I understand, of course. I'm sorry it's all gone so depressing.'

She put out a hand for his. There was a glint of what might have been tears in her eyes. 'I'm sorry, I feel a bit of a heel,

131

walking out on you when there's all this misery and everything. But honestly I don't think I'm being a help.'

'You're always a help to me, Liz.'

'Oh, sweetheart, of course, and in a way I want to stay, just to hold your hand – but you manage pretty well without having your hand held, and I feel . . . At the chateau, I felt like an intruder, you know?'

'Marie Guidon was grateful.'

'She was just trying to be polite.' She sighed. 'No, it's time for me to clear off, and that's what I'm going to do. And we'll meet again soon, next time you have to come to London for one of your musical extravaganzas.'

Her mind was made up. There was nothing to do but accept it. They cheered themselves up by talking about possible dates for a meeting in the future, ate the excellent food, drank some wine. In fact, Liz drank rather a lot, almost as if she was trying to drown her sorrows. He could tell that she was deeply upset.

When he drove her to her hotel, it was still early. He wondered how they would spend the rest of the evening but Liz gave him what was clearly a goodbye kiss in the foyer.

'I'm beat, love,' she said. 'And, you know . . . it just seems . . .'

He nodded. 'It's all right. What about tomorrow? Shall I come to take you to the airport?'

'No, better not. I don't know what flight I'll be taking until I've phoned the airline. I'll ring you when I get back to London.'

With a big hug and another little kiss on the cheek, she was gone.

He went out to the car, where Rousseau gave him a big welcome. 'Thank you, *mon ami*,' he said, 'but that's not really much comfort.'

His father and grandmother were watching television when he got back to Bredoux. They greeted him with only half their attention, but turned towards him when he began his account of his day.

'Good heavens,' sighed Nicoletta. 'So the poor soul was

there in the water all the time when they were enquiring for her in department stores and dentists' surgeries.'

'Those poor people, from what you've told us they must be devastated at the loss,' said Anton.

'Yes, Auguste is shattered.' He didn't say that other members of the household felt less grief.

'So what happens next?' asked Grossmutti. 'I suppose the jazz-band idea is completely abandoned now?'

'I really don't know. I'll see about that tomorrow.'

She shook her head in regret. 'I'm sorry now that I ever encouraged you to take that on.'

Me too, thought her grandson, but that too was left unsaid.

The next day, Friday, he felt depressed. Nothing like work to take your mind off your troubles, he reminded himself, so went to his office in Geneva to catch up with messages from his classical musicians. Amabelle offered him a list as soon as he came in the door. It was somehow comforting to have to deal with ordinary people and their ordinary problems – a choral group in Amsterdam had lost their luggage, an oboe-player in Chicago had developed a cough and needed to be replaced urgently, the wife of a timpanist was sending his birthday present and needed his next destination.

Around eleven he was thinking it might be time to ring the jazz players. He was almost reaching for his office telephone when it rang. 'Hirtenstein Agency,' he said.

'Monsieur Couronne, is that you?' It was Sasha, sounding jittery.

He was at once alerted by the man's tone. 'Is something wrong, Sasha?'

'Monsieur Couronne, Madame has asked me to ask you to please come at once. She doesn't know what to do!'

'About what?'

'About – about the message we've received. This morning.'

'What kind of message?'

'An email.'

'What does it say?'

133

'Madame has forbidden me to repeat it on the telephone. She asks you to come, monsieur, please. She doesn't know where else to turn.'

'I'll be there in an hour, Sasha.'

As he dropped the instrument into its receiver, Amabelle protested, 'But you haven't finished with the list—'

'Handle the rest yourself, Amabelle. I have complete confidence in you.'

He dashed out, rescued his car from the parking area, and drove off in a hurry. All the way to the chateau he was trying to imagine the sort of problem that had arisen. He made good time, although he felt the mountain wind buffeting the car as they climbed from the thousand-odd feet of the city to the little plateau of Chatcau Guidon. A wind like that usually meant very cold weather on the way.

Sasha was watching for him out of a window at the front of the house. He came into the hall as Greg was being shown in by the housemaid. Behind him hovered Rosanne Guidon. 'This way,' he said, and led him into a room across the hall from Auguste's study. Though furnished with less splendour, it offered comfort with all the assets for secretarial work.

In the bright light of midday he and Mme Guidon looked scared and anxious. Madame's careful make-up was smudged where she had shed some tears. As for Sasha, he was ashen. His hand trembled as he pointed towards his computer.

It was switched on. Greg leaned forward and read: 'Clearly Auguste Guidon has no interest in his son's welfare or he would have responded to our message. Tell him he has one more day to give us an answer.'

He straightened. 'What does that mean?' he asked, looking from one to the other.

'We don't know. It was just there when I switched on this morning about ten o'clock.'

'Has Auguste mentioned any message?'

'No, nothing,' his wife wailed. 'And Dr Perlerou says he is not to be disturbed or distressed so we can't ask him. The doctor is concerned for Auguste's heart, you see.'

134

'Have you looked among his papers? His letters?'

'Of course,' faltered Sasha. 'And we telephoned his secretary at the bank . . . to ask if there were any personal letters there, unopened. You see, things have been in a very . . . unsettled state over the last few days. Monsieur only went back to his office yesterday.'

'And then, of course, came hurrying home because of the news about Nounou,' Rosanne took it up. 'So we thought the message might be there – I mean in his office. But his secretary – that's Albert – he said there was nothing other than business correspondence.'

'And he's checked since then and rang back to let us know, there isn't anything . . . that seems like . . . you see . . . this message must be somewhere . . .'

Greg considered. He thought about his own office set-up. Amabelle dealt with ordinary business matters that came in by post, by telephone, and by email. Personal matters she left for his attention.

'You mean that since this message came to your computer . . .'

'Yes.'

'That could mean the unanswered message is at a private email address for Monsieur?'

'Yes, that's what we thought, Greg – but there's a password for that, and only my husband knows it.' Rosanne began to cry again, collapsing on a chair and hiding her eyes with clenched fists. 'Gilles!' she moaned. 'Oh, my poor boy! Where are you?'

Greg leaned over her for a moment, making soothing sounds, then said to the secretary, 'Someone should perhaps look after Madame – her sister, perhaps? Or her maid?'

'Mme Armonet went out to a committee meeting at Nyon this morning. I'll get Arlette.' He went to a telephone to call her.

'No, no, I'm quite all right. I'm sorry. I'm behaving like a child!' But Sasha made the call and in a moment the maid came hurrying in. Once she was leading her mistress out, Greg returned to the matter of the lost message.

'M. Guidon has a computer of his own?'

'Well, the house is a network. This is the main screen, but both Monsieur and Madame have access . . . Also Nounou had her own section for doing things about the household, ordering food or equipment, fetching in extra waiters . . . I do Mme Armonet's charity work mostly . . . Of course I have my own address on it and as you can see, the message . . . the message is addressed to me.'

Greg frowned. 'It's unsigned. Comes from . . .' He paused to read out the address. 'Openmarket@uniprop.com.'

'I never heard of it, sir.' It was an emphatic protest.

'How did they get your email address?'

'Oh, that's easy enough.' Sasha was eager to defend himself from any accusation that he knew the sender. 'You can find almost anyone you want on the Internet if you know how to search.'

Greg nodded acceptance. He was no expert. At his office, Amabelle handled the computer.

'So M. Guidon has his own email address for which there's a password. Is there anywhere we might find it? In his desk? His diary?'

'Not that I'm aware of. M. Guidon is a very discreet gentleman. I think he changes the password regularly.'

'What about the secretary at the bank? Does he know it?'

'No, we asked him.'

'So only Auguste Guidon can tell us?'

'Yes.'

They stood for a moment considering the problem. Sasha was fidgeting from one foot to the other, unwilling to make any suggestion that might involve him in later recrimination.

'We'll have to ask him.'

'But the doctor forbids—'

'Oh, talk sense, Sasha! What would Monsieur prefer? That we obey the doctor or that his son's welfare should be in question? Because that's what the message means, doesn't it?'

'It's a threat . . . It is, isn't it? That's what you think, sir?'

'It seems so to me.'

'And it means . . . Monsieur Couronne, does it mean that Gilles is . . . is . . . in danger?'

136

Greg left the question unanswered. 'Which is M. Guidon's bedroom?'

'Upstairs, of course – but you aren't going to—'

'Show me,' he commanded, and led the way out.

Twelve

They went up in the little lift. Sasha stood as far away from Greg as he could, as if to distance himself from what was about to happen.

When they stepped out into the corridor he muttered, 'I take no responsibility.'

'Very well.'

He tapped on a door. It was opened by a manservant. He walked in rather hesitantly, Greg following.

'Oh, Monsieur Resedeul,' the servant protested to Sasha, 'the doctor said Monsieur wasn't to be disturbed.'

He half-turned as if to leave. Greg blocked his movement.

Auguste was lying propped up on a pile of lace-edged pillows, eyes closed, cheeks unshaven, hair ruffled. A long way from the self-assured man who had first summoned Greg to lunch with him.

Hearing some slight disturbance in the room, he seemed to force his eyelids open. 'Ah, Monsieur Couronne . . . How kind . . .'

'How are you feeling, Auguste?'

'Not good . . . I keep picturing . . .' He coughed a little, then said, 'Sasha . . . ? Is there something you want?'

'No, sir, I was simply showing M. Couronne the way.'

'Oh, of course.' Voice faint, breathing uneven. Under some form of sedation. Greg felt guilty at troubling him but knew it must be done.

'Auguste, Sasha and I were just saying that after the item in the papers this morning—'

'In the papers? About Nounou?' He almost choked on the name.

'Yes, a little item, reporting the accident and mentioning

138

that she was a valued member of your household.'

'So she was, so she was . . .' A tear trickled out of the corner of one eye.

'We were thinking that many people would wish to offer their condolences.'

'Oh? Oh yes. Of course.'

Sasha caught the Prince's glance and caught up with the lie. 'Yes, monsieur, there have been several . . . telephone calls . . . already. And we think . . .' He was unable to go on, but nodded at the Prince.

'Sasha thinks there will be other messages in your email.'

Auguste blinked away his tear. 'Oh, you think so?'

'It seems likely, don't you agree?'

The invalid wasn't thinking clearly enough to wonder if anyone would really send condolences by email. He sighed deeply and closed his eyes as if to shut out all thought of his loss.

'But we can't access them, you see, Auguste, without your password.'

Auguste made a muffled sound. Then he forced himself to look at the speaker. 'You need my password,' he said, like a child repeating a new piece of learning.

'Yes.'

'Well, then, it's . . . it's . . . what is it? I can't remember.'

Sasha Resedeul drew in a breath and began to turn away, glad to have an excuse to abandon this attempt. Greg stood his ground. 'Did you change it recently?'

'I don't know. I think so. I change it often, don't I, Sasha?'

'Yes, sir.'

'And I make a note of it. I do, of course I do. And I keep it . . .' He coughed again, and the manservant came with a tissue to wipe spittle from his lips. 'I feel so woozy,' Auguste complained. 'As if my mind's got disconnected . . . What were we saying?'

'The password for your email,' Greg prompted, keeping his voice very quiet and calm. 'You keep a note of it in a safe place?'

'Of course. Foolish not to. In case I forget and try to use the one before. I did that once . . . A drink of water, Armand.'

The servant poured from a carafe and brought the glass to his master. Auguste sipped. 'Yes, of course, the password is written on the fly-leaf . . . of my copy of . . . wait now . . . the *Yearbook of Banking*. On the bookshelf that stands behind the door when you open it. In my study . . . Yes. Was that what you wanted?'

'Yes, indeed. Thank you, Auguste.'

Sasha Resedeul had already slipped out of the room. He was waiting in the corridor. He huddled into himself as they went together to the lift. 'I take no responsibility,' he repeated.

He went into the study with reluctance but found the book at once. The password was 'Stability'. He went to the computer and typed it in. There were indeed several messages that hadn't been read over the last few days: he ran the indicator down the list, but there was nothing from 'Openmarket'.

'Nothing,' he reported.

'Anything unusual?'

He selected a sender called 'Filial'. 'Most are from friends. One is from his vintage-car club. But I never saw that one before.'

'Try that, then.'

They had expected something dramatic. The message was almost humdrum. 'If you want to hear news of your son's chances of survival, ring 44.0800.662.3663.'

Each of them was accustomed to international correspondence. They said, almost in unison, 'That's a UK prefix.' Then they stood staring at the screen.

'Why are we asked to ring somewhere in Britain?' ventured Sasha.

'And why are both messages in English?'

Sasha shivered. 'Yes, what does it mean?'

'Perhaps it means that the sender is an English-speaker. I mean, speaks only English.'

'An English person is threatening Gilles?'

'Let's find out.' Greg indicated the telephone on the desk. 'Ring the number.'

Sasha edged away. 'You do it.'

140

Greg sat down at the desk. The number ran six or seven times. He was beginning to think it was a waste of effort when a voice clicked in. The words he heard were in English. 'This is a taped message. Please obey the instructions. Please be ready to take notes. I will wait.'

The voice was toneless, metallic. He felt sure some contrivance had been used to distort it. He glanced about the desk, saw a pen, and grabbed it. He made scribbling signs at Sasha, who snatched up a notepad and gave it to him.

'Are you ready? I will wait.' Another few seconds went by. 'Message begins. This is the account designation: it is 87PH-upper case-dash-alt-dash 63690414. I will repeat that. 87PH-upper case-dash-alt-dash 63690414. I will wait. If you have the number correctly written down, press figure one on your telephone pad. I will wait.'

He obeyed, saying quickly to Sasha, 'It's a tape.'

The voice on the telephone went on: 'You will give the password tomorrow in response to a telephone call which you will receive before noon. If you understand this instruction, press one on your telephone. I will wait.'

'Another message tomorrow,' muttered Greg, obeying.

'When the password is delivered, you will receive instructions concerning Gilles Guidon. The police must not be involved. This message ends but can be heard once more by redialling.'

There was a click then silence. He hung up the receiver, then picked it up again and handed it to Sasha. 'It says you can hear it again if you redial.'

'No,' Sasha said, drawing back.

'Yes. We need to be witnesses to each other.' And when the secretary still hunched his shoulders and half-turned away, he commanded, 'Do it,' and pressed the redial button for him.

At last Sasha gave in. He listened in silence to the message. Greg stood close to him, catching enough to know the words were exactly the same. At the end, Sasha let the receiver drop into its cradle and shuddered. 'Who could that be?' he gasped.

'Somebody expecting to speak to Auguste and asking for

a lost password. I'd say it must be for a bank account, wouldn't you?'

'But whose account is it? Is it an account at Banque Guidon?'

'How would I know? The only one who can tell us is Auguste.'

'Oh, God, no! He's too ill to be told about this!'

'We have to tell him. We're supposed to have the password ready for a telephone call tomorrow.'

'How can we? We'll have to explain to them that Auguste is—'

'If it's the same as what we just heard, there won't be a chance to say anything.' He paused. 'Wait. Let's try the number again.'

He did so. The phone rang and rang at the other end, but no one picked up. He held it out so that Sasha could hear before cradling it.

'This is terrifying! What are we going to do?' Everything about Sasha's demeanour told Greg that he wished he'd had nothing to do with the making of the call from the outset.

But what in fact were they going to do? It was a good question. After a moment's thought, Greg said, 'We have to tell Madame.'

'No, no! She's so upset!'

'There's no one else, Sasha. Come on, telephone Arlette and ask how she is.'

Sasha obeyed. 'Please tell Madame that M. Couronne and I need to speak to her urgently.' He waited. 'Yes, madame, we have . . . some news. Yes. In Monsieur's study. Yes. Thank you.' He replaced the phone to say, 'She'll be down in a moment.'

'Can you type out the message, Sasha? She's never going to be able to read my scribbles.'

Unwillingly Sasha sat in the chair by the desk, opened Word, then typed briskly. The machine was printing it out as Rosanne Guidon hurried in, flushed and anxious. 'What is this news? What?'

Greg knew that Sasha would never take the responsibility so began at once. 'We had to get access to Auguste's

142

email. We went to Auguste's bedroom to speak to him. I persuaded him to tell us the password for his email account and from that we got a telephone number.'

'A telephone number? And – you rang? Was it Gilles?'

'We got a recorded message.' He turned to Sasha, who unwillingly offered her the sheet of paper.

In a faltering voice she read it aloud. Sasha had typed the account number and then the words, 'Password for this account must be revealed. Information will follow re Gilles. No police.' She clutched it between her hands as she cried, 'Who was this? Who dares to do this?'

'There's no way of knowing, madame,' Greg said. 'All we can tell you is that all the messages have been in English, and the number we were given in the email had a UK prefix.'

'Ring it again! I must hear what they say about my boy!'

He shook his head but pressed the redial button. He held out the receiver so she could hear the continuous ringing. 'The recorded message said we could hear it over again once, but I think the tape machine has switched itself off now. I'm sorry, Rosanne. That's all we have, except the demand to have the password ready for a phone call tomorrow.'

Rosanne's mind was fixed on her fears for her son. 'He's in England? They've taken my son to England?'

'I don't think so. I think the telephone call was a set-up of some kind.' A thought occurred and he said, 'Wait. I can try to find out – may I?'

'Of course!'

He rang Liz Blair's number. She picked up after a moment and when she heard his voice said in welcoming tones, 'Well, that was lucky! I just walked in about ten minutes ago! Can't live without me, eh?'

'Liz, please listen. This is an important question. What town in England has the prefix 0800?'

'What? What on earth do you mean? Are you joking?' She was puzzled but laughing.

'Liz, please pay attention. You do business all over the country. Do you recognize that telephone code?'

'Of course I do, you idiot. It's a freephone.'

'A what?'

'A phone number you call when you want to place an order or make an enquiry. A commercial number that the caller doesn't have to pay for. What on earth is this about?'

'I can't explain now. Do I gather that anybody could hire a number like that on a short-term basis?'

'I suppose so. Why are you snapping at me like a school-teacher?' she asked, offended.

'I'll ring you later. Will you be at home this evening?'

'Yes, I suppose so. Greg, what on earth is the matter?'

'Later,' he said, and disconnected. He looked ruefully at Rosanne and Sasha. 'Ms Blair knows about that kind of tele-phone service. She says it's used by commercial firms. It had a machine connected but I think that's been switched off now. And even if the number is traceable, I think we'd find an empty office.'

'But that . . . that seems to mean . . . Greg, you're saying that this was all planned beforehand!' Rosanne straightened the sheet of paper that Sasha had given her, to study it as if it were Holy Writ. 'My son's been abducted.' Her voice was faint, disbelieving.

No one said anything.

Sasha sat down and brought up the screen with the tele-phone number. The cursor winked. Rosanne was still star-ing at the paper that Sasha had typed.

There were murmurs of sound from the hall, then a moment later Marie Armonet came hurrying in, with the maid at her heels catching the outdoor coat she was discarding. 'You're unwell, Rosanne? Has Auguste had another attack?'

'No, no, Marie, nothing like that.' Rosanne held out her arms as if to clutch at her sister-in-law, but held back until the housemaid had gone. Then she wailed, 'We've had a message. About Gilles.'

'Gilles?' Marie repeated, baffled that this was a cause for tears.

'He's been kidnapped, Marie!'

Marie gaped at her. 'Don't be silly, Gilles eloped with that—'

'No, no – look.' She thrust the sheet of paper at her. Marie accepted it, read its contents.

Greg said: 'We must get the password from Auguste some time before the phone call tomorrow.'

There was a stricken silence.

'That's impossible!' said Marie. And Rosanne was nodding agreement.

'But we must. Call the doctor, ask him if Auguste can be told what's happening—'

'No, no, you don't understand!' Rosanne broke in. 'My husband would never divulge the password of an account at the Banque Guidon!'

'Don't be absurd, Rosanne, we have to have it.'

'He won't!'

'He won't,' agreed Marie, grasping her hands together as if in prayer. 'And even if he wanted to, he couldn't.'

'But the criminals are demanding—'

'You clearly know nothing about banking security,' she interrupted with scorn. 'I've gleaned a little during a lifetime spent in and around it. Confidentiality is absolutely everything in banking. No details of an account may be revealed . . . except with the approval of other officers of the executive . . .' She hesitated. 'That's right, isn't it, Rosanne?'

'But in this case, of course, once Auguste is made aware of the situation, he'll get approval.'

Both women were shaking their heads. He stared at them. 'What?' he asked.

'I'm fairly sure proof of ownership would have to be supplied,' Marie said.

'Yes,' Rosanne confirmed.

Sasha began to say, 'Then we can ask them to supply . . .' but faltered into silence. After a moment he said, 'No. If it's a machine again, we can't ask them for anything.'

Greg looked from one to the other of the group. 'And in any case,' he said, thinking it out as he spoke, 'if they were the owners, they wouldn't resort to extortion to get at the account. *Pris dans leur propre traquenard!* They been too clever for their own good, haven't they? They just didn't know enough about how the bank works.'

'What are we going to do?' moaned Rosanne. 'My poor boy! My little angel! They have him, and we can't give them what they want. What are they going to do to him?'

Greg pulled himself together. 'Nothing, madame – I'm sure Gilles is all right.' He didn't give his reasons – that it would be foolish of the kidnappers to harm their victim because they might need him to turn the screws on the relatives.

'And you think he's been taken by that girl? That she was . . . what should we call it? Bait?'

'I think her brother Lou must be involved as well,' he returned thoughtfully. 'I look back now, and I think he picked a fight with Auguste after the elopement, so as to have an excuse to pack up and go.'

'But she seemed so ladylike . . . The brother, I never thought much of him, but Morena looked quite refined . . .' Rosanne was shocked, hurt. 'And so they came here, and . . . what then? They saw a chance to make money and seized it?'

Greg frowned. 'That can't be. The business with the answering machine on the phone . . . You said it yourself – that must have been set up some time ago.' He paused. 'It seems to me it must all have been planned in advance. Perhaps they didn't expect Gilles to fall in love – you could call that something of a bonus. But it seems to me . . . when I think about it . . . they came here with the intention of getting to know how the household works and then snatching Gilles.'

'But how could they plan it, Greg? Gilles engaged them because he was short of a musician. How could they possibly have known that would happen?'

He looked at Rosanne with no idea how to answer her. 'I don't know,' he said.

Marie Armonet made a move towards the telephone on the desk. She said in a tone of careful practicality, 'Rosanne, I think you should have a little something – we could have afternoon tea a little early, and then you ought to have a little rest. You look absolutely devastated. And I must admit that I need a drink.'

Rosanne put a hand to her head in confusion. 'I don't think we've had lunch . . .' She turned to Greg. 'What must you think of me? So neglectful—'

146

'Not at all, madame,' Greg said, but realizing that he was in fact hungry.

'Shall I ring?' asked Sasha, happy to have some return to normality.

'Of course.' Rosanne was the mistress of the house once more. She must ensure that everyone was looked after. 'Tell Cook we'll be in the dining room in about ten minutes. And ask for aperitifs to be brought here.'

'Certainly, madame.'

The meal had presumably been waiting in the kitchen for some time. They had their drinks in the study, then the house-maid appeared to say that lunch was served. Rosanne ate very little, Marie said she'd had lunch already but drank perhaps too much, Sasha and Greg paid the most attention to the food. Greg felt uncivilized to be thinking of his stomach but the fact was, seven long hours had gone by since breakfast.

Rosanne was persuaded to lie down for an hour or so. Greg wondered whether he ought to leave but the merest hint of that idea sent her into a panic. 'Oh no! Please don't leave us! You are the only one who seems able to keep his head!' And then, recovering her manners: 'But then of course you have matters of your own that need attention—'

'No, no, nothing that can't wait. I'll stay for a while if you want me to.'

'Of course we do, don't we, Marie? We've no one else to turn to!'

'Then perhaps I could make some phone calls? There are one or two things I'd like to check up on.'

'Certainly. Please – use Auguste's office. Anything you want, just ask Sasha – he's just across the hall. Or use the telephone – if you press eleven, you get the butler's pantry – we no longer have a butler but one of the staff will connect you with any of the rooms. And to get an outside line you press nine.'

'Thank you.'

The analysis had been forming in his mind ever since the demand from the kidnappers. Gilles had left the chateau with Morena Ferigiano and had written a note explaining why he

147

was going. The letter had been completely acceptable to the parents as something Gilles would write. It wasn't a forgery, it read as if he himself had composed it.

So Gilles had left willingly. He trusted Morena because he loved her. And Morena had come with Lou, whom Gilles himself had engaged.

Where had they come from? From Paris. They had arrived on a flight from Paris. Lou had originally called Greg from Paris.

Had he? Greg had never thought to check where the call originated. But Lou and Morena had had a stint at a club in Paris – le Jalon, he seemed to remember. He summoned up directory enquiries in Paris and asked for the number of the club.

The number rang and rang – somewhat like the number in England used by the kidnappers. After a time he disconnected and instead rang a friend in Paris, an Australian who earned a precarious living writing articles about musical performances of all kinds.

'*Grego, mon bon bougre, comment ça va?*'

'*Assez bien, assez bien, tu sais.* Listen, Arnold, do you know a nightclub called le Jalon?'

'Le Jalon? Lemme see . . . Wait . . . Oh, right, that's that place in the basement of the salsa school. Yeah, I've heard of it. Why?'

'I'm trying to ring it but I get no reply.'

'No, I don't suppose you will. Seems to me it closed up early in the year. There was a drug bust or something.'

'How long ago?'

'Oh . . . February? March? If I remember rightly, the owner of the salsa school was very upset about it and refuses to let anybody rent the place now.'

It seemed to Greg that Lou Ferigiano had claimed to be playing there only recently. He tried the name on Arnold. 'Ferigiano? Plays what?'

'Saxophone.'

'Good Lord, what are you doing making enquiries about a sax player? Not in your line of business at all, mate.'

'You don't know him?'

'Never heard of him, but that means nothing, takes me all my time to keep up with the bands at the top of the pops. All the same, if this feller had been rounded up in the drug bust, his name might have been mentioned. Don't think so, though. When they closed they had . . . lemme see . . . wasn't jazz, it was like . . . Nah, it was a disc jockey, Poppa Party, I think he was called.'

'Thank you, Arnold. That's very helpful.'

'Any time, *petit copain.*'

He sat thinking after he hung up the receiver. Then he called directory enquiries for Marseilles. Lou had claimed he played there with Wally Clifford in a band led by Pierre Vernon. He had to soft-talk the girl who took his call, for all he had was the name, but a white lie about having forgotten the whereabouts of the club resulted in Pierre Vernon's home number. There a recorded message informed him Vernon could be reached at the Salle Chicane, with the number supplied. He called it, and was answered by a brisk voice saying, 'Vernon.'

Greg introduced himself as agent for the late Wally Clifford. 'Oh, good heavens, yes, poor old Wally . . . That was a very sad thing. What can I do for you?'

'I'm trying to get in touch with another sax player, Lou Ferigiano. He was with you a couple of years ago.'

'Who?'

'Ferigiano – Lou Ferigiano.'

'No.'

'He didn't play in your band?'

'Never heard of him.'

'He told me he was a friend of Wally's, had learned a lot from him.'

'That's possible, but not playing with my combo,' Vernon said with perfect certainty.

'But Wally was with you, about two years ago?'

'Yes, certainly, and living out of a bottle when he wasn't playing. Then I heard he went on the wagon, great, I was very pleased, but when he was with me he was the only sax in the band and he worried me a lot because I thought he'd fall down on the stand one night.'

'So Lou Ferigiano never played with you at all?'

'Not at all.'

And probably never knew Wally. That had been pure invention. Simply a means to get an audition with Gilles Guidon, desperately in need of a saxophonist to replace the dead man.

After he'd said goodbye, he sat thinking. It was a continuation of the memory about Gilles being in great need of a replacement musician.

It seemed to him that somehow the criminals had known. They had supplied a replacement.

But wait. The preparation for the abduction must have begun long ago. Before Gilles had found himself lacking a saxophonist. The answering service with its demand for the password . . . How long did it take to hire a freephone number? He had no idea but he thought it probably couldn't be done overnight.

So had preparations begun as soon as Gilles started looking for band members?

The jazz world was quite a small one. Probably musicians who didn't want the job let others know. The news would come to the notice of people who were on the watch for any news out about the Guidon family. And then they had to find a musician who didn't mind going outside the law for a handsome fee.

Or perhaps the other way round – find a hoodlum who played sax. A lot of people were amateur musicians. He seemed to remember that a former President of the United States played the saxophone. So perhaps they hired Lou because he was a thug who could acquit himself reasonably well – for of course, he was never expected to have to play in public. All he had to do was get into the Guidon household.

But Morena? Why Morena?

Because she was beautiful? Because it was known that Gilles had a weakness for pretty girls?

But that argued inside information. Someone in the house, for example.

And that brought him to Sasha.

It seemed to him, looking back, that Sasha had been in a state of agitation ever since Nounou disappeared. He'd been much more affected than any other member of the staff. Almost immediately after, he'd gone to the musicians to order them to pack up and leave. This was done at the behest of Marie Armonet but without the consent or knowledge of Auguste, the head of the household. It wasn't the kind of thing a sensible member of staff would have done except under pressure.

Today, Sasha Resedeul had telephoned Greg for help. That had been done, on his own admission, because Mme Guidon had ordered him to do it. His attitude throughout had been of extreme unwillingness, as if he dreaded what might come out.

And then there was the big question that had been troubling Greg. Why had the email appeared on Resedeul's computer?

He'd said that anyone could find an email address if they looked hard enough. Then why, failing a response from Auguste Guidon, should the kidnappers look for the address of Sasha Resedeul, secretary to the victim's aunt? Why not go directly to the mother?

Rosanne Guidon should have received that email, by any ordinary reasoning.

Greg rose from his chair and went across the hall. There was no one in the secretary's office. He picked up a phone, pressed eleven, and asked for a maid to come to the office.

'Would you be so good as to show me to M. Resedeul's room?' he asked when she came.

'Oh, monsieur, if you just dial eighteen you'll get his room—'

'No, no, please show me the way.' No good getting Sasha on the phone. What he had to say had to be said face to face.

The maid, hiding a frown of irritation, took him up in the little lift, turned left along the passage, and on for several yards. Then she tapped on a door and opened it.

Greg walked in. He found Sasha with a suitcase on the bed, packing in a hurry.

Thirteen

Greg nodded at the maid to go. The other man looked up at him nervously.

'So, Sasha, what's the story?'

'I don't know what you mean,' Sasha said.

'Are you thinking of going somewhere?'

Sasha sat down on his bed, so that the items collected there for packing slid off on to the floor. 'I can't bear it here any more,' he cried. 'Bad things keep happening.'

'And then your conscience troubles you, doesn't it?'

'Nothing of the kind – it's just that I'm . . . I'm not able to . . . to keep going when the atmosphere is so . . . you know . . . so fraught.'

'Very sensitive and shy. So why did you agree to act as informer? Was it for money?'

'Informer?' It was a faint, shocked echo.

'You did give information to someone.'

'No.' But it had no conviction in it. He sighed wearily then said: 'There was no harm in it. It happened at a one-day conference in Milan. You know Mme Armonet takes an interest in several charities . . . well, this conference was about diseases of the thyroid gland . . . you know that there used to be a problem in Switzerland with that because of a lack of iodine but we've dealt with it . . . still in under-developed countries it goes on being prevalent . . . well, you don't want to know all that.'

He took a breath and went on: 'It's not a big romantic charity, doesn't get much publicity. But there were one or two journalists in Milan, and one of them approached me . . .' His voice died away.

'Go on.'

'Davie Daniels his name was . . . There didn't seem any harm in it!' he protested, colouring up. 'He said he was a freelance who sold pieces to a gossip magazine in London . . . *Talked About*, it's called. He said if I gave him anything about the Guidons that he could use, he'd split the proceeds with me.'

'And you agreed.'

'Well, you see . . . I thought I could sell him bits about Marie's charities. She's really keen on doing good things for them but in all honesty . . . she's not important enough and I thought it would be such a helpful thing . . .'

'So when was this?'

'First week in April.'

'And how did you contact him?'

'He contacted me. He'd ring me every couple of weeks or so and I'd tell him what Marie had been up to . . . and he seemed quite interested . . . and then he asked me about Auguste, and Madame, and I didn't see the harm so I told him when there was a party or if Auguste got an honour from some African country, things like that . . .'

'Did any of this stuff appear in the magazine?'

'How should I know?' Sasha cried. 'It's not the kind of thing I read, and you don't see it on the bookstalls here. But he was paying me, so I supposed the things got published.'

'So did you tell him about Gilles and his ambitions to form a jazz group?'

'Yes.' A very quiet assent.

Greg said nothing for a moment then asked, 'How did you get paid? Did he send you a cheque – anything like that?'

'No, money just appeared in my bank account.'

Greg sighed inwardly. No hope there of getting some trace of the culprit. 'Are you still being contacted?'

'No.'

No. Of course not. The plotters had got what they wanted – a way of coming into Chateau Guidon.

'Did Daniels ever contact you by email?'

'Never.'

'Did either Lou Ferigiano or Morena make contact with you?'

Sasha shook his head vehemently. 'No, no, I hadn't a clue!

153

But then, you see, Nounou went missing. At first I thought nothing of it, she'd done it before, you know . . . But I knew she'd been snooping . . .'

'Snooping?'

'Yes, in Morena's room. She did that . . . Nounou liked to know all there was to know about people who came to the house. And she disapproved of Morena so completely . . . everybody knew she'd be slipping into Morena's room when she wasn't there, she'd say she was checking that the maids had done their work properly but she was very keen on knowing about Morena. And though she never went across to the stable block to pry . . . at least I don't think so . . . but she kept an eye on everybody coming and going . . . So after she took off without doing her usual dramatic comeback, I began to think that . . . well, I don't know what I thought exactly.'

Sasha got up from the bed and began to pace about the room.

'You thought she might have learned something about Morena, perhaps?'

'Well, I did, yes . . . And I wondered if . . . but it seemed so extravagant to believe that anybody would do anything to her . . .' He shook his head at himself. 'Then Gilles and Morena took off. I was . . . honestly, I was staggered. I thought at first it was simply a money-grabbing girl taking advantage of a great chance . . . And then I wondered if Nounou had somehow got hold of something . . . Or had guessed something . . . I was worried, it just seemed to me that . . .' He faltered, staring at Greg as if asking for approval and understanding.

'Well,' he went on, 'I began to think that she and her brother turned up so . . . so à propos . . . I thought perhaps Daniels had given a hint to some grasping lady friend of his . . . I thought the band might have had some idea what was going on, might have helped her. I wanted rid of them so I told them to pack up and go.'

'That was your own idea?'

'Yes, but I said Marie had ordered it. Marie . . . you know, she gets a bit frank with her opinions when she's had a few, so I knew I could say she'd ordered me to get rid of them.'

'I got the impression they were genuinely surprised at the elopement.'

'I suppose so. I overreacted . . . But now, you see, after what's happened, it really does look as if Davie Daniels used me as an informer, and for all I know . . . Gilles . . .' He stopped, ran his hands through his thinning hair, and stared up at the ceiling as if beyond it he could see the great judge on his heavenly throne. 'I didn't mean any harm,' he wailed.

'No, Sasha, I understand.' He wanted the man in a calmer state, so as to get what information he could give. 'And you don't know how to contact Daniels?'

'No, no, if only I did! I'd get a message to him, explain that Auguste is ill, that he can't divulge the password without involving a lot of other people . . . Oh, God, poor Gilles!' He flung himself into a chair by the window and put his head in his hands.

Greg let him have a few minutes to recover then asked: 'Was that Daniels on the telephone this morning?'

'No idea. The voice seemed hardly human.'

'Well, the first thing we must do now is go back downstairs and send messages from both Auguste's email account and yours.'

'Saying what?'

'Something to the effect that M. Guidon is very ill and can't be informed of the instructions.'

'What do you bet we get a "Message Undeliverable" response?'

Greg sighed. 'I wouldn't take the bet. Both those addresses will have been closed down, I'm pretty sure.'

'You do it, then. I want nothing more to do with it.'

'Sasha, you can't wash your hands of it, just like that. You're involved. You may know something that could help.'

'I don't! I don't! I tell you, all I know is that some reporter paid me for what seemed ordinary gossip.'

'You can describe him, perhaps.'

'Oh . . . well . . . He was English. Middle-aged, but well looked-after, if you know what I mean – smooth tanned skin, good manicure, that sort of thing.'

'Tall, short? Dark or fair?'

'Tallish, dark hair but that might have been touched up. You know, the kind of man who gets invited to parties and first nights, as you'd expect if he was always trying to be friends with celebrities.'

So that wasn't much help. Greg groaned inwardly. Yet even if the man had some distinctive trait – a scar, a limp, something to make him stand out a little – what good would that be? They'd been told not to approach the police, but only the police had the resources to trace a criminal by distinguishing marks.

He said: 'Sasha, we have to tell Madame about this and ask her to call in the police. There's just a chance they might be able to find Davie Daniels.'

'But on the phone they said not to!'

'I'm pretty sure the police would do better than we can—'

'But if it endangers Gilles?'

'How would they know the police had been contacted?'

Sasha shook his head. And half an hour later Greg got the same negative reaction from Rosanne Guidon. 'No, no, we must do nothing that might endanger my boy! No!'

'But it's just possible this man Daniels has some kind of record—'

'Monsieur Couronne,' she said formally, 'I value your opinion, of course. You've been extremely kind and helpful. But my husband is the only person who could take this decision, and as you well know, he's not fit to be consulted. I must insist that the police are not informed.'

'Very well, madame.' He thought she was wrong, and his tone witnessed to the fact. Mme Guidon bridled a little.

Marie Armonet so far had been speechless. She had been glaring at Sasha, who was standing inside the door of the small sitting room, haggard with shame and anxiety. Now she spoke up. 'I was totally against having all those low-life musicians on the premises because I thought they'd be up to no good. It turns out I should have been looking at someone that I thought of as a friend!'

'Marie, I had no idea that Daniels might be—'

'Don't dare call me Marie! And the sooner you're gone, the better!'

'But, Marie—'

'To think I trusted you! To think I was fond of you—'

'For goodness sake, be quiet, Marie,' said her sister-in-law with asperity. 'This isn't about what you and Sasha might have been up to, it's about my son's life!' She paused to think what to do next. 'When this person rings tomorrow, we must tell him that Auguste is ill.'

'But if it's a machine again, madame?'

'Well, we'll – we'll tell the machine. After all, it wants us to speak to it – utter a password. We'll just say, "M. Guidon is too ill to speak to you." And then . . . and then they'll . . . I suppose they'll make some fresh contact about Gilles.' Her voice was shaking towards the end. She wasn't sure if she was endangering her son's life.

'Wouldn't it be better to let Auguste's condition be more widely known?' Greg suggested.

'In what way?'

'Well, Sasha has contacts with the newspapers because of his charity work – you have, haven't you, Sasha?'

'I hardly think the assistance of M. Resedeul is required any more.'

'Then perhaps Marie could do it.'

'But we can't do a thing like that!' cried Marie. 'What, tell everybody that the President of Banque Guidon has had a heart attack?'

'Oh, surely, in this case—'

'It would cause hundreds of people to transfer their accounts immediately! Auguste would be furious with us.'

'Monsieur Couronne,' said Rosanne, 'we are extremely grateful for all you've done. And of course you mean well. But you don't understand the responsibilities of a banking family such as ours.'

'And besides which,' Marie added waspishly, 'it was your fault that Ferigiano and his sister ever got to know Gilles.'

'I see.'

He had overstayed his welcome. And to tell the truth, he was very weary – physically, because it was now mid-evening and he'd been in the midst of this catastrophe now for nearly nine hours, and mentally because he'd had too many unknowns to handle. 'I'll take my leave now,' he said. 'If you should need me, you have my telephone number.'

He was shown out by the housemaid, who looked at him in puzzled hopefulness for some clue as to what was going on. He smiled and murmured goodbye.

On reaching Geneva he parked in his usual spot outside his office then ran upstairs. The place was locked up and Amabelle was long gone, but had left Post-it messages for him to remember this and do that. He disregarded them all. Instead he rang Liz Blair.

As soon as she picked up he began, 'Liz, sweetheart, I want to apologize for being so abrupt earlier—'

'No, no, I understand! I admit I was furious with you at the time but I've thought about it and I—'

'I shouldn't have barked at you. I'm sorry. But—'

'Something bad has happened, hasn't it?'

'Well, yes . . .'

'At the chateau? Is that where you are now?'

'No, I'm at the office, on my way home.'

'Tell me about it.'

'Liz, I can't. At least not on the telephone. It may seem silly, but—'

'No, no, darling, you know what you're doing. I feel terrible for walking out on you like I did.'

'Oh, you were quite right. You said the family was under a curse and you were right!'

'Is there anything I can do? Shall I come back?'

'No, no, this isn't a good place to be – at least, if I keep on being connected with them, and I don't see how I can just cut them off – they're in such trouble.'

'You're saying there's danger? Actual physical danger?'

He didn't reply. After waiting a moment she said: 'You know, I thought the whole thing with that family was beginning to be scary. There was the elopement, but before that Nounou went missing and now we know she's . . . well, I thought about it on the plane coming home and I wondered . . . I wondered if—'

'Did she fall or was she pushed?'

'Yes. My word, you're quick! That's what I was wondering.

158

And before that . . . that poor man Willie Clifford—'

'Wally Clifford.'

'Wally, then. He fell – under a train. Didn't he?'

'Yes.'

'Did he fall or was he pushed?'

'Liz!'

'Well, it seems sort of . . . You needed to hire Lou because Wally had died, and now Lou's cleared off, and Morena's gone off with Gilles, the heir to the family fortune, I imagine. And Nounou . . . well, I don't know about Nounou, really—'

'Sasha said she was known to snip. No, wait a minute, *fureter*—' He caught himself up, translating in his head. 'I mean snoop. She snooped in people's rooms. And Morena's room was just along the corridor from hers.'

'You think she found out . . . something . . . about Morena?'

'It's certainly possible.'

'My poor darling, you should never have got involved in setting up a jazz band. It just never was you, if you know what I mean.'

'Now you tell me.'

'I think I should come to Geneva—'

'No, no, don't, Liz.' He didn't want her anywhere near a place where kidnapping and probably murder was going on. 'But there is something you could do,' he suggested, with a sudden flash of inspiration. 'I've tried to find out about Lou and the jazz career and found out he didn't have one. Could you find out about Morena?'

'Love to. But how?'

'I thought . . . because of her clothes? You kept saying she dressed expensively – well, we tried to account for that, remember, we thought perhaps her family gave her an allowance but you know . . .' He was working it out as he spoke. 'If Lou wasn't a genuine musician, perhaps she wasn't either. So when we were trying to account for her expensive clothes, we limited ourselves because we thought she earned a living singing in hotel bars. Perhaps . . . I don't know . . .'

'Well, the dress by Anika Roth might not have been in the

159

very top range of dress prices because Roth is still trying to make her name,' she said, picking up his train of thought. 'But all the same, it must have cost quite a lot. The Donna Karan could have been bought off the peg, I suppose. All the same, we're not talking peanuts.'

'Is there any way of finding out about the dresses? Do dressmakers keep records of their customers?'

'Oh, you bet! And invite them to their shows, and serve them champagne, and send them little goodies at Christmas, designer scarves with the designer's name on them, that sort of thing.'

'So if you were to ask this Roth lady about Morena . . . ?'

'Now that's a good idea! Why didn't I think of that?'

'So will you do it?'

'Of course! And since America is five hours behind us, it's still early evening there, so I can try her on the telephone right now.'

'You know her number?' he said in surprise.

'Oh, certainly, my innocent! I was so intrigued about her, I looked up her website. Always keep track of the up and coming designers, you might be able to copy one of their frocks before they wake up to the need for security!'

'You really are a little shark, aren't you?' he said.

'Oh, Jaws Minor, that's me. Stay there, I'll get right on it and ring you back.'

Fourteen

But when the phone rang, Liz had no good news.

'I'm sorry, sweetness, I made the wrong approach. She just didn't want to know me.'

'What did you say to her?'

'I told her I was in the rag trade and might be able to do her some good in the British market. She froze me right out.'

She was so contrite he didn't have the heart to sound critical. Instead he said, 'Could you try again? Use a different attitude?'

'What, speak in a deeper voice and say, "I am ze Countess Goldenblock and I vish to buy zis dress"?'

'I suppose not.' He couldn't seem to think of anything helpful. 'Never mind,' he said. 'It was worth a try.'

'Which I made a mess of. I'm so sorry, Greg.'

'Let's sleep on it. We might think of something to try in the morning.'

'If only . . .'

They said their goodbyes, he went home, he excused his long absence by telling his grandmother that Auguste Guidon was ill, and that was that.

Next morning, Saturday, he was coming home from a pre-dawn walk with Rousseau when he heard the telephone in the living room. He hurried to it, hoping it might be Liz, and was astonished to find himself speaking to Auguste.

'I apologize for calling you so early, and on a Sunday too,' said the banker, not perhaps in his usual bank-regulating voice, but with some of his habitual firmness. 'And I also apologize for last night. I gather that there was some frigidity in your treatment.'

'Oh, no, not at all, not at all.'

'My wife, you know – she is under a great deal of pressure. And so am I, of course.'

'I'm glad you feel well enough to—'

'If I may, I'd like to ask you to come to the chateau. You understand that I – we – our situation is that we must make decisions for ourselves.'

Meaning he wasn't going to call in the police. Greg thought he was wrong but said nothing.

'You have been so helpful, Greg, I'm asking you – I'm – I'm entreating you to come back and help me to think things through.'

'Are you sure you're up to it, Auguste?'

'Yes, yes, not perhaps my usual self but I am not about to die. May I expect you here soon?'

'Of course.' Impossible to refuse. He felt somehow responsible for what had happened because, as Marie Armonet had said, he'd brought the evil-doers into the house. He went to the kitchen, where his grandmother was just starting breakfast preparations.

'Grossmutti, I have to go out.'

'Breakfast will only be a minute, dear.'

'No, I'm going now. That was Auguste Guidon on the phone.'

'Good heavens, not again,' she protested as he dashed out.

Daylight, as it slowly emerged, was hardly above steel-grey. The lake, as he drove past Geneva, looked sullen and dark. Snow was coming at last, much desired by the ski centres and to tell the truth, welcome to Greg himself. If there was a good snowfall and he could get a day free, he'd get out his skis and go cross country.

At Chateau Guidon, Roger was waiting to put his Mercedes under cover. 'No sense in getting snow on the old girl's bonnet,' he joked. He gave a keen glance at him. 'Monsieur's more himself and the household's in less of a scrum. Think everything's going to be all right?'

'Of course,' said Greg. They both knew he didn't mean it.

'Your little pals are up and about already, strange to say. And they weren't particularly late back last night. P'raps they're learning to be civilized after all.'

'I'll have to have a word with them later,' said Greg. He had little doubt that they were getting restless, but they couldn't be allowed to leave. For all he knew, they might be complicit in Gilles's abduction.

Rosanne was waiting for him in the sitting room. 'I'll take you up to Auguste in a moment, Greg, but first I want to . . . to apologize.'

'Good heavens, what for? No need for anything like that.'

'That's so kind of you. And of course, as soon as you had gone last night, I wished you were still here. Because, you see, the police telephoned to say they were releasing Nounou's body and asked if they should bring her belongings home to us. And I didn't know how to tell Auguste.'

He took one of her hands in both of his and gave it a little squeeze of encouragement.

'Then this morning, he felt so much better, and Dr Perlerou came first thing as he'd said he would, and while he was giving Auguste a check-up, a sergeant arrived with Nounou's things and I signed for them.' She gave a little shudder at the recollection. 'So before the doctor left I asked him if I should tell Auguste about . . . you know . . . these things and say should we start thinking about the funeral.'

'That was hard for you,' he murmured.

'Oh yes. I knew it would upset him, but he is the head of the family. He was very emotional for a moment . . .' She sighed and shook her head. 'But Dr Perlerou saw him through it. So then he seemed . . . resolute . . . determined . . . as if he got some strength from somewhere else . . .'

'Well, that's splendid news.'

'So then after the doctor left, I told him the rest.' She faced Greg with the news, head up, trying to be in control.

'About the telephone message you're expecting?'

She nodded slowly. 'I had to tell him. He is the only person who can make the decisions.'

'And how did he take it?'

'He's – he's really such a fine man, my husband!' she burst out. 'Sometimes he's thought of as being rather dull – oh, I know what people say! But he heard me out, and – well – it took him some time to regain his self-control but he –

he became quite calm and asked for the telephone to be brought to his bedside so that he could speak to you in person. I beg you to do all you can to help him.'

'That goes without saying, Rosanne.'

They went up in the little lift. He expected to be shown into Auguste's bedroom but instead they entered by a neighbouring door, which opened on to a pleasant room, rather feminine, with Dutch flower paintings on the wall and a chaise longue in soft pearl-grey satin. Madame's boudoir, he supposed.

From an adjoining door Auguste came in. He was in pyjamas and a handsome brocade dressing-gown. Rosanne rushed to help him to the chaise longue, although he really needed no help. He seemed well, his colour was good and he had been well barbered. Yet he wasn't quite the same Auguste that Greg had first met at the Cascade.

'Thank you for coming,' he said, shaking hands. 'Please, take a seat.' He indicated an upholstered armchair drawn alongside the sofa. 'Rosanne, our guest would like coffee, I'm sure.'

'It's coming, dear.'

'Good. Now, Rosanne, off you go and telephone to all our friends.' He paused to explain to Greg. 'We had invited guests for lunch today, but now Rosanne is going to cancel. Off you go, my love.'

Rosanne obeyed. When she had gone Auguste said: 'She's going to tell them that I'm unwell. They're not by any means chatterboxes but I think word will get round that Auguste Guidon is under doctor's orders.'

'But what if the kidnappers try to telephone meanwhile?'

'They will use the landline. Rosanne is calling our guests on a mobile. If the telephone on my desk rings, she'll pick up immediately.'

'And say what?'

'That I'm too ill to come to the phone.'

Greg pursed his lips. Was that a good move?

Auguste understood his hesitation. 'You told my wife and my sister yesterday that we ought to let it be known I'm hors de combat. They resisted the idea of letting the gossip columnists have the news but I thought about it this morning and it seems to me this way is quite reasonable.'

'Well, yes . . .'

'I know, you think it's too restricted. But when I don't go to the office tomorrow, that will extend the circle of communication.'

'But not as far as the criminals, perhaps?'

'I've given it considerable thought, Greg. They managed to get hold of someone in the house, didn't they? It seems to me they probably have some way of keeping an eye on the bank. Oh, not through my staff,' he added hastily, as his hearer looked rather shocked. 'No, no, I think my staff is utterly reliable. Yet you know, these brutes who've taken my son have shown themselves to be quite devious. They may have made friends with some financial adviser who keeps his ear to the ground so as to alert his clients about problems. Or they may have contacts in the newspaper world, where reporters are always watching the banks. So if he exists I'm giving him the chance to know that Auguste Guidon is at home in bed.'

'Not bad,' Greg acknowledged.

A manservant came in with a tray of coffee. He drew up a little table to place it near them. 'Armand,' said his master, 'bring me the package from the bureau.'

He went to an exquisite seventeenth-century writing desk to fetch it. It was a large container of sturdy blue plastic. 'Give it to M. Couronne.' Greg took it. It bore the logo of the canton police.

When the man had gone, Greg pulled open the zip fastening. Inside in separate plastic bags were the belongings of the late Josephine Bartelet, better known as Nounou.

He saw folded clothes: dark red padded jacket, wool skirt, underwear. Then a pair of maroon leather shoes, a pair of leather walking shoes. The other items were a backpack of waterproof tartan cloth, a brown leather purse, the coins and notes it had contained in a separate clear-view envelope, a credit card from the Banque Guidon, and a little leather notebook. Everything bore the signs of damage by water – even the contents of the backpack, whose seams must have parted during long immersion – but they had been dried.

Greg looked at Auguste for guidance.

'Look at the notebook,' he suggested.

He opened it. The pages contained lines of writing, mostly smeared beyond recognition. They were in Romansch. A word or two was readable: 'polish', 'curtain fabric', 'afternoon', 'funicular'.

'Look at the last page.'

He turned the leaves of the notebook with a careful finger. The last page was just as damaged as the rest. He could read a few words.

'*Ferien . . .*' Something about holidays? A visit to a travel office – was that why the town shoes?

No, it was a longer word.

He looked up. Auguste was watching him. 'You see it?'

'Ferigiano?'

'I think so. It's a note about the Ferigianos.' Auguste was nodding in satisfaction. 'Try the next line.'

'It looks like . . . *Klein* . . . no, *keine* . . . The next word's a mess.' He spelled out the letters aloud. '*B . . . e . . . ze . . .* No . . . *zie . . .* something . . . *nung*? No, that can't be right, *Bezienung*? There's no such word.' He tried again, saying the letters to himself as he deciphered them. All at once, as if he were solving a clue in a crossword puzzle, he saw it. '*Keine Beziehung*! No relation!'

Auguste leaned back among his cushions. 'And just before that, "Ferigiano". She's saying they weren't related.'

Greg recalled Sasha's words, that Nounou was known to snoop in other people's rooms. It seemed she'd found something that gave her information.

Not brother and sister. Somehow, now that it was put before him, he wasn't surprised. They'd been so different. Family members could of course differ – but Morena was elegant, well educated. Lou had the air of being raised in a bar-room. And although he and Liz Blair had tried to account for it by imagining a father who loved his daughter but disowned his son, he thought now that there was a simpler explanation. They came from quite different backgrounds.

Auguste gestured at the bureau. 'Put it aside for the moment. Pour yourself some coffee. Let us think about this.'

He put the items back in the container and set it on the bureau. He poured himself a cup of coffee and resumed his seat.

Auguste said: 'Your friend Ms Blair remarked on the town shoes. She claimed that Nounou was on her way to town to see someone. Do you know what I think?'

'What?'

'I think she was going to Banque Guidon to speak to the head of security.'

'About the Ferigianos.'

'Yes.'

'That makes sense. And . . . met with an accident?'

'The police sergeant gave us permission to claim Nounou's body for burial. They are satisfied.' He broke off, his voice dying away as he frowned at his own weakness. 'Forgive me. I still find it hard to think of her dying alone on the mountainside. The police are satisfied that it was an accident, that she fell and hit her head and then slipped into the stream. But she didn't drown, she was dead before she went into the water, they say.'

Did she fall or was she pushed? Greg repeated to himself. Auguste's expression told him he was thinking the same thing. Greg sipped some coffee.

'You know,' said Auguste in a wry tone, 'I dearly loved Nounou. But I have to admit she had her faults. She could be very critical, very outspoken. And I think that . . . on that morning . . . she . . . she . . .'

'She had a quarrel with Morena Ferigiano and told her she knew she wasn't Lou's sister.'

'Or told her at least that she suspected it.'

'And that Nounou is dead because of that.'

'Yes.'

Greg shook his head in regret. 'If only I'd checked their background story more thoroughly.'

'Oh, my dear friend, don't reproach yourself! If I hadn't been so indulgent to Gilles . . . But he got carried away. He acted so quickly when they came on the scene. Because, of

167

course, he's always been susceptible to pretty girls.'

'I tried to check up on them yesterday,' Greg remarked. 'The place in Paris where Lou said they'd been playing – it's been closed since the spring. And the band-leader that he mentioned – the one in Marseilles – he's never heard of him.'

'And Mlle Ferigiano?'

'Well,' he admitted with some reluctance, 'I asked Liz Blair to do that for me. I thought she might find out something through the dressmaker.'

'What?'

'Liz was intrigued by the quality of her clothes. She guessed at the designer of one of her frocks . . . Oh, well, it's a very feminine thing, Auguste, but the long and the short of it is, Liz had got a telephone number from a website—'

'A telephone number?'

'From a dress designer's website. The designer has an atelier in New York. But nothing came of it, I'm sorry to say.'

'I'm sorry, I'm not following you. What has the dress designer to do with it?'

'Liz thought she might find out who had bought the dress – might even get an address for her – something like that.'

'But she failed.'

'Because she made the wrong approach. You probably don't know, but Liz is in the fashion business, so she started – I think this was the idea – she started with an offer to do some kind of a deal with her – her name, if I remember rightly, is Roth. Well, Mlle Roth simply wasn't interested. I think she may even have put the phone down on her, to judge from Liz's reaction.'

'Ahh . . .' Auguste leaned back on his cushions, closed his eyes, and thought. 'Could she try again? Perhaps make a positive offer? The Banque Guidon would provide any references she might need.'

'No, no, the rejection wasn't about money. I think Mlle Roth was offended at being approached to do chain-store fashion.'

The banker was disappointed. Money, he clearly thought, ought to have more attraction. He remembered his role as host. 'Please,' he said, 'pour yourself more coffee. Try the little pastries.'

'No, many thanks, I'm fine.' He sipped what remained in his cup. After a moment he ventured: 'It might be possible to make a different approach to Mlle Roth.'

'In what way?'

'I haven't quite worked that out yet. But if one were to see her in person, have a conversation . . .'

'My dear fellow, we can't tell anyone about what the Ferigianos have done – we mustn't.'

'No, no, that's understood. But Liz says that Roth is sure to have Morena's name and address.'

'But I've just pointed out, we can't mention their name.'

'But we could talk about the dress – Liz had a very high opinion of it, Auguste. I don't know if you remember it but at the party to celebrate signing the contracts, Morena wore a pale yellow dress?'

Auguste shook his head. 'She did?'

'Yes, and Liz – who knows a lot about such things – said it was quite special, and by a new designer. If she were to go there and talk about the dress—' He caught himself up. 'No, that won't work, Roth would recognize her English accent at once.'

Auguste looked disappointed. They sat in silence. The time on the pretty little French clock on the mantelpiece was a few minutes after ten.

'They might perhaps be calling soon,' Greg suggested.

'It's possible. But I think they're more likely to leave it until later – so that my anxiety level will be higher and I'll agree to whatever they say.'

'That's inhuman!'

'Oh, criminals who are after very large sums of money are not soft-hearted.'

'So it is a very large sum of money?'

'No, my boy, I'm not going to discuss the account with you,' said Auguste with a wry smile. 'And the fact of the matter is, I don't know how much it contains – I haven't made any enquiry because I want discretion. I haven't contacted my security people. You see my point?'

169

'I know that the bank would want to respect the customer's requirements—'

'Had I called in the police, I would of course have co-operated with them to the fullest extent. But I want to stay within banking regulations as long as I can. And therefore I want to do all I can to get my son back without the police, although I know – I admit – that they have better resources, but my security staff are not without ability.'

'What about Sasha? Has he been able to think of anything helpful?'

'Oh, Sasha . . .' A shrug. 'When this thing is ended – one way or another – ' and here Auguste's voice trembled for a moment – 'Sasha Resedeul leaves this house with my curse on his head.'

Greg was worried for a moment. The man looked so choked with emotion that he feared he might make himself ill again. But Auguste forced himself to be calm, and said: 'Let's think. Sasha can contribute nothing. The information we were given about the former career of the Ferigianos was false.' He paused, frowning. 'Absurd as it may seem, the only clue we seem to have is the dress.'

This had been Greg's conclusion, but he'd hesitated to bring it up again. He waited.

'Let's suppose,' said Auguste, 'that an approach was made in person. Let's suppose that someone were to go to this couturier and ask to buy another copy of the dress.' A faint smile touched his lips. 'I know this can happen because my wife often buys clothes in that way. She sees someone wearing something she likes and asks for a copy made in her size.'

'But I just told you, Liz has this noticeable British accent.'

'But she need not speak!' said Auguste. 'You take her to the atelier, you tell the designer she doesn't speak English, and you ask about the dress on her behalf.'

Greg stared at the banker in admiration. 'That's very clever!'

'My friend, I am President of a Swiss bank. I don't hold the position because I'm the latest candidate from the Guidon family, but because I have some skill in negotiating and manoeuvring. Will you go to New York?'

'Of course, but will Liz? She has her own business to run,

170

you know.' He said this simply to be on the safe side; he thought Liz was likely to jump at the chance if she possibly could.

'Can you get in touch with her? I mean, now?'

'I can try. But I sometimes have problems in the mountains with my mobile.'

'Oh, dear boy, we have a system in the house that boosts the signal. All the same, be a little careful what you say. It's easier to listen in on a mobile call.'

He got out his Nokia and pressed the buttons. It was Saturday, so he trusted that Liz wouldn't be out on business somewhere. After a pause she answered. He could hear conversation in the background.

'Liz, it's me. Where are you?'

'In a department store. What's happening, duckie?'

'What on earth are you doing in a department store on a Saturday?'

'Looking at clothes, of course.'

What else? 'But surely it's your day off?'

'I'm having a review of Christmas party frocks before they go on the rails tomorrow.'

'How would you like to look at clothes in New York?'

'Huh?'

'We could make a little trip. To the workshop of the person you were speaking to last night.'

'What? Wait a minute . . .' There was a little pause while she caught up. 'Oh, I see. But . . . what would be the good . . . I got the brush-off.'

'Well, we've got a new approach. Listen, my precious, the only thing to settle at the moment is, will you come with me to the Big Apple?'

'When?'

'Soon as possible.'

'Oh. Oh, well . . . I'd love to, but I'd have to sort out a few appointments—'

'Do that. Start now, because we want to be on a flight very soon.'

'Gee, I'm being swept off my feet, aren't I? Lovely sensation. OK, lover, I'll work things out. When's H-Hour?'

'I'll let you know as soon as I've fixed it up. Stay tuned, as I believe they say.'

'Greg, you're so up on all the trends!' she laughed. 'OK, I'll be waiting.'

Auguste had heard his side of the conversation. He heaved himself to his feet and made his way across the room to the writing desk. He sat down, explaining over his shoulder, 'I'll write you a note for our travel agent. It's the firm that takes care of travel arrangements for the bank. I'm afraid you'll have to go back into Geneva to see them. I'll ring and tell them to expect you.'

'Thank you.'

He wrote busily, folded the sheet and handed it with an envelope to Greg. 'Please read it. See if there's anything I should add.'

'No, no, I'm sure it's fine. Thank you.'

'No, I'm the one that should be saying thank you. You are so good to do this for us. Please keep in touch – and please be careful.'

He made his farewells then went across to the rag room to tell the musicians he wouldn't be around for a day or two. Only Nils and Emilio were there. Nils was playing Debussy, Emilio was reading a Spanish paperback. They both seemed listless and fed up.

'So what's happening at the Big House?' Nils enquired, leaving the piano. 'Any word from Gilles?'

'Not so far.'

'We can't expect him to think of us,' said Emilio. 'In a way, he's on his honeymoon, no?'

Nils gave a thin smile. 'But we, as it happens, are not having such a good time. Listen, Greg, François is saying he's going to pack up and go to Brussels.'

'He can't do that,' Greg replied. 'He has a contract.'

'I believe a contract becomes invalid when one of the partners breaks it. François is saying Gilles has broken—'

'Not at all. The contract specifies that you remain under agreement until you've performed at the Montreux Festival. That's still the objective.'

'But we aren't going anywhere. With the music, I mean.'

172

'And François is saying the whole thing's over,' sighed Emilio.

'No,' said the Prince firmly, 'nobody's giving up yet.'

Fifteen

Madame Wildstren, the travel agent, wasn't in the least put out at having to give up her leisurely lunch. She waved away Greg's apologies and listened with attention to his needs.

'Well, then, if you have business to transact, it makes no sense to try for a flight today,' she observed. 'Here we are now, midday, so if you fly via London – and that is what you wish, yes? Well, then, there's very little chance now of two seats for a late-evening departure from Heathrow and even then, you see, you'd arrive in New York about midnight their time, which is bad for your body-clock.'

Greg was used to calculations like this. He travelled frequently to negotiate with singers' agents and concert-hall managers. 'Then let's say I stay in London this evening,' he said. 'Can you get us on an early flight tomorrow morning?'

'Let me see what I can do.' She turned to her computer and called up screens. After some investigation she nodded at him over her spectacles. 'Yes, that we can do. So shall I book you into a London hotel overnight? Or would you wish one adjacent to the airport?'

'Oh, I'll be staying with a friend. She's the one who's travelling with me to New York. But of course I shall be paying for the flight to London myself—'

'Not at all, not at all!' She was quite shocked. 'This letter from M. Guidon requests me to take care of all your travel needs. You and your companion, certainly, everything shall be arranged.'

She finalized everything neatly and quickly, handed him a folder full of tickets and instructions. He shook hands then hurried to his office to call Liz with the news that he'd be with her that evening. 'I can't give you any details on the phone,' he said, 'but get packed for a trip to New York.'

Then he contacted Chateau Guidon. Rosanne answered, and as soon as he identified himself began to speak in Romansch.

'They called just before noon,' she reported in a quavering voice. 'It was a machine, just as you described. It asked me to give details of the password and while I was explaining that I was Auguste's wife and that he was too ill to come to the phone, it simply began speaking again, asking me to repeat the password and verify that it was correct. So then I started with the fact that Auguste was very ill – and I'd more or less got to the end of my explanation when it all switched off. The line just went dead.'

Greg heard her out. He said, 'They'll call again.'

'That's what Auguste says. And so – to give authenticity to the story that he's very ill, you see – he arranged for a private ambulance to come for him and he's been taken to a clinic. He said that if we were under surveillance, they'd be more inclined to believe he couldn't do anything about the password. He says that gives us some leeway.'

'He's right,' Greg agreed.

'But ... but what's happening to my poor boy all this time, Greg? Where is he? What are they doing to him?'

'He's all right. I'm sure he's all right. He's their bargaining point. They're taking good care of him, Rosanne.'

He wasn't sure if it was true, nor if it would hold good forever.

She sniffled for a moment but pulled herself together. 'What time is your flight? Auguste told me to say that Roger will meet you at the airport with some useful telephone numbers in New York, things like that. And will you telephone to let him know you've arrived, and so forth?'

'Of course.'

He went home to explain he was going on business to New York. His grandmother merely shrugged. She was accustomed to his sudden departures. He packed a carry-on valise. At early evening a very handsome four-wheel-drive vehicle arrived at Bredoux to carry him to the airport. His father came out to wave him off. 'Mmm,' he said with appreciation when he saw it. 'We need something like that. The Mercedes is getting too old, poor old girl.'

'Costs a fortune, Papa.'

'You going to be away long this time?'

'Probably not. I'll let you know when I'm coming back.'

'New York,' murmured ex-King Anton with a sigh. 'Scared me to death the only time I ever went there. Well, good luck, my boy.'

At the airport Roger, looking gloomy, rose from a bench to greet him as he came into the main hall. 'Evening, sir. Madame sent me to give you this.' He proffered an envelope.

'Thank you, Roger. How are things at the chateau?'

'Not good,' was the doleful reply. 'Monsieur was carted off in an ambulance! And poor Mme Guidon looks as if the world is coming to an end. It's too bad of M. Gilles to stay away so long – I mean, a man's entitled to his little outings but what with Nounou's death and now this heart attack . . . You'd think M. Gilles would have seen the news about Nounou's death . . .'

'I don't think so,' Greg rejoined. 'It was only a little item in the newspapers. And for all we know, M. Gilles and Mlle Morena are in Austria or Italy, or anywhere, come to that.'

'Oh, yes, I hadn't thought of that.' Roger twisted his cap in his hands. 'Everything at the chateau seems weird these days . . .'

'How are my jazz band getting along?'

'Oh, they've left. M. Resideul arranged hotel rooms for them in Montreux.' He managed a little grin. 'The ladies didn't feel comfortable having fellows like that around at a time like this. What with Monsieur being ill and Nounou's funeral—'

'Oh, the funeral!' He hadn't given it a thought.

'Yes, M. Resideul is arranging it. It looks like it'll be Thursday, he's putting a notice in the papers but nobody'll come, you know – only us in the household and perhaps a few old biddies from her church. Monsieur isn't likely to be fit enough, I suppose, which is just as well.'

Greg shook hands in farewell and took himself to the

departure desk. He was surprised to find that he was greeted with respect and escorted off to the VIP lounge. There he opened the letter from Auguste.

Hand-written, it supplied the address and telephone number of the travel firm in Fifth Avenue used by the bank, the name and telephone number of the security chief at the Manhattan branch of Banque Guidon, and the telephone number at the clinic to which he'd consigned himself.

'Call me with any news. Rosanne and I will keep in touch also. I've instructed her to speak to me only in Romansch just in case anyone is intercepting calls to and from the house. With grateful thanks from both myself and my wife for all your help and concern for us, Auguste Guidon.'

At Heathrow a limousine awaited him. He was wafted off to Liz Blair's flat near Archway in London. He'd let her know he had landed so she was waiting at her door to greet him with a hug and a kiss. 'Come in, have a drink, and tell me what on earth's going on!' she begged.

When they were settled on the sofa with glasses in their hands, he gave her a full account of recent events at the Chateau Guidon. She listened with growing alarm.

'Greg, no wonder you sounded so worked up when you telephoned this morning. Poor Gilles . . . But listen, love – these people are saying no police – but the police have been to the chateau already, haven't they – about Nounou?'

'That's true, but if they're watching – and I suppose they must be – they know that was just about Nounou. After all, our thesis is that they caused her death. And there was an item about her death in the newspapers. You can bet they saw that – they'll be watching like a hawk for any mention of the Guidons.'

'This has turned a lot more serious, hasn't it?' she said with evident anxiety.

'Deadly serious. And because of that, I have to ask you now – do you still want to go to New York and try to find out things about this Ferigiano woman?'

'Just explain to me again why it's so important to speak to her dressmaker,' she countered, frowning in the effort to organize her thoughts about what had happened.

'It's the only clue we have. Nounou's messy notebook seems to imply they're not brother and sister and, though I've tried, I can't find out a thing about Lou. So Auguste wants us to try to find out anything we can about Morena.'

'And how will that help?'

'Well, there's a security staff at the bank, you know. I dare say they have quite a lot of expertise in tracking people down. But it wouldn't do any good for a Swiss ex-policeman to try interviewing a New York dressmaker, would it?'

That brought a smile to her lips. 'Oh, I see.' After a moment's consideration she said: 'I'm to be a rich woman wanting to buy a dress—' She broke off. 'But she's going to recognize my voice!'

'No she's not. Because you're going to be a sweet little foreign lady who can't speak a word of English.'

'I am?'

'Could you be French? You've got some clothes by French designers.'

'Well, copies from French designers,' she amended. 'But, sweetheart, she's probably able to speak French herself – French is the language of couture, you know.'

'Oh. Well, then, you'll have to be German—' He checked himself. 'But her name's Roth. That's perhaps derived from a German family name ...' He thought about it. 'Hmm ... You're too fair-skinned to be a Latin. You could be Polish, I suppose. Or Scandinavian. How would you like to be Finlandaise?'

'What?'

'Finn? Finnish?'

She laughed. 'What does it matter, since I'm not going to say anything in case she realizes I'm the woman who telephoned?'

'Well, of course, that's true.'

'So how's this going to work? You're going to take me to this studio and try to buy me a dress, and you're going to translate what Anika Roth says into Finnish.'

'That's the idea.'

'Don't tell me you actually speak Finnish as well as everything else!'

178

'Well, I know enough to hire a hall in Helsinki and complain about the draught. Stuff like that.'

'Can you talk about a yellow voile evening dress in Finnish?'

'No. But I'm going to ask about it in English, aren't I? And then translate for you.'

'Oh . . . Yes . . . So . . . wait . . . I'll have to reply. So I'm the one that has to speak Finnish – to you.'

'Ye-es.'

'But here we hit a snag, don't we, genius. I can't speak Finnish.'

He rallied. 'But you'll only have to say yes or no, and look shy.'

'But I don't know how to say yes and no in Finnish.'

'You will by the time we get there.'

'Is this going to be Method Acting?' she enquired.

And though it was a serious matter, they found themselves chuckling at each other.

Liz set her alarm and they went to bed. Of course there was an interlude before they went to sleep, but they tumbled out obediently well before the crack of dawn. They had finished a quick breakfast and were ready when the buzzer summoned her to her entry-phone. It was the driver of the limousine, as previously arranged.

Greg wasn't altogether surprised when they were conducted to the VIP lounge. Liz was enthralled. 'I could get used to this,' she told Greg.

'Me too.' Despite his princely status, he usually travelled standard class.

They were shown to seats in the first-class section of the aeroplane. They spent some minutes examining the comforts and amenities but when the flight took off Greg said: 'Are you wide enough awake to learn a few words in Finnish?'

'No, I'm still half asleep but never mind – *en avant!*' She nudged him. 'That was to show you that I speak French so I'm really quite a linguist.'

But she had trouble with Finish. '*Jo reggelt.*' He pointed to the words he'd written down on a pad conveniently supplied by the airline. 'It's a more open sound – yoh – say yoh – more like yoh raggalt.'

'Then why have you written it with "e"?' she complained.

'Because that's the way it's spelled in Finland. Why do you write down e-n-o-u-g-h in English but say "enuff"?'

'You got me, pal,' she said.

By the time the airline breakfast was over, she'd learned a few words and phrases. 'But what if I get stage-fright and it all goes out of my head?'

'Oh then . . . just shrug and say nothing.'

'I think I'll be doing a lot of shrugging.'

They landed at mid-morning New York time. Greg consulted the itinerary provided by Mme Wildstren. 'Look for someone holding a placard saying Coulter Travel,' he told Liz as after the necessary security checks they emerged into the concourse.

'There he is, in the tan uniform.'

An elderly man was holding the placard. He hurried up to take their travel bags. 'If you'll just wait a moment outside the exit, I'll bring up the car, sir,' he said.

Another limousine. This one was a Cadillac de Ville. 'Oh, I'm so glad I know you,' said Liz, hugging Greg's arm.

They were wafted away to a hotel a little way north of the Guggenheim Museum, not ostentatious but beautifully furnished in a somewhat minimalist style. The desk clerk greeted them as if they were honoured guests. 'Mr Crowne! Ms Blair! Your flight was on time, I gather – everything is ready for you. Rupert!' An underling in black jacket and striped trousers hurried up. 'Please show Mr Crowne and Ms Blair to their room.'

A bellboy appeared to take their travel bags. The chauffeur relinquished them before turning to Greg. 'I'm told you'll be wanting me again, sir? At what time?'

Greg looked at Liz. 'How long to freshen up?'

'Half an hour? Forty-five minutes?'

'Make it twenty minutes, *Kätzchen*. If we leave it too long they might all be out to lunch. Remember, it's Sunday, the studio is only open till lunchtime.' To the driver he said,

'Can you wait for us? We need to get out to this address as soon as possible.'

The desk clerk provided him with a pen and a pad. He wrote down the address of Anika Roth's design studio. 'Sure thing, sir,' said the chauffeur, 'I'll just take a turn or two round the block and be back for you in good time.'

In the hotel room Greg asked for coffee immediately and while Liz took over the bathroom telephoned Auguste Guidon to say they had arrived.

'Everything is to your liking?' Auguste asked.

'Yes, splendid, thank you. We'll be on our way to the dress designer in a few minutes.'

'May you have good luck. Let me know the result.'

Liz sat down at the dressing table while Greg showered. When he came back into the bedroom he found her transformed.

She had rearranged her light brown hair so that soft little curls framed her face, and with a little magical gold spray had somehow lightened their colour. Her make-up was gentle, her lipstick rosy and her eyes enhanced so that their hazel seemed more enchanting. She looked about eighteen years old. She had changed from the silk shirt, slacks and cowboy boots in which she'd travelled to a short skirt and matching knitted top of hazy lilac. Her long legs showed to great advantage.

Greg stopped short in amazement. She laughed at his expression. 'Do I look young and shy?'

'You look good enough to eat!'

'Well, don't fall in love with this version, chum, because it's too much trouble to do every day. Come on, get dressed, the car will be here in a minute.'

He had decided to be his princely self for this occasion. People were often impressed at speaking to a Highness, and he wanted to do everything he could to get Anika Roth to talk to him.

He had brought a suit made in Savile Row and a shirt by Dior, a birthday gift from his grandmother. His tie bore the stripes of the regiment to which he belonged on his annual military service. In his buttonhole he inserted a little gold

181

shield bearing the logo of a conservatoire at which he'd studied for a time.

'How do I look?'

'Very royal.'

The phone tinkled. 'Your car is here, sir,' said the desk clerk.

The chauffeur had the door open for them. If he noticed a startling difference in the lady's appearance, he made no sign. He said: 'I've got the navigation system engaged, sir, we'll be at the address in fourteen minutes.'

He took them south to Tribeca. Liz gave a muffled exclamation of horror as they passed the great gap caused by the attack on the Twin Towers. They eventually drew up in front of a former factory or warehouse in a turning off Reade Street.

The chauffeur announced, 'This is it, sir. I can't park here, so I'll drive around.' He handed Greg a card. 'When you're ready to leave, just ring me on your cellphone.'

'Thank you.'

The building had a facade of old wrought iron. At the side of the entrance there was a list of occupants. The first floor held a firm offering 'Sculptured Leather', whatever that might be. Immediately above was 'Munera, Lotions and Salves'. Anika Roth was on the third floor.

The lift had clearly been for freight originally, but was now painted a gentle leaf green. 'Hmm,' said Liz, examining it. 'Very arty. Are we actually going to buy a dress?'

'I hope not. I don't know whether "expenses" would include that.'

The lift groaned upwards. 'By the way, what's my name?'

'What?' It was a matter to which they'd given no thought. 'Esa Kuopio,' he said quickly.

'Is that a real name?'

'Yes, she's a Finnish harpist performing at a festival in Ireland at this moment.'

'Esa,' she said to herself. 'I'm thinking myself into being Esa – it's my Method training.' She gave him an amused glance as they emerged into a huge open space lit by enormous windows.

Immediately to their right and left were narrow platforms on which shop-window models displayed dresses – all in soft colours, all made with soft materials. A few yards down this improvised channel was a desk, with a girl listening to music through little hooks in her ears, nodding her head in time to the rhythm while she read a magazine.

They approached. She was too wrapped up in the sound to notice. 'Ahem,' said Greg, tapping the desk. She looked up.

'Oh! Hi – wasn't expecting anybody this morning.' She put down the magazine but kept listening to her earphones. 'Did you have an appointment?'

'I'm afraid not. We came just on the off-chance. We'd like to see Mlle Roth.' He had adopted a faint accent, Germanic, very dignified.

'And you are . . . ?'

'Prince von Hirtenstein and Ms Kuopio.'

'Huh?' She'd heard only imperfectly and was bewildered.

'My card.' He'd provided himself with a few of the embossed visiting cards that he occasionally found useful. She took it, read it with amazement, then said, 'If you'd just . . . er . . . wait a minute.'

Unhooking herself from her sound system, she took off down the vista of the loft, tracking through a further display of dresses and round some partitions that gave the notion of separate sections. They could hear indistinct conversation. She emerged without the card, hurrying to say to them, 'Ms Roth will be with you in a moment.'

They stood in expectation. Greg explained to Liz in Finnish that Ms Roth was coming. '*Miellyttaa*,' said she, feeling she should show approval of whatever he was saying. This used up about one-tenth of her recently learned vocabulary.

Anika Roth came out from behind the farthest screened area. She was a tall, robust figure in tight velvet pants and a sweatshirt bearing the logo 'Beargarden'. She had charcoal dust from a sketching pencil on her fingers. Clearly she hadn't been expecting clients.

'Good morning,' she said, holding out her hand. 'Mr . . . er . . . Sir von Hirtenstein?'

'And Ms Kuopio, from Finland. It's very good of you to

183

see us without prior arrangement. Unfortunately Esa and I
are only in New York for a few days so we . . .'

'That's quite all right.' She led them to an area laid out
as a conversation module – steel-and-leather seating round
a low blond wood table. On the table lay big folders tied
with tape, which Greg deduced to be sketches of her work.
'Please, sit down, Your . . .' She floundered. 'Mr Hirtenstein,
sir. What can I do for you?'

They sat. Greg said to Liz in Finnish, 'I'm going to explain
a little,' which was a phrase he had often heard and used in
the Finlandia Hall in Helsinki.

'*Oh, kylla,*' said Liz, nodding agreement.

Greg smiled at Ms Roth. 'Esa doesn't speak any English,
I'm afraid. I don't suppose you speak Finnish?'

She gave him a smile that veiled irritation, but only just.
'I'm afraid not.' She was probably thinking, 'What a nitwit.'

'Ah? Well, we manage, nevertheless, yes?'

'We'll do our best.'

Greg and Liz had taken their seats on a settee with their
backs to the windows. Liz leaned towards Greg and murmured
into the crook of his neck, 'Get on, love, she doesn't suffer
fools gladly.'

'*Kutos,*' he said to her, and to the designer, 'Esa urges me
to ask you about the dress.'

'Which dress?'

'We saw a very pretty dress a few days ago. When we
asked about it, we were told that you were the couturière
and so as we were coming to New York we thought that
perhaps we—'

'You didn't see any dress of mine in a shop!' Ms Roth cut
in, with some alarm at the thought of being copied. 'I design
for clients only.'

'Certainly, certainly, we saw the dress being worn.'

'Worn? In Europe, did you say?' She was frowning. He
thought she probably knew each of her clients very well
and was trying to think who might be in Europe at this
time.

'Yes, we were at a little gathering.'

'But where? I don't understand.'

'In Switzerland,' said Greg. 'Do you know the ski resorts? The lady was playing the piano.'

'At a gathering in a ski resort? Après-ski, you mean? That doesn't sound much like Morena.' She'd identified a wearer of her clothes who might be in Switzerland.

'Morena – yes, I believe that was the name.' He turned to translate that to Liz, who was already nodding agreement at the name. 'Yes, Morena, she was so kind as to give us the pleasure of her talent, at a little gathering, but no, not après-ski, it was just a little party, she played for us, and Esa very much admired the dress she was wearing. So a lady friend who was also there was so kind as to enquire on Esa's behalf, because of course Esa couldn't converse in English and it would have been . . . let me see, I think it would have been improper, would it not, for a man to speak to her about what she was wearing.'

'Yes, yes,' urged Ms Roth, impatient at all this flowery verbiage. 'So she told your friend that I was the designer.'

'And Esa would very much like to have the dress made for her, in the same colour . . .' He paused to check with his lady-friend in Finnish and the lady-friend obligingly nodded and said, '*Kylla.*'

Ms Roth was looking less delighted. 'I'm very sorry, but everything I design for Morena Tullo is exclusive,' she said.

'Oh, don't say that!' protested Greg, catching Liz round the shoulder and holding her close to hide her dawning smile of triumph.

Liz pulled away to say: '*Exclusif?*' Clearly she felt the word would be universally understood. She pouted and looked upset. She hung her head.

He understood the message.

'Oh, Esa has set her heart on it – haven't you, my angel? Please, Ms Roth, telephone to Ms Tullo and ask for permission to—'

'But she's abroad, you just saw her there, and even if I had her cell number it wouldn't be any good because she'd just say no.'

'Perhaps you could ring her home number – leave a message.'

185

'No, no, we've always had this arrangement, she gets first look at everything I do and makes her choice, and after that the rest can go to the general clientele.' She gave a tiny shrug. 'Sad as it is to disappoint your little friend, Morena is one of my backers. I can't afford to annoy her.'

Liz leaned towards him so as to murmur, 'We heard she was coming home. Can we go see her?'

'But my darling,' he replied, and went on to tell her in Finnish that the concert would begin at eight o'clock, which was the only sentence in Finnish he could muster just then. To Ms Roth he explained, 'Esa says she heard Ms Tullo was coming home. We really don't want to miss this opportunity.'

'*Ei, ei,*' said Liz. The word for 'no' was the one she'd learned best because it was the shortest.

'Ms Tullo lives in New York? Perhaps we could drop by?' Greg persisted in dignified entreaty.

Ms Roth shook her head. 'You'd have to head for Philadelphia and anyway I don't divulge details like addresses or telephone numbers.' She pushed one of the big folios towards Liz. 'Perhaps your friend would like something else from my fall collection.'

Liz got up in a petulant flounce. 'No, no,' she cried again in Finnish, and headed for the reception desk.

'Esa!' cried Greg, hurrying after her as if to stop her. She shook off his hand and marched to the lift.

He turned back to the designer. 'I'm very sorry. She had set her heart on the yellow dress.'

'You can't win 'em all,' she shrugged in response. 'Thanks for coming. Tell your friend my new collection is out soon.'

'Thank you. You have been most kind. Esa, Esa!' And he made a flustering pursuit so as to catch up with Liz just as she was about to pull on the apparatus that opened the freight lift for them.

'Morena Tullo of Philadelphia,' she whispered, grinning in triumph as they descended

'Yes, and I'll tell you something – Brother Lou told me he started out with some jazz combo in Philadelphia.'

He got out his mobile to call the limousine. While they

waited outside for it he told her, 'We can look up Philadelphia telephone numbers in the Central Library – get her address that way.'

So that was where they went. But their feeling of triumph faded when they saw that Tullo took up nearly a whole page of the Philadelphia directory. There were two with the initial M – one Mario and one Martin Tullo.

Liz was dismayed. 'Not in the phone book!'

'No-o. I'll ask the desk to try enquiries when we get to the hotel.' They had themselves driven back to the Bonhomme, dismissed their driver, and went up to their room. While Liz sat down to get rid of her eighteen-year-old's image, he sat down to the telephone.

'No luck?' she asked when he set down the receiver with a dispirited click.

He shrugged. 'I think I expected that.'

'You did? How come?'

'I'm beginning to think . . . You know, Morena seems to have money. She's well educated, she dresses well, she actually backs a new dress designer . . . Perhaps she's not your ordinary gangster's-moll type.'

'Gangster's moll!' Liz stifled a giggle. 'Where do you get these archaic phrases? No, she's certainly not a gangster's moll, I never thought she was. She struck me as being rather brainy – more a career-woman type.'

He looked at the bedside clock. 'It's more or less lunch time. There's a friend I might be able to contact . . .'

'Somebody in Philadelphia?'

'No, on a newspaper here in New York.'

'Another of your Musical Mafia, I suppose.'

'He's a reporter on the *Gazette*, writes the Tell-Tale column.'

'But he loves music.'

'Well . . . He does, yes,' Greg said rather defensively. 'And I'm going to try to get hold of him and then we'll go to see him.'

'Just give me a minute to get rid of this eye-shadow.'

'Oh, must you? I rather like it.'

'Listen, buster, I'm not going around looking like a teenage bimbo just to please you.'

'Well, let me at least have a little taste of what it's like to kiss a teenage bimbo before she vanishes.'

She signalled agreement by getting up and hugging him, but then she held him off. 'Oh, Your Highness, you let down your loving little Esa over that frock and she's just never going to forgive you.' The little husky voice and the pout that went with it made him grin. She kissed him then said, 'Come on, we haven't got time for this. We're here on serious business.'

'You're right. Let me just say that when you chose to go into the fashion trade, the stage lost a bright star.'

'How true. One more minute while I get out of this skirt, the temperature's too low to be out and about with my legs exposed.'

While she changed he got the New York telephone directory out of the drawer in the bureau and dialled a number. He was answered after a few moments by a friendly voice but not the one he'd hoped for.

'Is Mitch there?'

'Sorry, he's out to lunch, can I take a message?'

'Would you tell him Greg Crowne called? And ask him to ring me back? It's fairly urgent.'

'Oh, Mr Crowne – oh, yeah, I've heard Mitch talk about you – this is Iris Miles, I'm on the desk next to his. He's at the Portico 'cause it's Sunday and that's their Milanese day. He's a nut for Italian food.'

'The Portico – where is that? I'd like to have a chat with him. Would he still be there if I tried to catch him? I'm at the Bonhomme, off 89th Street.'

'Sure – ten minutes in a cab. I'll call him on his cell, if you like – tell him you're on your way, how about that?'

'Thank you, that would be great, Iris.'

Liz had donned slacks and suede boots. 'So – we're off to see the wizard? At the newspaper office?'

'He's out to lunch and we're going to join him.'

'Oh, Greg, I don't know if I want to eat . . . What meal would this be for us?' She hadn't yet worked out her transatlantic time scale.

'We don't have to eat, sweetest. Come on, let's go.'

Getting a taxi was no problem outside a hotel like the Bonhomme. Fifteen minutes later they were entering an unpretentious restaurant where a grey-haired man in a somewhat rumpled suit rose to wave a welcome.

'Greg, my bucko, I didn't know you were in New York! Something attracting you at the Met?'

'Nothing like that, Mitch.' A waiter had arrived and was drawing out a chair for the pretty lady. 'Liz, this is Mitch MacDougal, an opera buff. Mitch, I'd like you to meet Liz Blair, a friend from London.'

'Sit, sit,' urged MacDougal. 'So what's your line, then Liz – singer? String player? – no, you've got no calluses so you can't be a violinist.' His sharp eyes were checking on her hands, where he'd noted the ring she was wearing – white-gold with a single diamond, a gift from Greg earlier that year. But it was on her right hand.

'I'm in the fashion business, Mitch,' she replied. 'Greg tells me you have a newspaper column.'

'Oh yes, for my sins. But listen, have you had lunch? Aldo – ' he beckoned to the waiter, who had withdrawn a little – 'give these hungry folk the menu.' And to Liz and Greg, 'I recommend the *vitello alla Milanese*, it's today's special.'

'No, no, thanks, Liz doesn't eat meat and besides, we're still not quite on New York time – our next meal ought to be dinner, I think. What about some mineral water, Liz?'

'Perfect.'

The waiter might have been resentful at such an order during lunch hour, but when Liz smiled at him he smiled back. Mitch ordered coffee and grappa for himself.

'Now,' he said, settling himself comfortably to listen, 'what's up? You don't chase me into my lunch-room all hung over with jet lag just to exchange the time of day.'

'Do we look hung over?' Liz asked, rather put out.

'Dear girl, you look gorgeous. But you're avoiding my question. What's this about?'

'No hiding anything from you, Mitch. Well, it's true, we've come to ask for help.'

'To do what?'

'To find out about a lady called Morena Tullo.' Mitch

189

raised an eyebrow and pursed his lips, but nodded at him to go on. 'It seems she lives in Philadelphia and of course if we had time we could follow that up, but the fact is we're on rather a tight schedule. So I thought you might help.'

'Morena Tullo, eh?'

'You know her?'

'Not exactly. I wouldn't have thought she'd interest you. She plays piano, yes, but not to any level that would impress you, Grego my dear old buddy.'

Greg tried not to stare in surprise. 'You know that much about her?'

'I know of her. Why not? She's one of the Tullos.'

'And who are they?'

Mitch took a sip from his nearly empty wine glass. 'They're a family. You know? A family. Once very important but now they've slipped down the league table.'

For a moment both Greg and Liz sat looking at him, working it out. Then Liz mouthed the word she'd used as a joke only half an hour ago. 'Mafia?'

'Dear girl, we don't use that term any more,' Mitch chided. 'Except in a slang sort of way to talk about groups of evil-doing Russians and Colombians. Because now all our former friends of the Italian persuasion are highly respectable businessmen, running law firms and public-relations companies and investment enterprises.'

The waiter came with the drinks. Conversation ceased until he had gone. Then Greg asked: 'This lady we're talking about – has she got a brother, Lou?'

'A brother? No, don't think so. There are two girls, as far as I recall. Morena and Felicia – Felicia's called after the mother, Felicia Ferigiano, who used to sing in the chorus at the Met.'

'Ferigiano!' sighed Greg.

'You've heard of her? That's odd – she wasn't anything much, as far as I recall. Her only claim to fame was that she married Benny Tullo.'

'And he was important enough that you remember the fact?'

'Important . . . Well . . . He was one of the family, he had his place in the pecking order . . . Not particularly important

190

except that I think he did most of their book-keeping.' He studied them. 'What's this about?'

Liz gave a subdued chuckle. 'It's about a dress,' she said. 'We came to New York to find out the real name of someone who wore a pretty dress. And to find out about her brother, who doesn't exist, it seems.'

'Can't help you there,' Mitch said. 'But there's one thing I've got to say – I wouldn't go around asking too many questions about anybody connected to the Tullo family.'

'I thought you said they'd lost their standing?'

'But that's relative, Greg, it's comparative! No, maybe they couldn't put the squeeze on a Federal Court judge any more, but they could sure find someone to beat you up if they took a dislike to you.'

Liz poured mineral water into her tumbler and drank deeply. Greg glanced at her and wondered what he'd brought her into.

Mitch said: 'Tell me why you're interested in Morena Tullo.'

'Can't do that,' Greg said. 'It's classified, if you know what I mean.'

'But we'd really like to hear about her,' Liz added.

'Well, let me see . . . She studied music fairly seriously, I think I heard, and I'm sure she plays the piano because there was a charity concert last year for some orphanage or something, and she was one of the performers. I didn't go to it, got a local stringer to do a paragraph. I've seen occasional mentions about her, seen photographs – she's got the looks and she's around, if you know what I mean. Wants to count for something, I imagine.'

'And the family? You said they'd retreated into the background.'

'Yes, in the sense that they're highly respectable now. I'm not really a good source for this kind of stuff, crime isn't my beat, Greg. But I do kind of remember some of the gossip about Felicia Ferigiano's wedding. Let me see . . .' He took a sip of grappa. 'I was about twenty then, and I thought I was in love with a girl who'd auditioned two or three times for the chorus, so she was interested in Ferigiano's departure from the Met. There was a big splashy reception, some

191

of the dons turned up or sent their minions ... But really you don't hear anything about the Tullos any more. They used to have power and money, but not so as you'd notice these days.'

'Do you mean they might be short of funds?'

Mitch frowned and shrugged. 'Not in any sense that we'd recognize! The Tullos are never going to have to beg for their bread.' He paused, thinking. 'But on the other hand ... They're not in the same league as before, that's for sure. If I heard somebody had bought Rhode Island, I wouldn't think of the Tullos. Bill Gates, yes, the Tullos, no.'

There seemed nothing more to be learned from the reporter. They stayed to chat a little longer, Greg promising to get Mitch tickets for a performance of *L'Africaine* at the Metropolitan Opera. As they left Mitch detained him with a hand on his arm.

'She's wearing a ring. Anything in it for the column?'

'God forbid,' groaned Greg. 'My grandmother would kill me.'

'Oh, come on – just a line to say a certain European royal is romantically inclined?'

'If you print a word, those tickets for *L'Africaine* go to someone else.'

The reporter held up his hands in surrender.

'What was that?' Liz asked as he rejoined her. 'He thought of something helpful?'

'Just chitchat,' Greg said.

Once back in their hotel room, Greg sat down to ring one of the numbers in the letter from Auguste. A secretary answered. 'May I speak to Mr Lederer?' he asked.

'Who's calling, please?'

'This is Gregory Crowne, from Geneva.'

'Ah, yes. One moment, please. I'm going to connect you.'

A moment later a deep baritone voice greeted him. 'Mr Crowne? M. Guidon told me to expect your call. How can I help you?'

'Mr Lederer, could you drop in at the Bonhomme Hotel? There's something I'd like you to do.'

'Certainly. When would be convenient?'

'Well . . . now, really.'

'I'm on my way. Where will you be?'

'In the bar – it's to the right of the entrance.'

'See you in fifteen,' said Lederer.

Liz, sitting on the bed and taking off her suede boots, looked up. 'Who was that?'

'That, my love, was a security man from the Banque Guidon. And because he knows the scene in this part of the world a lot better than me, he's going to do the follow-up on the Tullo family.'

'In Philadelphia?'

'Wherever it takes him.'

Sixteen

Philippe Lederer was tall, muscular, and looked rather like an American ex-marine. He shook hands like a Swiss, however. He set his laptop bag on the floor before taking a seat alongside Greg. He said in slightly German-accented American: 'Now. What's the buzz?'

'I want you to find out about two people. One is Morena Tullo of Philadelphia' – at which Lederer screwed his lips together in concern – 'and a man who might be a minor member of the family, or perhaps a hanger-on.'

'Ah . . . Why are you interested in the Tullo family?'

Greg hesitated. 'What did M. Guidon tell you?'

'Not much. To give you the use of our resources, stand by to do whatever you require.'

'I see. Well, in that case I have to tell you that this is a confidential matter for M. Guidon and so I'm not empowered to give you any details.'

Lederer looked vexed but accepted it. 'OK, then, I'll do some background on the Tullos. But they're a bit of a forgotten tribe these days.'

'You know something about them?'

'Before my time on the post, really. But I've read up on them – they're in our files. Has-beens, I would have thought.'

'Perhaps not. We need to think about them. Morena, she's one of the daughters of Benny Tullo, I gather. And there's a type who's in some way connected. Lou Somebody-or-other. He's about twenty-four, twenty-five, tallish, pale, dark, plays the saxophone—'

'The saxophone?' Lederer said, raising his eyebrows.

'He's posing as a jazz player. Morena is claiming he's her brother.'

194

'And they're . . . where? In New York?'

'I was told Morena lives in Philadelphia but the last time I saw her was in Switzerland. The brother too.'

'What else?' Lederer said, taking notes.

Greg gave him what he could recall, starting from the first time he heard from Lou Ferigiano from – he had thought – Paris. Lederer opened his laptop to key in some instructions. After a time the screen lit up, then reformed, then reformed again. He turned the screen so Greg could see. There was a photograph of Morena Tullo looking out at him.

'That's her!'

'A recent photograph from *Exceptional* magazine. Dated September, taken at the premiere of *La Forza del Destino* in Houston. I'll do a trace through our picture files, see if I can find anyone like your man Lou among her escorts.'

'Oh, I don't think . . . Lou didn't strike me as an opera fan. In fact I thought he was . . . a fairly rough type.'

'That makes it harder.'

'I'm sorry. Do the best you can. Let M. Guidon know as soon as you have anything. You know where to contact him?'

'Sure thing. Anything else? You'll be around, will you – should I let you have any contacts, any leads?'

Greg shook his head. 'I think I'll go back to Geneva. I'd be more use there, I think.'

'If you're sure . . . OK, then, I'll get on to it.' He closed up his laptop, shook hands, and left. Greg finished off yet another glass of the mineral water that he believed helped dispel jet lag, then went up to the hotel room to discuss plans.

Liz was lying on the bed, fully dressed but fast asleep.

He stood looking down at her. Sleeping Princess – should he awaken her with a kiss? Not yet. First he ought perhaps to do some telephoning.

First he called Auguste in his nursing home. He spoke as arranged in Romansch. 'How are you?'

'Still "on the brink of death", as we planned. The telephone caller has been in touch again with Rosanne, about two hours ago.'

'And what did he say? Was it a machine?'

'Rosanne says it was a real person but the voice was

distorted. He said he wanted to speak to me but Rosanne cried and sobbed – no acting required, she was very frightened. So he told her he'd be in touch again and would want to speak to my doctor. We don't know what to do.'

Greg took a moment to think before he responded. 'I think the call was good. It means we've got them on the back foot.'

'You think so? I wish you were here, Greg. Rosanne is doing her very best but she's terribly scared.'

'I could come back. Lederer is going to do all the work now, I've just had a talk with him. He was able to summon up a photograph of the lady in question – we've been able to identify her as a member of a well-known family. Well known but not admired.'

'What does that mean?'

'Criminal.'

'My God!'

'But we were already thinking they must be organized, now weren't we, Auguste? Lederer has the contacts here to find out more about them.'

'So you don't feel you can do any more yourself?'

'I could come straight back – if that's what you want?'

'Of course, of course – it would make a world of difference to Rosanne – oh yes, my boy, you are our rescuer, we'd feel so much better if you were here!'

'I'll see about a flight at once. Don't give up, Auguste. And tell Rosanne I think she's a heroine.'

When he'd disconnected he contacted Coulter Travel to ask if they could get him on a flight. The clerk who replied to his call recognized his name at once. 'But Mr Crowne, you only just arrived this morning, sir?'

'That's right. And I need to get back to Geneva as soon as possible.'

They discussed possibilities. When he'd heard them Greg said he'd call back in a few minutes.

He then went to wake Liz. He shook her very gently and reluctantly. It took some time before her eyelids slid open and when they did she gazed at him groggily.

'Wha-at?' she asked.

'Sweetheart, are you awake? Can you take in what I'm saying?'

'Course I'm awake. Wha-at?'

'I'm thinking of leaving. Do you understand?'

She blinked two or three times, sat up, swung her legs off the bed, and tottered to the bathroom. When she came out she was mopping her face with a hand towel.

'Is it still Sunday?' she asked.

'Yes, it is. But it will soon be Tuesday in Geneva and I want to be back there as soon as possible.'

She sat down on the chair by the dressing table. She got a glimpse of herself in the mirror and hid her face for a moment in the towel. When she emerged she said, 'How soon do you want to go?'

'This evening.'

'Oh.'

'But you don't have to come. You could stay on, take a look at Saks Fifth Avenue . . .'

'Why have you got to be back so soon?'

'Well, Auguste sounds very . . . unsupported. And there are some things I want to discuss and it would be better to do it in person. And lastly, Nounou's funeral is on Thursday. I'd want to be there.'

'Oh, good Lord, yes, Nounou . . . I was there when she was found . . . I ought to be there too.'

'No, Liz, it's asking too much, to drag you back to Geneva.'

'Nonsense, I want to be there. I mean it, Greg.'

He nodded. 'All right. The travel firm is in contact with the airline, they're holding a couple of seats. Shall I tell them to confirm?'

They were booked on a flight at mid-evening. With a stopover for a much-needed sleep and some food in Paris, it meant they'd arrive around midday Tuesday in Geneva.

Snow had fallen since he left. Everything glittered below them as they landed. Liz exclaimed at the beauty of it, and he wondered if it was a good omen. Certainly, they could do with one.

Wildstren Travel had an SUV there to meet them. The

driver took them to the Hotel Belle Cascade, where he seemed to expect Liz to disembark.

'No, no,' she protested, 'I'm usually in a little hotel on the edge of the Old Town.'

Greg stifled a chuckle. 'No, Coulter Travel made your booking – they had instructions from Auguste to look after us. So it appears they've booked you in here.'

'Oh, joy,' she said, reading the elegant brass plate at the entrance. 'It has a spa.'

'*Per te, mi amante, la luna e le stelle.*'

'You what?'

'For you, anything you want – it's an old Italian love-song. Prepare to have a good time. I'm going on to the clinic now to see Auguste and I'll ring you by and by. OK?'

'Great. I'll get my hair done – I didn't do it any good with that goldy-goo hair spray. If they can't find me in my room when you ring, tell them to try the beauty salon.'

The hall porter took their bags then escorted her in with ceremony. She turned to blow a kiss as the revolving doors took her out of view.

Auguste's room at the clinic verged on the dreamlike. It had walls of crème-caramel silk, lamps with shades that had the appearance of thin alabaster, carpet underfoot as deep as a duvet, and about twenty pillows on the bed. Auguste was among them, but not incapacitated – he sat upright at Greg's entrance. He was in green silk pyjamas and freshly barbered. Greg, travel-worn and with a shave accomplished in the men's room on the plane, felt distinctly outclassed.

The patient began a stream of questions while the nursing attendant was still closing the door.

Greg gave him an account of what had been learned. 'Lederer recognized the family name the moment I said it,' he reported, 'but his opinion was the same as MacDougal's – that they'd faded out of the picture to a large extent.'

Auguste had a contribution to make. 'Lederer called while you were on your way home. He told me the man playing the part of Morena's brother might well be a small-time criminal who deals drugs in the nightclubs of Philadelphia – a man called Lou Ellis, who does in fact sometimes play in a band and when he does, he plays the saxophone.'

'Ah.'

'And something more. He says it's been rumoured that the Tullos would like to become what he called "players" – that's to say, to have a part in big-scale moneymaking. And the opportunity is there in new gambling casinos that may soon be licensed in the UK.'

'And with the money in the account they're after, they could bid for a share in a casino?'

Auguste agreed. 'I imagine that the contents of the account they're trying to access must be . . . well, considerable. Let's say, perhaps it contains millions of dollars.'

'You think so?'

'Let's just take that as a possibility,' he replied, wrinkling up his nose as if to say, 'Can't you take a hint?' The rules of Swiss banking of course forbade him to tell Greg anything concerning the account.

'Very well, I'm imagining some millions of dollars in the account.'

'And let's say the account was opened some years ago in Philadelphia by an elder of the family Tullo.'

'Yes.' The number read out by the mechanical voice stayed more or less in his memory. It had begun with the figures and letters 87PH. 1987 Philadelphia? 'Almost twenty years ago in Philadelphia,' he suggested.

'Perhaps. And let's suppose – and this, my dear friend, is *so far* pure guesswork – let's say an elder Tullo has since died. And has died without telling his heirs where to find the password to the account.'

'Ah. That's a very possible possibility, Auguste.'

They let a moment go by. Then Greg resumed: 'Let me do some imagining now. From the way people spoke about the Tullos, they had gone downhill. But MacDougal said he thought Morena wanted to "count for something", and Liz thought of her as the career-woman type. So perhaps we could think of Morena as wanting to start some project for which the money in the Banque Guidon account would be very useful.'

'And they want the money now. They may have tried every

199

legal method to get at the account and been refused . . .'

'Have you asked at the bank to find out if there have been enquiries?'

'No, no, and of course I wouldn't be informed because there are many enquiries after latent accounts – they're dealt with by the staff. The general method is to inform the enquirer that to have access to an account all the formalities must be carried out – and that includes the password, full documentation in case of a deceased client, and so on.'

'And we're supposing that Morena and her friends are doing this without the approval of the rest of the family?'

'That's my view. So these plotters decide to find some bargaining counters. They study the Guidon family . . .' Auguste faltered, shaking his head. 'Well, well, they found a chink in our armour, and the name of the chink was Gilles. Gilles and his longing to run a jazz band.'

'I'm afraid so.'

'And . . . it seems they arranged for a vacancy in the band by disposing of the poor soul from Bristol—'

'Wally Clifford.'

'Yes.'

'And arranged an accident for Nounou because she got suspicious.'

Auguste said: 'We must get Gilles back. We must do everything we can to get him out of their clutches. They seem so . . . so ruthless!'

'I still think you should go to the police, Auguste.'

'No police!' It was said with such horror that Greg was taken aback. Auguste had gone pale, his breath seemed to leave his body for a moment. Against so much anxiety there was no more to be said.

'Very well. But we must at least confide in your doctor.'

'No!'

'But, Auguste, we must! You said they're demanding to speak to him—'

'No, the more people who know what's happening, the more likely it is that somehow it will get into the newspapers! No, I forbid it!'

'But, Auguste—'

'So far no one but the five of us know about the kidnapping – my immediate family, Sasha, and you. I want to keep it that way.'

'Liz Blair knows. That was why she agreed to go to New York and speak to the dress designer.'

'Of course, yes, and I greatly appreciate what she did. But you see? Little by little, as more people know for what seems good reason, there's a danger of word getting out to the press.'

'But we must tell Dr Perlerou – you told me on the telephone that they're asking to speak to him.'

'We must think of some excuse.'

'Such as what?'

'I don't know,' wailed the banker. He lay back on his many pillows, looking stricken and desperate.

The Prince had the feeling of being trapped in some kind of maze. Why was he sitting here trying to deal with a problem that needed resources far greater than he could summon up? The police should be here, planning what to do. If not the police, the bank's security staff.

A faint suspicion stirred. Why was Auguste so unwilling to ask for expert help? Could there be some problem at the bank? Someone – Rosanne, perhaps, or Mme Armonet – had murmured something about trouble ... but that was to do with economics, surely, with international finance.

He shook off the thought. 'Did Madame learn anything about the kidnappers in the latest call? Is the caller still speaking English?'

'Yes, and though Rosanne was too flustered to do much except weep, Sasha said he thought he recognized the voice.'

Greg was startled. 'It wasn't disguised?'

'Yes, and of course Sasha may be wrong. But he thought the speaker was the journalist who approached him in Milan.'

In his mind Greg heard Sasha's faltering voice when confronted with the accusation that he had been an informer. 'Davie Daniels,' he murmured. 'He supposedly sold articles to a magazine in London. *Talked About*, I think it was called.'

'Something of that sort.'

'Speaking perhaps from Milan?'

'There's no way of knowing. And as far as we know, there was no publicity in the magazine – Sasha says he asked for copies when this person Daniels telephoned him but never received any. And the telephone contact only continued for some six weeks. Sasha was quite hurt about it at the time, so he says, but let it go. You know, trying to get publicity for Marie's little charity is a very uphill task.'

'I'm afraid I can feel no sympathy for Sasha,' Greg said grimly.

Auguste sighed. 'So they got enough information to know that Gilles was the best target.'

'But Auguste, if we were to contact the police in Milan, they might—'

'How often must I say it?' cried Auguste. 'No police!'

Greg decided not to argue. In the end he hoped to persuade Guidon to call in the only force with the resources to handle the matter. He sat thinking.

'Sasha heard this man speaking?'

'Yes, of course, otherwise how would he recognize—'

'He was listening on another phone?'

'No, Rosanne had it on the speaker-phone in my study. All three were there listening – Rosanne, Marie and Sasha.'

'Your wife has to agree to have Dr Perlerou available to speak to the caller?'

'Yes.'

'When is that to be?'

'We don't know. The last call ended with Rosanne in floods of tears and the person at the other end said he'd call again. We still haven't heard.'

'So . . . when he calls again, Rosanne can say she's arranged for him to speak to Dr Perlerou.'

'Greg, haven't you been listening? I don't want Perlerou involved!'

'If it's Davie Daniels or whatever his name is, he doesn't know what Perlerou sounds like, now does he?'

'Well . . . no . . .' Auguste was gazing at him in uncertainty.

'Sasha can't be Dr Perlerou, because Davie Daniels knows

202

Sasha's voice. But Davie Daniels has never heard me speak. I could be Dr Perlerou.'

There was a long, long silence. Auguste Guidon lay back among his pillows, eyes closed, lips tightly compressed.

At last he said: 'But you don't know anything about medicine, do you? How can you talk about my heart condition with any authority?'

'I can buy a book. And since Davie Daniels probably doesn't know any more about medicine than I do, he's likely to believe what I read out to him.'

Once again the banker was reduced to silence. After a moment he remarked, with something that was almost amusement: 'You're wasted in the world of music. Would you like a job at Banque Guidon?'

'No, thank you.'

He was caught up now by enthusiasm. 'Greg, this might just work! And you really are prepared to do it?'

'Why not? At least it would give us time to find out more about the Tullos, to think of some way to get at them . . .'

'Then all I can do is thank you once more. You've been so . . . such a good friend . . . I'll never forget this, Greg.'

Greg nodded. It embarrassed him to hear this banking magnate stammering his gratitude. He began to plan, thinking on his feet.

'So now I must go. I have to find a bookshop with an easily understood description of heart trouble. In the meanwhile, tell Madame that when the kidnapper rings again, to say that Dr Perlerou will be available . . . let me see, give me some time . . . I have things to do . . . Let's say at nine o'clock this evening. And make sure she has my mobile number so she can let me know if the ruse is going ahead.'

He borrowed a car from the ranks in Roger's garage and was on his way to Montreux a few minutes later. He had to catch up with his musicians who, no doubt, were fuming at being boarded out to a hotel and left to their own devices. Though the Guidon family had forgotten them, they were still Greg's responsibility.

Snow had fallen on the slopes all along his route by the lake, which meant that the ski resorts in the higher cantons of Switzerland would be getting ready for the eager influx of skiers. The canton of Geneva wasn't famous for its ski slopes but all the same, skiers often started from there as they headed for Zermatt or Verbier. Traffic around midday and early afternoon could often be a problem.

He reached Montreux just as the winter sun was beginning its descent behind the peaks. The first thing he did in the town was to find a bookshop where he bought a chunky volume: *Your Heart and How to Live With It* by a pair of authors, one of whom had a string of qualifications after his name.

The establishment to which Mme Guidon had consigned the band was an 'hôtel garni', a place where comfortable rooms were available with kitchen facilities so that the occupants could make their own meals. The suite of rooms was probably more ample than those they'd had at the chateau but it was immediately clear that the players didn't like catering for themselves. François and Nils greeted him with an immediate flow of complaints.

'. . . And what's more they don't like us to practise—'

'And they don't like us coming in late—'

'Wait, wait,' begged Greg. He was staring at the pair of them. 'Where's Emilio?'

'Oh, Emilio, poor baby, he began to miss his Mamecita and all his brothers and sisters the minute we got here. So he's split.' François was scornful.

'Gone?'

'Gone home.' This was Nils, determined to make everything clear and not waste time being sarcastic. 'And to tell the truth, Greg, I too would like to go home. After all, it will soon be Christmas, and although this isn't a bad place, it lacks the charm of home.'

'Of course. I understand.' Greg was rather surprised that it was Emilio who had taken the initiative. He'd have expected François to be the first to go, to the engagement he'd always talked about in Brussels.

'He left a note for you,' Nils went on, picking it up from a clutter on the table. Greg read it. Emilio was sorry to let him down but it was so cold in Switzerland and the chance of playing at the Montreux Festival became more and more unlikely all the time, and the accident to the old lady had made him so sad, and he had spoken on the telephone to his mother and felt it best to leave. Sympathy and good wishes to the Guidon household. Any fees due to him should be forwarded to the attached address.

All quite understandable.

'So that's that,' François said. 'Nils and I have tried to contact you at your office but either got a recording or *une petite employée* who said she'd pass on the message. So now you're here, and we're laying it on the line – we're leaving.'

There was nothing to be done about it. He took them out to a nearby café for a farewell drink. The musicians had intended to be cold and businesslike, but in the cosy atmosphere their chilly determination melted and they began to look back with tolerance and amusement at the days just gone by.

'I wonder if Gilles is having the wonderful time he was expecting,' mused Nils over a Molson. 'He and Morena have been off in the romantic nowhere for . . . how long . . . seven days.'

'Still moon-struck,' François grunted. 'I give it another three weeks or so before they turn up again, with a gold band on Morena's finger and a marriage certificate in her purse.'

Nils nodded. 'And then she'll persuade him to move to the States where they can live in one of the really sophisticated cities—'

'Yeah, New York or Los Angeles – where the shops and the celebs are headquartered – she's never going to stay in little old Switzerland.'

'You think not?'

'I would agree with that,' Nils said. 'At one point Gilles was trying hard, poor soul, to explain to her how wonderful life can be here. He was saying the bank would probably give him a post in the Zurich branch, and he was telling her Zurich was very cool, lots of fine shops, lots of café society . . .'

'But she still preferred the States. So if they tie the knot I'd take a bet she'll get him to the Big Apple before very long.' François grinned. 'Papa will not be pleased. Papa

205

was grooming him to be the big noise in Geneva.'

'Oh, Morena will talk him round,' Nils declared.

Talk turned to business matters. Greg promised see that they got the salaries they'd been promised for the weeks spent at the chateau and a bonus for ending the agreement amicably. He left them ordering their evening meal.

He himself was hungry now but wanted to eat with Liz. He drove back to Geneva but at a better speed because now the traffic was the home-going rush hour, and he was driving city-ward.

Liz greeted him with warmth. 'How's tricks, sweetheart? You look worn. It's time you had some rest and recreation.'

'You on the other hand look lovely.' She twirled for his inspection. 'New hair style?'

'Just a few tweaks here and there. And I had a massage, and then I went shopping – I had a thought, tell me if I'm wrong but I had the feeling that for Nounou's funeral everybody would be wearing black?'

'Oh yes. Certainly.'

He didn't need reminding that Liz had only brightly coloured clothes with her. She said, a little shamefaced: 'I went shopping. Just for a black coat, darling. You don't think that's frivolous, do you?'

He laughed and hugged her, showered, changed, shaved again, and felt halfway human. They had dinner sent up to their room while he got Liz to help him rehearse his heart-specialist role.

He set *Your Heart and How to Live With It* on the table between them to decide on what sort of heart condition Auguste should have.

'It has to be something serious,' he said. 'I've got to convince him – whoever he is – that Auguste is too ill to do anything about getting the password.'

'I'd go with angina,' Liz said. 'I'm sure you're remembering that this chap who's telephoning isn't an expert, so he's only going to know the things we all know. And even I know that angina is serious.'

'OK, Auguste has got angina. Here we go.' He read aloud,

translating as he went: '"Angina is caused by obstruction of the flow of blood to the heart"—'

'Tell him he already knows that. Start by saying something like, "I'm sure you're aware". It might make him more receptive.'

'You just did that to me!' he cried. 'This is your sales technique, is it?'

'Believe me, people like to be told they're bright enough to know something, Try: "I expect you know angina is caused by" . . . whatever it is you just read out.'

'"Angina is caused by obstruction of the flow of blood to the heart, as I expect you know . . ."'

'That's it, but say "I expect you know" first – then he's already softening up for the rest of your lies.'

They practised for the rest of the meal. Then they found other things to do for a while. But by eight o'clock he was back on the well-known road to Chateau Guidon, repeating to himself the phrases he was going to use.

Rosanne was waiting for him in the hall when he arrived. She burst into anxious speech. 'I told him nine o'clock. He said that was too long a wait but I told him Dr Perlerou had other commitments and I said . . . I said that unless I'd told him all about it, the abduction I mean, he wouldn't be likely to make himself available to come sooner. So he growled and threatened but he agreed.'

'Well done!'

'But, Greg, he insisted I give him the doctor's telephone number so I knew he was going to check!' She was breathless as she remembered her panic. 'So I quickly called Dr Perlerou on his private line and asked him to come.'

'What? Here?' Auguste had been urgent that Perlerou shouldn't be involved.

'Yes, I asked him to come at nine. But an hour later I cancelled – I thought by that time that wicked wretch would have been in touch with Perlerou, and do you know? – the doctor said to me it was too bad I'd asked him for a house-call because someone had wanted an urgent appointment at his office and he'd had to say no. So you see? – they think very fast, they act at once!'

207

'They certainly do.'

'Do you think we should give up the idea of tricking them?'

'And do what instead?' he countered. 'Tell them that Perlerou couldn't come after all? They've checked back once, they'd do it again.'

'And find out I'd cancelled.' She clutched at her hair in dread. 'No, no, we must go on. But be very, very careful, Greg!'

She led him into the study. Sasha was there, sitting on a chair alongside the desk. The managerial chair used by Auguste was vacant. Greg sat down, opened his advisory text, and waited. Rosanne paced up and down in slender-heeled shoes. Her lips were moving. She was silently praying.

At exactly nine o'clock the phone rang. Sasha leaned forward to press the button that activated the speaker-phone.

Rosanne stepped towards the desk. 'This is Rosanne Guidon.'

'Good. Is your doctor there?'

The voice was distorted, as if the man was speaking into a metal tube. Sasha, listening intently, nodded at Greg. He was confirming that he thought this was the man calling himself Davie Daniels.

And that was a man who had never heard Greg speak.

Rosanne gave Greg an agonized glance. 'I'm handing you over now to the doctor,' she said, her voice wavering.

Greg took up his role. 'This is Dr Perlerou,' he said in a very testy tone. 'What can I do for you?'

Seventeen

At the other end there was a grunt of satisfaction. The man they thought of as Davie Daniels said: 'Right. Let's hear the info, then, Doctor.'

'I first must say,' Greg began, in accented English and sounding affronted, 'I find this highly unethical. I have the consent of the patient's relatives, but information between doctor and patient should be confidential—'

'Never mind all that. Get on with it!'

'This is the first time in my experience that I have ever—'

'Mme Guidon, are you there?'

'Yes, of course,' faltered Rosanne.

'Tell this old fool to do as he's told!'

Greg was modelling himself on the real Dr Perlerou, whom he'd met for a few minutes at the time of Auguste's collapse. The doctor was elderly, expert and authoritative. Greg now said, as if in indignation over Daniels's manners but in Romansch, 'Rosanne, tell me to stop speaking to him.'

She gaped at him. 'In Romansch,' he urged.

She said, bewildered but obedient, 'Please don't say another word to him.'

'Good,' said Daniels, taking her intervention to be an order to behave. 'Now let's get on. What's wrong with our banker friend?'

Mindful of advice from Liz, Greg now launched into a lecture. 'You probably know that angina pectoris is a very serious condition. The patient must be given medication to relieve the intense pain – you're aware, perhaps, that the word angina means "strangling" in Latin?' He was thinking meanwhile: 'One little thing we now know. He doesn't understand Romansch. So we can talk to each other and he'll be in the dark.'

'I'll strangle you if you don't get a move on!' declared Daniels. 'He's got a pain, OK. But you've got him sedated?'

'Of course. That is the first step, to relieve the pain, and also the anxiety that goes with it.'

'So he's not in pain and he's under medication. So he's doing OK. I want to speak to him personally.'

'But, monsieur—'

'He's got a phone by his bed, I suppose? And if not, he can have one brought toot sweet.'

'But, monsieur, he has to wear an oxygen mask! It is impossible for him to use the telephone, and may be so for some days.'

'Umm . . .' There was a hesitation.

Greg said to Rosanne in Romansch: 'Ask to speak to your son.'

Once again she was taken aback. But as the words sank home, she seized on the idea and cried in English: 'Oh, monsieur, monsieur, please let me speak to Gilles! Please – just to know he's all right!'

Greg said in astonishment and in his Perlerou English: 'Gilles? How does he come into it?'

'Shut up, you!' shouted Daniels. 'Mrs Guidon, mind what you're saying! Get that old nuisance off the line.'

'Oh – yes, yes, of course, I'm sorry, Dr Perlerou, if you would be so good – please, you've been very kind . . .'

Greg made muttering sounds, went to the room door, opened and closed it. There was a pause. He nodded at Rosanne to carry on with her plea.

'He's gone, I'm sorry, please forgive me, he knows nothing, I told him you were a business colleague, but I implore you to let me speak to Gilles, monsieur!' She wasn't acting. She had been entirely captured by the idea of hearing her son's voice.

'No can do,' grunted Daniels. 'And that's not what I'm here for. I want to speak to your husband so that he knows what he's got to do—'

'But he's too ill, it's impossible, and meantime my poor

boy – who knows what's happening to him? And it's not his fault, you mustn't punish him just because we can't obey your orders, monsieur! Please, please put Gilles on the line.'

'That's just not on,' Daniels said in a less aggressive tone. 'He's not here – I mean, he's not where I am, but he's OK, and he'll stay OK as long as you do what you're told.'

'And we will, of course we will, as soon as my husband is well enough to go to the bank and deal with your – your request. But you must understand, monsieur, that it cannot be done by instructions over the telephone and he is much too ill to be driven to the bank.'

'Eh? What?' He sounded taken aback, even though the distortion made his tone to some extent flat.

Rosanne put her hands together as if she were pleading with the unseen enemy. Greg gave her a wave of his fist as a victory sign. 'Go on,' he mouthed.

'May I speak to Gilles at some other time?' she ventured, her voice shaking. 'I've obeyed you, I got Dr Perlerou to speak to you and it wasn't easy, monsieur, he is a very conventional man, so, please, don't you feel that I'm showing goodwill? I'll do all I can, but I want to speak to my son.'

'No, no, I'm not going to agree to that.'

'But all I want is a word or two, to let me know he's all right.'

'Ummm . . .' Once again that hesitation which meant he was thinking. 'Well . . . I'll see what I can do. Something might be arranged,' he said. 'So long as you stay on message and don't let anybody know the situation, get what I mean? That doctor, for instance – you'd better think up some way of keeping him shtum.'

'Oh, I promise, he knows nothing. Oh, monsieur, if only I can be assured that Gilles—'

'OK, right, don't go on about it, Ma! There could be a way. But I expect full cooperation, get me? And as soon as your husband's out of bed, I'll want action. Is that clear?'

'Yes, yes, I understand. I can persuade Auguste, once he's feeling better.'

'OK, I'll be in touch.'

211

There was a click, then that deadness that speaks of a broken connection.

Rosanne sank down on a chair to bow her head into her hands and cry helplessly. Sasha rose, but didn't know what to do. 'Can you call Mme Armonet to look after her?' Greg suggested.

'Er . . . well . . . Marie is . . . shall we say she's under the weather.'

'Drunk?'

Sasha flinched at the term. 'It's how she deals with stress. I'm sorry, she'd be no help here.'

Greg knelt at Rosanne's side. 'Don't cry,' he soothed. 'You did very well. You were marvellous.'

'No I wasn't, I went to pieces!'

'No, no, you kept your head, and we learned something.'

She raised a tear-stained face. 'We did?'

'Yes, we did. Come now, let's get you a drink, and we'll talk it over.'

Sasha produced a box of tissues form the desk drawer, she mopped her eyes, and submitted to being placed in the more comfortable desk chair. Sasha went for brandy. When he came back she was more or less recovered. She sipped, looking questioningly at Greg.

'For one thing, he doesn't speak Romansch.'

'Oh, that! Who does, outside of Switzerland.'

'For another, he doesn't sound to me like an educated type, and his English sounds as if he comes from the northern part of the country – I believe perhaps Lancashire or Yorkshire.'

'You can tell that about him?' she asked, surprised.

'Well, it comes from my musical training. I have a very acute ear. I'd say Mr Daniels comes from somewhere like Manchester.' He knew Manchester from business visits concerning music.

'Good God!' cried Rosanne. 'Do you mean they've taken my boy to England?'

'No, no, Rosanne, quite the reverse. I think he might have been speaking from England, but he specifically said Gilles wasn't there. Of course there's no way of knowing where he is, but I'd take a bet that he's somewhere a long way off from Daniels. Do you remember that he said, "I'll see what I can do"?' Rosanne nodded. 'I think that meant he had to consult someone – someone with more authority.'

'He doesn't have the power to bring Gilles to the phone?'

'He doesn't have the power, nor perhaps the possibility. Gilles is somewhere else, probably with someone Daniels is working for. And I think – don't you? – that is probably Morena.'

'Morena,' she wailed. 'If I ever meet her again, I'll kill her!'

'No, no, think of her as a good thing. From what I gathered in New York, she's not a career criminal. She's turned to this method because she wants to raise money urgently for a business venture – a legitimate business venture. And she didn't abduct Gilles to call for a cash ransom. All she wants, in a way, is what may in fact belong to her family – the password to an account that was opened some twenty years ago and that has been lost.'

'You're excusing her?'

'Not at all. I'm just trying to show you that Gilles is perhaps not in mortal danger.' He wanted to give her what comfort he could, because she was chief player in this drama while her husband was supposedly out of action. 'And now because Daniels was impressed by what you said, he's thinking it might be a good idea to let you be in touch with him.'

'Oh, if only, if only that could be!' She was looking better, the rouge on her cheeks standing out less because her natural colour was coming back.

'So what do we do now?' Sasha enquired rather moodily.

'We wait.'

'How long and for what?'

'As long as it takes, and for some way of learning how Gilles is getting on.'

'Humph,' said Sasha, and mooched out.

'If you please,' Rosanne said, managing a smile, 'I should like to be alone, so as to speak to Auguste. He told me when I spoke to him this afternoon that he won't sleep tonight unless he hears what happened.'

213

'Of course. Tell him I think it went well.'

'I will. And I believe we did gain something. I might be hearing from Gilles. To think that . . . that I might actually hear his voice . . .' Tears threatened again but she set her lips and blinked two or three times. 'Thank you, Greg. You must be relieved that your impersonation went so well. Please let Sasha pour you a drink.'

He smiled but shook his head. 'No, thank you, I'm really rather tired and it would have too much effect on me. I have to drive back to Geneva, you know.'

'Not at all, you must stay overnight with us.'

'No, no, it's good of you, but I have things to do and Mlle Blair is waiting for me at the Belle Cascade.'

Rosanne managed a shaky laugh. 'Of course. I'm getting to be a silly old woman. Of course you must go – but Roger shall drive you.'

Roger was delighted to be called out. He clearly knew something big was going on with the family but, like the rest of the household, was in the dark.

'Madame holding up all right?' he began as they sped towards the city.

'Mmm,' agreed Greg, who was fading fast and feeling as if he had the sands of the Sahara under his eyelids.

'Is Monsieur going to have a heart op, then?'

'No idea, Roger.'

'That clinic he's gone to – does it do surgery and stuff?'

'Yes, of course. All that stuff . . .' He yawned. 'Roger, I've been on the move constantly for forty-eight hours. Let's not talk, eh?'

'Oh, just as you say, sir,' said Roger, offended. But within seconds his passenger was asleep, so he had to admit the excuse had been genuine.

He woke him as he drew up outside the hotel. 'Night, sir,' he said as he helped him out. Greg stared around in bewilderment for a moment then navigated himself into the foyer.

He had enough hold on consciousness to get himself to the door of Liz's room, where he knocked rather weakly. She opened, wearing a teasing smile and a very pretty negligee.

214

But her smile changed to concern when she surveyed him.

'My poor angel, you look like death!' she pronounced, and gathered him in her arms.

He was aware of being helped off with his jacket, of his shoes being taken off and then his tie. He fell into bed some minutes later, to sleep like death for twelve hours.

When he at last came to, bright daylight was streaking through the chinks of the Venetian blinds. For some moments he considered what day it might be, then decided it was Wednesday. It had snowed overnight, hence the brightness outside. He was in a very comfortable bed in a very handsome hotel room and was naked but alone.

Liz was nowhere to be seen. Presumably she was out on one of her morning runs, in trainers and jogging suit perhaps. He dragged himself up to look at the bedside clock. Nearly ten.

With a groan he reached for the telephone and called Bredoux. Luckily his father answered, so it was easy to convince him that after landing from his New York trip he'd been kept at Chateau Guidon overnight and would be busy for some time this morning.

'Of course, of course,' said the ex-King Anton. 'Your grandmother is constantly saying she should have discouraged you from taking up this business engagement, it's taking up so much of your time.'

'Well, it's rather important,' sighed his son, stretching. 'How's Rousseau?'

'Oh, he's fine, fine, I took him for a long walk yesterday, he loves playing in the snow.' His father was very much at leisure during mid-winter; getting a van with a valuable competition horse up to Bredoux wasn't exactly easy, so he did very little teaching.

He sent his love to his dog and his respects to his grandmother. He was thinking to himself how angry she'd be if she knew he was sharing the luxury of the great hotel with 'that awful woman'.

He indulged himself in a long hot shower and a leisurely shave, so that he was in one of the hotel's bathrobes when

Liz came in. He was addressing his second croissant and had a cup of steaming coffee before him.

'Baby-love!' she cried, dashing to him across the room and flinging herself upon him. 'I was so worried about you! You were totally unconscious, you know! Except that you were snoring.'

'I don't snore.'

'No, of course not.' She hadn't been jogging. Her wet hair was sheathed against her head and there was a swimsuit under her dressing gown.

'You smell of eau de swimming pool,' he told her. She looked up in indignation. But she decided to let it pass.

'Tell me how your performance went last night.'

'Pretty well. Sit down, have some breakfast, you're making my chest damp.'

She rose, made a face at him, and departed to the bathroom. After re-showering at length with scented shower gel, she returned clad in a matching bathrobe to take her place opposite at the little breakfast table. She poured coffee for herself and after selecting a brioche began pulling it to pieces and spreading strawberry jam. He began his account of the telephone dialogue.

'So they're going to put Gilles on the line, then?'

'Seems so. But what they'll let him say remains to be heard.'

'Hmm.' She gave it some consideration. 'Gilles didn't strike me as the kind who, if given the chance, you know, would get some sort of message across. I mean, not quick-witted.'

'I agree with you. But it will do Rosanne a world of good to hear him, and she's the star player in this team.'

'Poor soul. And poor Auguste, what he must be going through!'

Greg shrugged.

'What? Not poor Auguste? Come on, Greg, he must be suffering.'

'Yes, he's suffering, and he's worried about Gilles – of course he is. But there's something else that's making him suffer.'

'What?'

'I don't know. Something about the account, or the bank
... There's something odd about his desperation any time I
mention bringing in the police. It's what you'd call stodgy.'

'No I wouldn't. Stodgy? Dull and conventional?'

'Oh, confound it – what's that word you use when something peculiar is going on.'

'Oh – dodgy.' She stared. 'You're not saying Auguste
Guidon is up to something naughty with the bank's money?'

He took a bite of croissant and chewed it before he replied.
'No, of course not. He's a pillar of society.'

'Uh-huh,' agreed Liz, with recently acquired scepticism.

They were dressing when the telephone rang. They both
stared at the instrument. Should anyone try to ring Liz, the
caller would try the little hotel in the Old Town. No one so
far knew that she was in the folds of the Belle Cascade. 'It
must be for you,' she sighed. And that must mean trouble,
because only the Guidon family knew he was at the Belle
Cascade.

He picked up the receiver. The voice of Rosanne Guidon,
scared and shaky, greeted him. 'Greg! Greg, we've heard
from the . . . the people . . . the people who . . . You know
who I mean!'

'Yes, of course. Calm down, Rosanne. What's happened?'

Liz, in the midst of putting on her suede boots, looked up
in alarm at his words.

'They've sent us a CD. Sasha put it in the computer and
it shows . . . it shows . . .'

'What, Rosanne? Go on.' Her terror was infecting him.
He simply didn't know what to expect.

'It shows that those wicked people have taken my boy to
New York!'

Eighteen

Greg asked the desk to summon a taxi. They were off to Chateau Guidon within minutes. Liz made sure that the dividing glass was closed between them and the driver before she asked: 'Is it bad?'

'I don't know. She says they've got a CD that shows Gilles in New York – which must mean a photograph, I suppose.'

'New York?'

'It's possible. Don't forget, we believe Gilles went with Morena willingly – in fact, eagerly. She could have taken him anywhere. If only Auguste would let us bring in the police, we could check that because he'd have had to show his passport.'

'But . . . am I right? These are a clever bunch. You told me they had false papers, those they gave you to get their work permits. So they could have false passports.'

'Yes, so they could.' He stopped to shake his head. 'No, they couldn't. Why would Gilles agree to using a false passport?'

'Umm . . . Well, what if by that time – airport departing time – he wasn't going along so willingly? What if he just had to agree to travelling as Joe Bloggs?'

'You're thinking . . . A knife in his ribs?' Another pause. 'But you can't get a knife on a plane these days.'

Only too true – not even a metal nail file, if the security checks were strict. 'Well, then . . . maybe just threats? "We've already killed your old nurse, we'll kill you if you don't behave"?' She tried to picture Gilles under duress, and found it discouraging.

They were making speedy progress up the snow-bordered road. 'A CD?' she ventured after a while. 'Did she say they have a CD?'

218

'I think so.' He recalled her words. 'She said they'd been sent a CD.'

Silence between them. Then she went on: 'That's odd, isn't it? Why not email it?'

'I don't know,' he said again.

Greg would have been the first to admit that he was no computer expert. Liz had some experience, often using a digital camera to record fashion ideas she'd seen worn by young women in the cities and towns she visited. She'd told him her method: she stored the images on her computer and printed them out if she needed to. She sometimes used a CD to record images she wanted to send to a colleague, because that was in her opinion the safest way against hackers. She liked to remind him that the fashion business was a cut-throat world; she wanted to be on the safe side where something important was concerned.

'How did the CD get to them?' she demanded.

'Liz, I don't know!' he said in exasperation.

She disregarded that. 'Because, you know, if they took a picture of Gilles in New York and transferred it to an actual disc . . . There's no way the disc could be here now.'

'No?'

'Well, how would it get here? It could only come by plane, couldn't it? And Thingummy-bob – on the phone last night—'

'Daniels.'

'Yes, Daniels, didn't you say he sounded as if he had to consult somebody? So then they decided to take a picture – because it seems they didn't want to put Gilles on the phone. Am I making sense?'

'They decided in New York to take a photograph – yes – go on.'

'So they put it on disc. They didn't email it – or perhaps they did, and then somewhere else they put it on a disc – no, wait – I don't know, Greg.'

'That's what I keep saying. I don't know.'

They tried their reasoning two or three times over and kept being baffled. Had Gilles been taken to New York? Did that make sense? If not, where had the disc come from?

When their taxi drew up at the chateau Rosanne ran out to greet them. She threw her arms around Greg. 'Oh, please, come and look – there isn't much time!'

They hurried in at her side. They went at once to Auguste's study. There glowing on the computer was a photograph of Gilles Guidon.

He was sitting in the corner of a settee of fine cream leather. He was holding up a copy of the *Wall Street Journal*.

Greg stifled a little groan of dismay. It seemed to make all their efforts worthless. He was so far away, with an entire ocean between them.

'You see?' whispered Rosanne, and began to cry.

Liz was taking off her coat. She hurried to get rid of it then put an arm around Rosanne. It seemed Rosanne had just been waiting for a woman to offer her some sympathy for she sagged against Liz, and had to be led to an armchair near the window. There she sank down, put a handkerchief to her face, and struggled for control. Liz knelt beside her to pat her gently and murmur kind words.

'Explain this to me,' said Greg to Sasha, who was sitting in the swivel chair at the desk. 'You got an actual CD?'

'Yes. I put it straight into the computer.'

'It came by mail?'

'No, that's what's so weird – it was in a little carrier bag hanging on the gates this morning. There was this little slip of paper with it, saying "1pm".'

'What? On the gate?'

'You know things have been a bit disorganized around here since Auguste was taken ill so Roger was rather late going down to the post-box. He went about nine thirty and there it was.'

The force of Greg's surprise had made everyone look at him. While the explanation was being given, Rosanne took the handkerchief from her face to stare at him.

Greg took hold of himself. They were agog, waiting for his next words.

'Don't you see . . . It was delivered by hand.'

'Yes,' Sasha said, as if to let him know he'd already worked that out.

'So that means there's someone nearby who's a confederate.'

'But we always suspected that,' Sasha protested. 'We always thought we might be under surveillance or being spied on somehow.'

'Yes, but this is an actual physical contact. And it seems to me it was done because they didn't want to waste time. Perhaps . . .' He paused to glance at Rosanne. 'Perhaps they're afraid Auguste's condition means he'll have to have a heart bypass and then take – how long, days? – perhaps weeks, to recover.'

'Which might mean,' Liz suggested, 'that they need the money urgently – for something that has a time limit – bidding for a contract, something like that.'

'Yes. So let's say Daniels in England telephones them here in Geneva and says that you want proof Gilles is safe and well. So they . . . so they . . .'

'Why don't they let me just speak to him?' cried Rosanne.

Liz left her side to come and study the picture on the screen. Gilles was looking out of it with what might have been a faint smile on his lips. He looked . . . what was the word? Contented. Certainly not under compulsion. She leaned down to peer at his face. His eyes looked odd.

'Greg,' she said, and leaned close to murmur, 'that's a goofy smile. He's doped.'

'What did you say?' Rosanne exclaimed, jumping up. She was beside them in a moment. 'Oh, no, don't tell me they've drugged my poor little boy!'

Sasha hunched away from them. He seemed shocked and unhappy, aware that to some extent they held him responsible for what had happened.

'Be calm, Rosanne,' Greg urged. 'I think Liz is right. It looks as if he's being kept under tranquillizers or something. So that's why they couldn't put him on the phone – he probably can't speak properly, can't be relied on to say what they want him to say.'

Rosanne tried to accept this suggestion without lamentation. She shuddered and moved away. She said: 'They're inhuman! They take him across the sea and they keep him stupefied. How are we ever going to—'

'Wait,' Greg interrupted.

'What?'

'Perhaps he's not in New York.'

They all gaped at him.

'But he is!' wailed Rosanne. 'The newspaper is today's date, and we've been working it out. It means they must have taken the photograph within the last five or six hours, because it's early morning now in New York.'

'And then you see,' Sasha took it up, 'they transmitted it to somebody here to put on disc and bring to us.'

'That's possible, of course. But why couldn't they just transmit it straight to this computer?'

'Because it's possible to trace which computer sent it—'

'But that computer, you're saying, is in New York. Why would it bother them all that much? If they're in New York, they're out of our reach.' His mind was racing. 'Let's think this through. Roger went down to the gate about nine thirty, you say. But let's suppose the person who delivered it didn't want to be seen. He or she would deliver it before it got light – that's before eight o'clock. Which means, if Gilles is in New York and the photograph was taken there, it was taken before three a.m.' He paused. 'You'd have to be in daily business with stocks and shares to know where to buy the *Wall Street Journal* at that hour in the morning, don't you think?'

No one replied to this question. All three were thinking over what he'd just said. It seemed true. If the photograph had originally been taken in New York it meant someone had to go out and find a copy of the newspaper at an unearthly hour. Even so, it was still possible. They looked at him for more.

'But if it's a computer here,' he said, 'somewhere nearby, and we could trace it – that would be a danger, wouldn't it?'

He glanced at Liz to see if this was correct, and she gave him a nod but said: 'Tracing it would take time, though, I think.'

'Let's say they don't want to take the chance. They've been very wary up till now – distorted voices on the phone, automatic messages to start with. So they're still being careful, and I'll tell you why – I think they're holding Gilles somewhere not far off.'

'What?' It was a chorus of mixed response– incredulity, hope, bewilderment.

'Perhaps even in Switzerland,' Greg added.

Rosanne gave a gasp. Liz frowned at him for making such a rash statement on scanty evidence. He held up a finger and then pointed at the screen.

The newspaper Gilles was holding was face outward to the camera, with the blue banner of the *Wall Street Journal* clearly visible and the day and date of publication below in sedate capitals. He had his fists folded down from above, holding the paper against his chest, somewhat in the manner of a child showing off his drawing.

'May I use your telephone?' Greg asked Rosanne. At her anxious nod, he pressed buttons to summon his own office in Geneva.

Amabelle, his faithful assistant, picked up. 'Hirtenstein Agency, how may I help you?'

'Amabelle, this is Greg. Have you got today's *Wall Street Journal*?'

Amabelle was one who took her secretarial and book-keeping duties seriously. 'Yes, I have.'

'Would you mind bringing it to the phone?'

A short pause while she did so. 'Here it is. Now what?'

'Read me the main headline.'

'Ahem.' She read: 'Corolan's Board, Still in Disagreement, to Meet Today.'

He was gazing at the newspaper in the computer photo-graph. He had just heard her read out exactly the same words. 'Amabelle – that's the *Wall Street Journal* Europe?'

'Yes of course. Why do you ask?'

'Do you ever buy the New York edition?'

'Yes, occasionally, why?'

'When you get it, does it have today's date on it?'

'No, as a rule it's available a day late. And of course it's not about European finance in anything like the same degree.'

'It's published in Europe?'

'Of course. It tells you so beneath the banner – "Edited and published in Brussels".'

'Whereabout is that?'

223

'Whereabouts? Brussels?' she repeated, puzzled.

'No, the information about publishing. Where would I look for the words if I wanted to find them?'

'I told you, beneath the banner, on the right-hand side.'

And that would be the left-hand side to the viewer looking at the picture of Gilles. Gilles's left hand was clutching the paper so that it was crumpled. The word 'EUROPE' in the blue banner and the words 'Edited and published in Brussels' were hidden under his fingers.

'Thank you, Amabelle.'

'Are you coming into the office today? There are letters—'

'I'll see you later, soon as I can.'

He disconnected. He turned to find the three others waiting in suspense.

'That paper Gilles is holding is the European edition of the *Wall Street Journal*, published in Europe and available in any of the cities of Europe probably from about five o'clock this morning.'

They were speechless. At length Rosanne clapped her hands with a cry of delight. 'He's not in New York?'

'I don't think so. Rosanne, that picture might have been taken as soon as the paper became available to use as window-dressing, and immediately put on disc and delivered to your gates – before it got light, as I was saying, so the messenger wouldn't be seen. So . . . it gets light about eight o'clock, give or take. Let's say it got to your gate just before eight. That could mean the photograph was taken somewhere about three hours away by car.'

She glanced at her watch. It was past noon. Her whole demeanour changed: she was alert and encouraged. She was once more the mistress of her household. She said formally: 'Thank you, Greg. And as they're going to call me at one o'clock, we ought to have something to eat and decide what we're going to say to them.'

She ordered food then went to repair her make-up. Greg asked Sasha to print out some copies of the photograph. When the first one emerged he took it up to study more closely.

The largest image was of Gilles holding the newspaper. Behind him was a window. Shutters had been thrown back so that they now flanked the window frame. Beyond that was a vague blur but it was a white blur – snow outside under lamplight?

They're in Switzerland, he said to himself.

Liz came to join him. 'An old house?' she remarked. 'Because of the shutters.'

'Lots of Swiss houses have shutters.' He nodded. 'I think they're here – or perhaps just across the French border in the Jura. I'm sure it isn't New York, at any rate!'

Rosanne reappeared, bringing with her Mme Armonet. Her sister-in-law looked rather wan, as if she were in the throes of a hangover. Almost immediately behind them came a servant wheeling into the study a trolley which opened out to make a reasonable-sized dining table. The servant was dismissed, the covers were removed from the dishes, to reveal a steaming ragout and a meatless risotto for Liz.

By wordless agreement they drank mineral water: they had to keep clear heads. Marie Armonet ate almost nothing. Sasha looked at her with concern and seemed just as averse to food. The others ate dutifully, while Rosanne tried to keep up social standards by asking after the musicians in Montreux.

'Oh, they'll be leaving, madame,' Greg told her, 'as soon as they sort out the cancellation of their work permits and so on. You know, there's no prospect now of their ever performing at the Festival, and they were unhappy . . .' He paused, wanting her to understand that they hadn't defected. 'I felt it was unfair to keep them here, and in any case we had no legal right to detain them.'

'I suppose not.' She'd never really liked the jazzmen being connected with her family. She dismissed the topic by asking Liz if her hotel was agreeable.

'Oh yes, marvellous, it's so comfortable and so efficient. I got all the things we took to New York cleaned and pressed within hours.' She hesitated. 'And it has some lovely boutiques in the lobby so I . . . I bought a black coat—' She broke off, sorry she'd mentioned it but ended lamely: 'For the . . . for, you know, the funeral.'

'My dear, that was very thoughtful of you. Auguste will appreciate that.'

Marie burst out: 'You know Auguste insists on coming to the funeral?'

'What?' Greg said.

'Yes, insists – he says he couldn't live with himself if he didn't pay his last respects to her.'

Greg turned to Rosanne. She nodded despondently. 'I tell him he's not really quite recovered from his little attack, and the cold weather—'

'Rosanne!' Greg interrupted. 'What happens to the fiction that he's not able to come to the telephone if he's seen attending a funeral service?'

She gave a gasp. That clearly hadn't occurred to her. 'You mean they might be at the service?' Her tone was tinged with horror. She hadn't thought how close they might be.

'We don't know that, but we ought not to take chances. He mustn't leave the clinic.'

She shook her head. 'He's determined, Greg.'

'But it's upsetting our whole plan of action.'

She looked a little ashamed but held her position. 'He's the head of the house, you see. And Nounou was the oldest member of the family, and greatly honoured.'

Marie snorted at the last word, but didn't argue.

'So what are you going to say to Davie Daniels when he rings?'

'I – I'll just see what he demands and I'll – I'll think of something.'

He knew she was quick-witted. He had seen her in action. All the same, she couldn't go on declaring that her husband was practically at death's door if next day he was going to be seen out in the cold and the snow.

'You could perhaps say his condition is improving,' suggested Sasha.

'And then Daniels will immediately demand he goes to the bank and gets the password.'

'Perhaps when he goes out tomorrow Auguste could be in a wheelchair, with . . . you know . . . a little portable oxygen thing,' Liz put in.

Marie was astounded at the idea. 'And let the whole world

226

believe that Auguste Guidon is dangerously ill? The press will be there and at the merest suggestion he's not in control, clients would be besieging the bank. Auguste isn't going to let them see him in a wheelchair!'

They all stopped to look at each other in consternation. After studying the mutinous expression on the faces of Rosanne Guidon and her sister-in-law, Greg shrugged.

'Well, then, you're going to have to tell Daniels that your husband's getting better. Then he'll say he's to go to the bank and get the password.'

'But Auguste will never divulge the password,' she protested, throwing her arms wide to show the greatness of his determination.

'You'll have to persuade him.'

She met this with a glance that said: 'I've been married to him for nearly thirty years and I know I can't do that.'

They were still arguing when the telephone on the desk rang. They almost started in surprise, they'd been so intent on their argument. It was a little before one o'clock; the kidnapper had rung early to take them off-balance.

Sasha pressed the button for the speaker-phone. Rosanne said in trembling tones, 'This is Mme Guidon.'

'Are you pleased with our little present?' To the surprise of everyone listening, the sound was perfectly normal. It seemed Davie Daniels had decided he had nothing to fear if they heard his real voice.

'Oh yes, yes – thank you so much!'

'So now you're happy. You know your son is safe and well and living in New York.'

'Why did you take him so far away?' she cried as if she believed him. 'My poor darling! Please, please, bring him home to me!'

'Yes, of course, that's how it's going to be. No problem, if you just behave yourself.'

'I will, I will, I promise.'

'You owe me now, don't you, Ma? I let you see your kid so's you won't worry about him any more. He's not gonna come to any harm if you just do what you're told. Right?'

'Yes, I understand, thank you, of course . . .' She was stammering, for she knew the dreaded moment was approaching.

'Right. So you're gonna get that password from your husband.'

'But all that kind of thing is in safe-keeping at the bank.'

'So he's got to go there and get it.'

'But he's not well enough . . .' The words died away. Tomorrow that would be shown as a lie. She hesitated, tears welling up and over on to her cheeks, then she said: 'But he's improving a little. Yes, he's improving.'

'Uh-huh. That's what I want to hear. So he's going to cooperate, isn't he?'

'Yes. But—'

'No buts.'

'Please, let me explain. Yes, he's getting better, but the doctor says . . . well . . .' She was floundering.

'That old ninny! You don't want to pay any attention to what he says. Your old man's got to go to the bank and sort this out for us, hear me?'

'Well . . . in a day or two . . .'

'What?'

'The doctor said he might go in on Thursday just for a day, to see if he was fit—'

There was a grunt from Davie Daniels. 'Day after tomorrow?'

'Yes, we thought that seemed—'

'Listen, Ma, you better get this straight. We're not going to play nice forever. I'll ring him at the bank Friday, right? And if he's not there ready with you-know-what, then it's whistle-time, you understand – no more play allowed after the whistle, Sonny Jim gets a taste of the hard life if you don't come up to scratch. Are you with me?'

'Please don't hurt him,' wept Rosanne.

'That's up to you, lady.' And the line went dead.

Rosanne looked around at the others, seeming uncertain of their reaction to what she'd done. Her sister-in-law merely shrugged. Sasha said, 'At least, Madame, you've accounted for his appearance tomorrow at the funeral – you said

Monsieur was improving. If he can act a little, look as if he's under the weather—'

'Sasha, he won't have to act. That's his beloved Nounou in the coffin.'

Sasha looked ashamed, Marie Armonet huffed a little as she always did at mention of the old nurse. Greg and Liz thought this the moment to take their leave, promising to see them next day at the little chapel where the services would be held.

Roger drove them to the Belle Cascade. It was mid-afternoon. Greg said he ought to go to his office to deal with the matters Amabelle had mentioned and Liz said she ought to telephone various business contacts in London to explain her continued absence. They parted for the time being.

At his office he found Amabelle about to leave for the day. 'Letters there, notes of phone calls there, cheques to sign there.' She was pointing at little piles on his desk. 'One urgent message about Laszlo Grima – he's got mumps.'

'Mumps?' The flautist was fifty years old.

'He's got a substitute lined up – call him to OK the money side. Goodbye, I've got to collect my kids.' And she was gone.

He made the call about the mumps-stricken musician but let the rest slide. Instead he looked in his pocket for the telephone number of Phillipe Lederer in New York. It was morning office-hours there. Once again there was a secretary to enquire his name before he was put through.

'Hi! What's the buzz?' came the cheery greeting in Americanese. Then a change-over to Swiss-German. 'Was that stuff I put through to M. Guidon of any use to you? I've got a little more, if you'd like it.'

'Of course.'

'Someone in the Tullo family has been dealing with a law firm in England about licences for a casino. The British government hasn't set any time limits but some of the lawyers are trying to weed out the no-hopers so they're making conditions about money up front.'

'Aha,' murmured the Prince.

'Any help?'

'It backs up what we suspected. Thank you, Lederer. But it was something else I wanted to ask. Can you find out something about Morena Tullo for me – something quite recent?'

'I'll try. What?'

'I heard she lives in Philadelphia. If she goes travelling, presumably she uses a travel agent there. Would you say that's likely?'

'More than likely. These old Mob families, they have their followers and supporters that they turn to for menial tasks. I'd say Fräulein Morena probably uses one particular firm to sort out her travel arrangements.'

'Well, I was wondering ... Morena has been here in Switzerland. Before she left the States, she may have done some forward planning. She might have arranged to rent a house.' He was looking at the photograph of Gilles and the newspaper as he spoke.

'A house. Yes?'

'It might be a chalet. It might be not too far from Geneva or Montreux, for instance.' Because someone had had to purchase that morning's edition of the *Wall Street Journal*, take the photograph, and then deliver the disc to Chateau Guidon by about 8 a.m. 'It would probably be a high-class sort of place.' Because the sofa of cream-coloured leather must have cost a great deal of money. 'And it might quite possibly be not too far from some resort town.' Because Morena wasn't the type to be stuck way out in the sticks with no place to go for relaxation and enjoyment.

'Let me check that back with you. You're saying east of Lake Geneva and west of Canton Bern?'

'Something like that. And probably not rented under her own name ...' He was about to explain he knew she'd been using a false name and identification papers but decided that wasn't necessary.

'And you want me to do what? Find out which travel agent Morena Tullo uses and ask them who's rented a place in those areas?'

230

'Not straight out like that, Lederer! Can you just . . . you know . . . say you're trying to hire a place yourself, and you've heard . . . you understand . . . spin them a yarn?'

'How do you think I get information about *die Schwindlern*, eh? Leave it to me, *Genoss*. How soon do you want this?'

'Yesterday, Philippe.'

'Shall I ring Guidon as before with this information?'

'No, no, that information is for my ears only. But it's for M. Guidon in the end, and it's very important.'

'*Versteh'n*,' said Lederer briskly and disconnected.

Having reached a stage where they were calling each other chum or by their first name, Greg was satisfied. He'd get prompt action, and the sooner the better – for if Gilles Guidon was being kept continually under drugs by his captors, it couldn't be good.

At the chapel belonging to the hamlet of Vereche the gathering for the funeral of Josephine Bartelet, otherwise known as Nounou, was sparse, even with a few reporters and photographers. The Guidon family clustered around Auguste, who looked wan enough to convince any spy that he was ill. The parson had known Nounou personally so was able to pick out her good points and ignore the bad.

Within thirty minutes it was over, Auguste and his wife alone accompanying the coffin to the crematorium.

Marie Armonet was in floods of tears, to her own and everyone else's surprise. She clung to Liz Blair as if she were her dearest friend, leaving Sasha dangling. Several of the cars under Roger's care were in use to take them and the servants back to the Chateau Guidon.

There a buffet luncheon was waiting. A few inhabitants of Vereche who had known Nounou as a fellow-worshipper arrived, partly out of respect for the departed but partly out of a desire to see the luxury of the house.

When it seemed polite, Greg suggested they should leave. Liz hesitated. 'I think I should stay on, love,' she told him. 'Marie's in a real old state. And that means that when Rosanne gets back from seeing Auguste safely to the clinic, she'll have to cope with her. You see what I mean – she's having a hard time, poor soul.'

He argued against it but only weakly. He wanted to get to his office and then home to Bredoux. He had things to do.

As it was growing dark in Geneva, his mobile phone rang. It was Lederer in New York. 'How's tricks, dude?'

'Don't ask. Have you got something for me?'

'That's an insult. Lederer always gets results. You got a pencil and paper?'

'Go on.'

Lederer enunciated very clearly the names and locations of four possible houses within the designated area. 'One of those, the one at Villars, isn't so likely. It's a six months' rental and I was told it's to a botanist who studies Alpine flowers – but who knows what evildoers will say! The others seem more likely.'

'Thank you, Philippe, you've done wonders.'

'The possible we do every day. Wonders are more unusual. *Zum Wohl, mein Freund!*'

So now he had targets. He went home, got out maps, and measured distances. Then he rang Liz on her mobile.

'Where are you?' he enquired.

'Still at the chateau. Marie is awash, Sasha is sulking, and Rosanne quite understandably has a migraine. She's asked me to stay overnight and I've said yes.'

To tell the truth, he was quite glad to hear it. 'So do you think you'll be there tomorrow too?'

'Well . . . at first, I suppose. Why?'

'I've got something to do tomorrow – might take me all day.'

'One of your looking-after-my-musician trips?'

'Something like that.'

'OK, then, I'll hang around here until they seem a bit recovered. See you at the hotel for dinner, yes?'

He agreed, although he was by no means certain. He was going hunting, and it might take a long time.

Nineteen

No one is more innocuous than a cross-country skier. There he goes, slogging along on trails safely removed from the traffic, nothing gaudy about him, no luminescent jacket, no fashionably slanted snow-goggles. Nobody is going to give him a second glance.

The Crown Prince had thought well about his expedition. He had his route planned. He took an early-morning train to Gstaad and by efficient use of cable-ways and ski lifts got himself above and to the west of Saanen. Here there were two addresses in outlying areas that he wanted to inspect.

The Bernese Oberland is not the highest region of the Alps but it attracts many visitors, for both the skiing and the scenery. Chalet Beilerein, his first port of call, had skis parked outside its door in large numbers, all recently used as he learned on close inspection. That seemed an unlikely home for the kidnapped Gilles Guidon. He glided in close, to be greeted with a cheery wave from a hearty young man drinking his morning coffee on the porch. He waved back and turned away.

He descended about a thousand feet then trekked another two miles along a *Langlauf* track. As befitted a route for keen cross-country skiers this took him to a secluded valley with a little lake. Here he found Chalet Grünsee standing by itself on an inlet, where children were building a snowman on the lakeshore.

He was pretty sure Morena and her minions wouldn't be holding Gilles captive in a house with children. He paused to tell the children he admired their work. They rewarded him with a few badly made snowballs.

So he travelled on to the last address on the list provided

by Philippe Lederer, Villa Bienfaite, on a little road off the main highway out of Chateau d'Oex. Something over two hours' drive for someone who needed to deliver a package to the gates of the Chateau Guidon halfway between Montreux and Geneva.

The villa was a more capacious house than the others. It had in fact once been something like a large country house, built perhaps for a rich merchant of the Victorian era yet still in the style of the local architecture. It was three floors high, had gables and cornices of wood but with the ground floor faced in local stone. Lovingly restored and extended, it was rather a courtly residence.

Here there was no conglomeration of skis; no child was playing in its snow-covered garden. A handsome lamp-standard would light the drive at night. It stood alone in a pasture, the nearest house about half a mile further up the mountain road. A good place to store a prisoner, and elegant enough to attract Morena Tullo. The town of Chateau d'Oex not far off was pleasant, with some nightclubs and good restaurants. Compensation for a city-dweller like Morena.

He skied past the place. The house further up the road appeared unoccupied at present. He took himself round the side of it, found a bench set for the view of the Alps and perhaps the hot-air balloons if they were in the skies. He shed his skis, sat down, and got out his vacuum flask of coffee and his raisin bars, for he'd been out a long time now and it was necessary to keep up one's energy.

It was a day of bright light, not exactly sunlight but almost blinding as it reflected up from the snow. So he was still wearing his old snow-goggles. When a car came around from the side of Villa Bienfaite and turned in his direction, he flinched, but then remembered the goggles. He was unrecognizable. So he stared at the car as it went past just as any snow-hiker would.

And what he saw was an off-road vehicle with the familiar high-riding chassis, giving a clear view of Lou Ellis driving Morena Tullo. They were headed towards the cable car that would take them up to a restaurant at something over five thousand feet.

'*Hola*,' said the Prince to himself.

A cable-car journey isn't very fast, and then there was lunch, a leisurely Swiss lunch in a good restaurant – say four courses and liqueurs afterwards. They might be gone for a good couple of hours.

Quickly he put away his snack and put on his skis. He glided down the slope to Villa Bienfaite, went past as if he had a long way to go, turned at right angles then toiled up a hill that would give him a good view of the house. He got binoculars out of his backpack. He found himself a shallow ledge of snow and sat down. Then he prepared to keep the villa under observation.

Ten minutes went by, twenty. He moved position so as to see the back of the house. Twenty-five minutes. No sign of any movement. No one opened a door, no figure passed a window. No sound of music from a radio, of a talk show from a television.

Could it be that the kidnappers were so sure of themselves that no one was keeping an eye on Gilles? That's to say, if Gilles was there . . .

He had to find out. He put away his glasses. He skied down to the house door in five minutes. He rang the bell.

No answer. He rang again, three rings, urgent. He was going to say, 'Please, I'm lost, can you tell me if this road leads to the cable-car station?' But nobody came.

Well, let's say there's nobody home, he said to himself. Nobody on guard over Gilles, because Gilles was out for the count with drugs. So he ought to go inside and look.

The villa was an old wood frame reinforced with bricks, and it had an oak door that wasn't going to yield to pushing and shoving. He slipped off the skis, tucked them out of sight under a snow-laden bush, put his goggles in his pocket, and took a quiet walk round the house. Some of the windows had shutters thrown back, so he shielded his eyes to gaze in. Very handsome furniture, a modern stove gleaming with warmth, a low ebony table with magazines and a discarded iPod. A massive television and a rack of DVDs. A fixed-line telephone with a pad and pencil alongside.

A big extension was built on the side, solid workmanship; its door wouldn't budge. The inside shutters of these rooms were closed so it was no use breaking a window and trying to climb in. He walked on, to find a garage attached to the building at the back.

And the driver of the car he'd just seen had obligingly left the garage door up.

He walked in. There ought to be a door connecting the garage with the house. Yes, there it was – nothing like as substantial as the outer doors. He found a chisel on the tool shelf, inserted its blade between the door and the jamb, and leaned on it hard.

The door gave way.

He returned the chisel to its shelf. He got out of his boots and, carrying them in case he had to throw them at an unexpected warder, stepped into the room behind the opened door. It was a utility room, the kind of place where you could leave snowy coats and galoshes. He parked his boots there, unnoticeable among two or three other pairs. He went out the door opposite and found himself in a corridor.

He'd looked in through the window at the big living room. He turned in the opposite direction. A minimalist dining room, a beautifully equipped kitchen with almost every pan and bowl gleaming unused on the shelves. A few dishes in the dishwasher, a toaster with a few crumbs suggesting that the occupants had made some toast for breakfast. But nothing else seemed in use. No wonder they'd headed for the mountain restaurant for lunch.

The only other room on the ground floor of the main house was a games room. It was well equipped with a billiard table, shelves of boxed games suitable for children in bad weather, a card table and comfortable chairs. But no sign of Gilles Guidon.

He went out into the hall and began to ascend the stairs. He moved soundlessly on his wool-clad feet, thinking how his boots might have betrayed him had he worn them.

He looked in at the first door. Very pretty nightwear strewn across the unmade bed, expensive creams and lotions in disarray on the dressing table – this was the room Morena was using. There was something very reassuring in a sight so feminine and unthreatening.

The next one was Lou's room, even more untidy and without the decoration of pretty things. The wardrobe door was open to show a couple of suitcases but only an empty rail with a few coat-hangers.

There was a half-open door in the far wall, not a wardrobe or a cupboard because light was pouring from the gap from unshuttered windows.

He went through the door. He found himself in an adjoining room. Gilles Guidon was lying fast asleep in bed. The bedclothes had slid off to one side, revealing that he was clad in under-vest and boxer shorts.

The room was perhaps meant for a child, though it was still furnished in the handsome minimalist style of the others. There were night tables on either side of the bed but none of the usual accoutrements – no clock, no lamp, no radio. The only lighting seemed to be an angular standard lamp by the small dressing table. On this stood a water carafe with a glass up-ended on its neck.

The air in the room had an odd smell. He stepped to the bed. Gilles wasn't asleep, but under deep sedation. His skin colour was very pale, made almost grey by a day's growth of beard. Although the room was warm from the efficient central heating, his skin was cold and clammy to the touch. His breathing was very slow, there was a white crust about his lips, and when he felt his pulse, it seemed weak.

Auguste Guidon kept saying he was anxious to avoid bringing in the police. Yes. Well, nuts to that, as Liz was wont to say.

Greg went downstairs to the telephone in the living room. He picked it up. Dialling tone. He felt a great surge of relief. Help was on the other end of that line. Not the police, the ambulance service.

He dialled the emergency service number. Yes, it was urgent, yes, the subject looked very ill, in fact was unconscious. He gave the name of the villa and its location.

'And you are, sir?'

'Gregory von Hirtenstein.' Not likely to be known by a

paramedic but when it reached someone further up the chain, it might have its effect.

'We'll be with you as soon as possible. Keep the patient warm and safe meanwhile.'

Warm and safe. He went upstairs, thinking he might try to get him dressed. But there were no clothes in any of the drawers or fitted cupboards. He went back to the outer room and opened the first drawer in the bureau. And drew in his breath at what he saw. A 9mm automatic in a clip-on holster.

He shut the drawer quickly. That couldn't have been brought into Switzerland on a plane. Someone must have supplied it here. An accomplice. Which meant he ought to get Gilles out of here as quickly as possible, for the accomplice might walk in.

He snatched up a tracksuit slung over the back of a chair, and trainers from a jumble by the bed. He was just discovering the trainers were too small when he heard a car approaching. He looked out of the window but it faced out on the back of the house. He could hear the car coming along the mountain road. It was turning in at the drive to the villa. It was at the front door.

So much for criticizing the kidnappers for being sure of themselves. He'd been guilty of the same fault. Just because people head towards a cable-car station, it doesn't mean they're going to go up in the cable car. It perhaps only meant they'd gone to buy a magazine or a litre of milk from the shop adjoining the station.

The front door was being unlocked. They came in, arguing loudly and angrily. 'You had it last, it should be in your pocket-book.'

'Well, it isn't, I've only got the Ferigiano one.'

'For God's sake, you know we can't use that one any more.'

'Let's use cash, then, you know we've got enough.'

'Cash is for emergencies! Find the card, Lou.'

They were arguing about a lost credit card. He could hear them moving about in the living room, picking things up and throwing them down. In a house with a wooden frame and wooden floors, sound travelled clearly.

'OK, it must be in the jacket you were wearing yesterday.'

'That's upstairs.'

'Then for the love of Mike go up and look! By the time we get to the restaurant they'll have stopped serving lunch!'

Heavy footsteps on the wooden stairs. Lou was coming to his room to look for the credit card.

Greg held his breath. With luck, he'd find it and straight-away go downstairs.

Lou was walking about next door. Grunts of irritation as he took up and shook one or two garments. Then: 'Got it!' he shouted down to Morena.

'I'll start the car,' Morena called, and he heard her cross the hall and go out, leaving the front door open for Lou.

A pause. Then footsteps across the room, coming towards the inner bedroom. He was coming to check on Gilles.

Greg stepped quickly to the wall behind the door. Lou pushed the door open enough to glance in at the captive.

Alas. The man he'd left unconscious lying in bed in vest and boxer trunks was now propped up against the headboard wearing a tracksuit.

'What the—!'

At that moment came a sound from outside – the sound of a helicopter approaching overhead and from the east. Lou gave a cry of alarm and darted to one of the windows that faced east in this room.

After one glance he rushed to the outer door. 'Morena! Morena! It's the cops!'

Greg couldn't see the helicopter. But he guessed it bore the logo of the Air Rescue Service, REGA. Meaningless to someone who wasn't a Swiss citizen. Threatening to some-one who expected trouble.

Morena's voice came from below. She'd tumbled out of the car to call instructions. 'Get the goldfish! Come on, grab him and let's go!'

Lou didn't hear. Or he was in a panic. Greg heard a drawer jerked open and then the sound of the safety catch coming off the automatic.

A crash of glass. Lou smashing a window so as to take aim.

Next moment there were six shots, rapid fire. The helicopter zoomed away and out of reach behind the house. Greg could imagine the astonishment and alarm of the crew.

'Lou!' Morena was shrieking from below. 'Don't be a fool – let's go!'

But Lou was beyond logic now, beyond reason. In a strange country, against opponents he couldn't estimate, he seemed to think attack was the best form of defence. He rushed across his room to get to a window where he could aim at the helicopter as it hovered now over the back of the house, probably reporting 'Shots fired' to headquarters.

'Lou! I'm going!'

It brought Lou to his senses. He surged towards Gilles's room to carry him away. As he came in, Greg stepped from behind the door wielding the water carafe by its neck. He brought it down in a crash on Lou's head.

Lou went down like a log. Greg snatched the pistol out of his unresisting hand. Below, Morena gave one last despairing wail. 'I'm off, Lou!' The door of the car banged, Greg heard its engine revving.

He took the stairs four at a time with his long legs, ran out to the drive, the ground icy beneath his woollen socks. Morena was lurching away in an mishandled racing start. Greg steadied himself and took careful aim with the pistol.

Two calculated shots each side. He wrecked her back tyres.

Twenty

From the hospital he rang first Auguste at his clinic, and then Liz on her mobile. He felt he needed her to handle the breaking of the good news to Rosanne. Luckily she was still at the chateau. She gave a whoop of delight at his information.

Auguste arrived first, then ten minutes later Rosanne and Liz. Both parents barrelled past Greg to be taken to the bedside of their son. Liz stayed back, and when they'd gone tried to get to Greg. He, however, was still engaged with a policeman, trying to explain what had happened. Luckily the conversation was taking place in French, so that she was quite unaware there had been something of a shoot-out.

He waved to her, and the police sergeant glanced round. He softened in his manner at sight of the *belle anglaise*. 'Shan't be much longer, sir,' he said. But it was another fifteen minutes before he declared himself satisfied for the present. 'I think the commissaire will have to be in touch, but I believe I should let you go for the moment. Where will you be this evening?'

'I'm not sure.' Either at the hotel or home at Bredoux. 'I'll give you my mobile number. You know my home address.'

'Certainly, sir.' He made a little salute and turned to Liz. 'A very brave affair, mademoiselle. And your *ami* is a very good shot.'

She frowned as he left. She said to her *ami*: 'A good shot? You shot somebody?'

Greg laughed. 'Not somebody, something – the tyres of the car that Morena was driving.'

'Morena? You found Morena?'

241

'Yes. And Lou as well,' he said cheerfully. 'He's in another ward with a suspected concussion.'

'And did you do that too?'

Something in her tone warned him that he had nothing to be cheerful about. 'Well . . . yes.'

'What on earth has been going on?' she cried. 'Where did all this happen?'

'At a villa up in the Oberland.'

'That's where you went?' When he nodded, looking wary, she said: 'You lied to me! You said you were going to look after one of your music clients!'

'Well, Lou and Morena were my clients—'

'Stop it! It's no joking matter! You shot something – you went out with a gun?'

'No, I took it from Lou—'

'Took it from Lou! Took it from Lou, who's a thug and a criminal, and you went off to the Oberland without me and—'

'Liz, I couldn't possibly have taken you. It's rough going up there.'

Auguste and Rosanne came through the doors of the waiting room. Rosanne surged up to Greg, to throw her arms around him and kiss him resoundingly on both cheeks. 'My dear, dear friend,' she sobbed. 'How shall we ever repay you? You've given us back our boy. He might have died!'

Auguste was beside his wife, trying to pat him on the shoulder. 'I'll never forget this, my boy. Never, never.'

'How is he?' he asked, to prevent any further gratitude.

'Umm. Very unwell, but stabilizing. They tell us he's been under haphazard dosage with some form of morphine, for several days. Much longer and . . . well . . . it doesn't bear thinking of.'

'But he's going to be all right?'

'Yes, thank God. However, it's going to take time. Yes, it will take time . . . but he has that now, thanks to you.'

'They say he'll probably recover consciousness some time this evening,' Rosanne put in, 'so we're going to stay here so as to be the first people he sees – not those dreadful brutes who – who—' She broke off, unable to name their crime.

242

Greg and Liz said goodbye. Each had had a long day so far, though in different ways. Liz had been shut up in the chateau with the aftermath of Nounou's funeral – a weepy, repentant Marie and an anxious Rosanne. Greg had been in action since five in the morning, and it was now five in the afternoon.

In the taxi to the hotel, Greg kept up a conversation about the prospects for Gilles. He would need some weeks of treatment: 'I suppose so,' said Liz. He would probably never like to get involved in jazz again: 'I suppose not,' said Liz.

She was still indignant at not being told where he was heading today. She demonstrated this by stalking away from him and into the hotel entrance while he was delayed paying the taxi. He caught up with her in the foyer. The young man behind the desk called her name as she was about to walk past. She stopped, turned to him expecting perhaps a message from London.

He said: 'A lady is asking for you.' He nodded beyond her, towards the lounge.

'Really? Who?' But without waiting for his reply, fearing that it might be Marie Armonet, she went on into the lounge, with Greg at her heels.

And there, rising to meet them from an armchair in an alcove, was ex-Queen Nicoletta of Hirtenstein.

Her grandson gave a stifled gasp. Liz caught the sound and guessed who it was, although she looked older than in press photographs.

'So!' said Nicoletta, staring at her with a gaze of stone. 'This is what you are like!' She shrugged. 'I had expected a great beauty.'

'Grossmutti,' said Greg with indignation, 'what are you doing here?'

'I am meeting the girl who bewitches you, or so it seems. You do not ever introduce me, no, of course not, because now I see her I find her quite common, quite unworthy.'

'Hey!' said Liz.

'You were quite right to keep her a secret, my child. All the same, I would have preferred to learn that she was present here – here on my home ground – from your own mouth.'

'How did you find out?' Liz enquired caustically. 'Hired a private eye, did you?'

Nicoletta gave an icy smile. 'From little housewifely duties. Polythene bags for clothes cleaned by this hotel, when I emptied the wastepaper basket. So I ask myself, why is he staying at a hotel, and learn that you are here, taking advantage of the generosity of M. Guidon while you – while you—'

'Grossmutti, that's enough. You should leave before you say something we'll all regret.'

'I shall not regret what I say. I am here on purpose to say it.' She turned to Liz, in all the splendour of a Givenchy dress and her pearl choker. 'You are a bad, wicked girl to keep clutching at my grandson. Let me tell you, you waste your time. He will never marry you, no matter how you coax him. His sense of duty will always overcome—'

'Madame!' Greg said. 'That's enough! Let me escort you to your car.' He was attempting to take her by the elbow to lead her out but she jerked herself free.

'I intend to tell her—'

'Don't bother,' Liz interrupted. 'I get the gist. His sense of duty to your tin-pot little kingdom would prevent him from marrying me. Great! Who'd want to have anything to do with a place like that, four acres of nowhere—'

'How dare you! You have no manners!' When in the grip of emotion, Nicoletta sometimes reverted to the High German of her early years. She went into a tirade now: Liz was a hussy, a temptress, a deceiver, out for her own ends, uneducated, unmannered, and . . . and . . .

'Grandmama, you're getting hysterical,' Greg intervened in the same language. 'Calm down.'

'I am calm. I perfectly calm and composed. I speak of things to which I have given much thought.'

'Oh, this is great!' cried Liz. 'If you want a fight, let's have it in English so that I can have fun too!'

'There you are,' said Nicoletta in triumph but in English. 'Speaks only her own coarse language! Uneducated – I told you so. And selfish, out for her own gain—'

'Gain? Gain? What do I gain by being with Greg? If you

had any decent human feelings you'd know that—'

'I know that you take my grandson from his proper standing in the world. I know that it would suit you very well to have his name linked with these tawdry clothes you sell.'

'Tawdry? Listen, you old witch, I lose out by spending time with him.'

'Oh, yes, you use him to meet important people, and if you could only get him to marry you.'

'I wouldn't marry him if he got down on his knees.'

'So? And what is that, then?' Nicoletta directed a glare at the ring on her right hand. Even if it was the wrong hand, it did have the look of an engagement ring.

Liz snatched it off. 'It worries you? There it goes!' She threw it at Greg. It hit him in the chest and fell to his feet. He ignored it.

'Liz!'

But she was stalking past him. He made to follow her, but his grandmother seized him by the sleeve.

'Oh!' she panted. 'Oh, let me sit down, Gregory. I . . . I . . .' She tottered towards the chair which she'd been occupying. He had no choice but to support her, and when he turned back Liz was going up in the lift.

Nicoletta was leaning back in the chair, making little moans, whether of pain or emotion he couldn't tell. She looked pale. Her make-up, usually unnoticeable, stood out against her skin. 'Take me home, my darling,' she gasped. 'I . . . I don't feel well.'

An under-manager, alerted to the brouhaha in the lounge, hurried forward. 'Madame is ill? Is there anything I can do?'

Greg said inwardly: 'Please, not another victim of a heart attack.' He'd dealt with Auguste, he didn't want another. Aloud he said, 'Thank you, a little upset. A glass of water?'

'Certainly, sir.' The assistant waved at a bellboy. He stooped to retrieve something from the floor. 'Yours, sir?' It was the diamond ring.

'Thank you,' Greg said, and shoved it in his pocket.

Nicoletta continued to be unwell. He had no choice but to ask for her car to be brought round and to drive her home.

Before leaving he asked the desk to tell Mlle Blair that he would telephone.

In the Mercedes, Nicoletta lay in the corner of the back seat, saying nothing, and from his occasional glances at her in the mirror, seeming genuinely afflicted. But whether from a heart flutter or from indignation at hearing herself called an old witch, he couldn't tell.

Getting his grandmother settled at home on a sofa with a pile of cushions and a glass of Madeira took time. So did giving some sort of explanation to his father. When he could get away he hurried to the office next to the stables so as to ring Liz and have a sensible private conversation.

'I'm sorry, sir, Mlle Blair has checked out.'

'What?'

'Yes, sir. She wanted to catch the nine o'clock flight.'

He dashed out to the Mercedes, left out in front of the house door. He intended to drive like the wind to the airport, but as often happened after he'd been away and Nicoletta had been using the car, it was low on fuel. He had to stop for a refill. When he got to the airport the nine o'clock to Manchester had taken off.

'Why is she going to Manchester?' he asked himself, and the woeful answer was: 'To get away from you.'

Would she take a train home to London? Or would she stay overnight in Manchester? He tried her mobile when he knew she had landed but got no reply. He rang her flat and got the answering machine. He was still trying to contact her at midmorning on Friday when he got a polite call from police headquarters inviting him to the offices in Geneva.

He went, somewhat in trepidation. He'd fired a weapon at a moving vehicle, which was a crime. But he'd handed over the automatic to the emergency-response patrol that had quickly turned up.

A genial commissaire greeted him. 'Quite recovered from the excitement, monsieur?'

'More or less. Have you any news of Gilles Guidon?'

'Oh, yes, his father has kept in close touch.' This was said with a smile. Greg understood that some diplomatic exchanges had taken place.

Banking was a serious matter in this country. If possible, nothing should happen to bring it into disrepute. If a pillar of the banking community had been the target of criminals, that had to be remedied at once and with extreme discretion. In this case, the problem had been attended to not by the police but by something like divine intervention; the super-intendent let it be known that he was quite satisfied at how things had turned out.

'But Morena Tullo and her accomplice?'

'They were interviewed by a judge earlier today and have been remanded in custody.'

Greg gave a little frown. That might mean a long time before the case was ever tried. But his next thought was: why should I care?

'So there we are,' the commissaire said. 'As the English say, all's well that ends well.'

'Ye-es.'

'So you should be able to get back to your music, monsieur, and I wish you well in that.' This was a polite way of saying, 'Leave the shooting matches to us.'

'Thank you.' He accepted the reproof. He rose.

'And of course your belongings are with Sergeant Huss – if you ask at the reception desk, he'll give them to you.'

'My belongings?'

'Your skis and boots, sir – they were at the villa, you know.'

'Oh. Thank you.'

And that was the end of the affaire Villa Bienfaite, it seemed.

But not of the affaire Guidon. Auguste invited him to lunch at the bank, in a private dining room on the first floor – panelled walls, a table of figured walnut, French crystal, Swedish silver, four courses of exquisite food and wines to match. Greg attended in the same suit he'd worn to their first meeting. It was less old than the twelve-year-old décor, but not much.

When the liqueurs were offered, Auguste came to the point. 'You must know,' he said, over the smoke of a cigar, 'that I'm deeply in your debt forever.'

'Not at all, sir.'

'But yes. You saved my son. You save my reputation. You perhaps saved my bank. I can never do enough to repay you.'

'Ah, well, speaking of the bank, Auguste.' He had to settle this point, for it kept nagging at him. 'Was it something about the bank that was worrying you when you kept saying no police?'

Auguste was surprised and a little put out. This wasn't how he'd expected this meeting to go. 'Well, of course, it's never good for a bank if the public see the police taking an interest—'

'But was there something for them to be interested in? Something a little . . . out of order?'

The banker flushed and pursed his lips. 'Certainly not!'

Greg looked at him. He wanted to know what Auguste had been up to. An offer of a life-long friendship was remarkable – but he couldn't be friends with a swindler. 'All right, then. If you don't want to tell me . . . But I'll always be curious, you know.'

Auguste was silent for a long moment. Then he said: 'You perhaps know that the bank has had to make reparations to descendants and relatives of customers who entrusted funds to us during the Nazi era?' Greg was nodding. 'It put Banque Guidon under a lot of strain. And so . . . well . . . this is in strict confidence . . . we used money from accounts that had lain dormant, accounts that had never been accessed for many years.'

'You mean you used the Tullo account?'

'As a matter of fact, no,' said Auguste in obvious relief. 'We used accounts opened long before that – some as far back as eighteen-ninety. And that, of course, is something we didn't want known.'

'But, Auguste . . . What if some great-great-grandchild finds the details and in the end asks for the money?'

'Oh, we'll pay up. So long as he has the password and legal papers to back his claim. It's happened once, and we reopened the account. But on the whole . . .' He shrugged.

'And is this legal?'

'We-ell . . . there is a procedure that should be followed to close a dormant account . . . but . . .'

248

'You didn't carry it out.' When Auguste gave an embarrassed smile, Greg went on: 'And the Tullo account? It's Mafia money, isn't it?'

'Er . . .'

'It has to be notified to the agency that deals with international crime?'

'Well, yes.'

'That's been done?'

Auguste huffed a little. 'It will be done, in due course. But the authorities would prefer to have it done with discretion.'

That was the best he was going to get out of Auguste concerning the bank. So he turned the conversation to news about the family. He had already heard that Gilles was recovering his health, but he asked how he felt about Morena.

'Poor boy. He . . . he finds it hard to believe,' said Auguste. 'You see, they managed matters so that he was still under the impression they were eloping.'

'What? Even when Lou was manhandling him and shooting him full of dope?'

'He doesn't remember that. I imagine they gave him something in a glass of wine or a cup of coffee early on, which knocked him out while he was still in the land of romance. After that it's all a blank.'

'So he can't offer any evidence against them?'

'No, it seems not, and Morena is saying that if he had drugs in his system, he put them there himself.'

'So they are being charged with – what?'

'We-ell . . . Gilles went with them of his own accord. The only hard evidence against them is possession of a firearm and firing it at the Air Emergency helicopter. I gather Lou is pleading temporary insanity and Morena is saying she didn't even know he possessed a gun.'

'Auguste! You mean she's going to get off scot-free?'

The other allowed himself a grim smile. 'I hear from Lederer in New York that the Tullo family in Philadelphia is very annoyed with Morena. It seems that these days they want to be considered very law-abiding and respectable. They might take measures to prevent her from doing anything else to damage their reputation. That's once our slow legal system lets her go home.'

'And the voice on the telephone? The man we think of as Davie Daniels? Have they caught him?'

'Not so far, and it seems unlikely. The police tracked down the location of some of the telephone calls – one of them was a deserted office in London, and another was one of those apartments in Le Touquet that people rent for a holiday – only someone had broken in and had been using it without permission. Some seemed to come from a mobile, but the detectives say that's probably been put through a crusher in a scrap yard by now. Another loose end is Gilles's car. He and Morena set out in it, but where it is now may never be known.'

'But look here!' cried Greg, indignant at this easy acceptance of defeat. 'How about poor Nounou? And the death of the saxophonist in Paris – Wally Clifford?'

'My dear man, those are already accepted by the authorities here and in Paris as accidental.'

Greg stifled a groan. 'Poor, poor Wally Clifford. I was the one that hired him . . . And poor Gilles. You probably think it's for the best, but he's lost both his plan to play at the Festival, and the girl he thought he might marry. What's the outlook for him?'

'He's taken it hard. But he's getting help . . .' Auguste hesitated before admitting, 'He's seeing a psychotherapist. It will take time.'

'Did you tell him the band had gone home?'

'Yes, and he was to all appearances indifferent. It all seems to have ended in a messy but final discord, if you see what I mean. And if he resumes his interest in it, Greg, it can only be as an amateur, not a professional.'

'I see.' He nodded in sympathy with this decision. 'And Madame Guidon? She's happy at how it has turned out?'

'Oh, delighted, delighted. Only one thing . . .'

'What's that?'

'You know, I could never allow Sasha Resedeul to remain in my household after the way he sold gossip items. And Rosanne completely agreed . . . So I dismissed him.'

250

'Quite understandable.'

'But Marie rushed to his defence, and things got very contentious, and . . . and, well –' he looked put out – 'they're getting married.'

'No!'

He shrugged. 'Sasha needs somewhere to go, and she needs someone to keep her more or less sober, and they are fond of one another. So they're going to live in Basle and they'll be gone by Christmas.'

'In Basle? Far enough away to be good for family peace?' Greg asked with some irony.

'Oh, well, I own property here and there, you know. As a wedding present I'm giving them the lease of a flat in a good part of the city.'

Greg smiled and let it pass. But later he thought about it.

He'd had to move out of Bredoux. Relations between himself and his grandmother were strained. He couldn't forgive her for her behaviour at the hotel, nor did she even attempt to apologize – quite the contrary, she seemed to feel he ought to admit being at fault. Ex-King Anton of Hirtenstein had been living a miserable existence between these two icicles.

So Greg was sleeping in his little office in the Old Town. It couldn't be a permanent solution because the rooms weren't intended as living accommodation.

To move out of Bredoux was a serious matter. His contribution to the family income was quite large: Anton's earnings as an instructor in fine horsemanship and dressage were seasonal, and though Nicoletta was paid well, it was only intermittently. Greg was rather hoping for some substantial payment from the Guidons as a winding-up operation of Project Jazz Band. If so, he'd invest some of it for the Bredoux housekeeping account. And some of it, for a place of his own.

He thought now that he should have moved out long ago. If he ever repaired his relationship with Liz, he had to be free to come and go as he wished, to see her here in Switzerland or anywhere else in the world without the interference of his autocratic grandmother. Auguste Guidon might be able to point him in the direction of some not too expensive property.

Whether he and Liz would ever get together remained in doubt.

As he walked back to the office he took her ring out of his pocket to give him encouragement. He carried it with him wherever he went.

One day, he hoped to give it back to her.